STAR TREK®
INTO DARKNESS

STAR TREK®
INTO DARKNESS

A NOVELIZATION
BY ALAN DEAN FOSTER

BASED ON THE MOTION PICTURE SCREENPLAY
BY ROBERTO ORCI, ALEX KURTZMAN, & DAMON LINDELOF

BASED UPON *STAR TREK*
CREATED BY GENE RODDENBERRY

SIMON &
SCHUSTER

London · New York · Sydney · Toronto · New Delhi

A CBS COMPANY

First published in Great Britain by Simon & Schuster UK Ltd, 2013
A CBS COMPANY

This paperback edition, 2013

1 3 5 7 9 10 8 6 4 2

Simon & Schuster UK Ltd
1st Floor
222 Gray's Inn Road
London WC1X 8HB

www.simonandschuster.co.uk

Simon & Schuster Australia, Sydney
Simon & Schuster India, New Delhi

A CIP catalogue record for this book
is available from the British Library

Paperback ISBN 978-1-47112-890-5
Ebook ISBN 978-1-47112-891-2

Printed and bound by CPI Group (UK) Ltd, Croydon, CR0 4YY

STAR TREK®

INTO DARKNESS

I

CLASS-M PLANET
NIBIRU

It seemed as if not just the supervolcano, but every square meter of solid ground on the planet was on the verge of shaking itself apart. The serpentine smoke cloud that emerged from the enormous, towering cone stretched far out to sea, retaining its ominous coherence even as it cast much of the ocean's surface in shadow. Struggling to escape the noxious gases that rose from the planet's interior, troubled flying creatures sought clearer air to the north and south. Meanwhile, landslides periodically thundered down the volcano's slopes as its insides continued to swell, while the magma-clogged throat coughed and rumbled threateningly. Far below the outer planetary crust, something was building, something that portended far more than a mere series of Strombolian eruptions.

Designed by its builders to withstand intermittent quakes and recurring tectonic stutters, constructed of hand-hewn stone, the massive temple situated not far from the mountain's base violently trembled but did not fall. Mute and immovable at the convergence of multiple pathways that had been laboriously cleared from the red-leaved forest, it had stood thus for many hundreds of cycles.

The bipedal figure that burst from the bas-relief framed entrance was moving as fast as possible. While the simmering volcano appeared the greater threat, the more immediate one took the form of dozens of figures who emerged from the interior of the temple in hot pursuit. The bright yellow cowls and loincloths they wore stood out in sharp contrast to their skin, which more than anything resembled the cracked and splitting clay that might be found at the bottom of a long-dried-out lake bed. Primitive, simple symbols and lines of painted vegetable dye marked their otherwise bare bodies. Their yelling and screaming formed a nightmarish cacophony that contrasted with the lead figure's heavy breathing.

The gray cloth wrappings James Tiberius Kirk wore had disguised him. Now they interfered far too much with his breathing as he struggled to stay ahead of his pursuers. Whipping them off, he sucked in one desperate lungful of alien air after another as he dodged primitive spears that would terminate his life as surely as any phaser. Around him, the deep red Nibiran forest seemed intent on deliberately impeding his flight.

Emitting a howl of outrage in memory of the desecration that had just taken place in their most holy temple, the high Nibiran priest shook the weapon he was carrying as he urged on his fellows. Though the Nibirans were decidedly humanoid, their rounded facial features, ritually marked clay-colored skin, and black pupil-less eyes marked them as genetically and evolutionarily different from the humans they otherwise closely resembled.

As the object of their fury, Kirk fought to lengthen his stride as he ran. He knew that if he was caught in possession of the scroll he had snatched from the temple, his pursuers would show him no mercy. He would be dead before he could explain that his intentions were wholly benign. He had to just keep running—if all went according to plan, that would not be much longer.

It *couldn't* be much longer, he knew. His legs were turning to rubber while his lungs threatened imminent surrender.

The branches and tendrils of the surrounding forest whipped at him; every second they slowed him, allowing the furious Nibirans to draw that much closer. A foraging mother and child gazed up at him with wide eyes as he bolted past. Sitting on a red branch, a creature that resembled a yellow anemone drew tentacles back into its sack-like body as he sped by. He didn't know if it was plant, animal, or a combination of both, and at the moment he didn't care. Down a slope blanketed in red foliage, across a stream, and into a small clearing he raced—where, startled by his sudden emergence from the thick undergrowth, a massive fanged quadruped reared directly and unexpectedly in front of him.

The phaser Kirk drew was as technologically out of keeping with his surroundings as a ram hydrofoil would have been in a traditional sailing regatta. Before huge paws could come down on him, he hit the animal with a full blast from his weapon. It promptly collapsed in a pile of legs, fur, and dismay, revealing another masked biped behind it. Facing Kirk but weaponless, this second figure fumbled to remove its own facial wrappings. The face soon revealed was contorted, but no more so than usual.

"Dammit, man," Leonard McCoy sputtered, "that was our *ride*! You just stunned our ride!"

Confronting the ship's doctor and still breathing hard, Kirk barely managed to mutter a frustrated "Great" before the babble of the pursuing mob of enraged Nibirans rose above every sound except the dangerously deepening growl of the looming volcano. Gesturing in lieu of speech, Kirk beckoned for McCoy to join him as he resumed his flight. With a last regretful glance at the immobile local riding beast, the doctor followed.

Taking note of the rolled tube of local parchment that Kirk clutched like a relay runner's baton, McCoy nodded in its direction.

"What the hell is that?"

"I don't know." The captain was fighting for breath now, each lungful demanding an increasingly painful effort. He motioned in the direction of the bellowing native throng behind them. "But they were bowing to it." As a second glance showed the lead Nibirans continuing to close the space between them, he drew his communicator with his free hand and snapped the instrument open.

"Kirk to *Shuttle One*: Locals are out of the immediate kill zone. I've . . . given them something else to focus on. You're clear to proceed as we discussed! I repeat, you're clear to proceed! Operation's a go now!" Lowering the communicator, he looked to his left. "You know, for someone whose expertise resides in what is essentially a sedentary profession, you move pretty good." A spear slammed into the tree just to his right.

Behind them, the immense volcano was beginning to spill streams of lava down its flanks, bleeding bright red-orange against the dark basaltic slopes.

McCoy's gasping reply was as dry as the chief engineer's

favorite gin. "Being chased by howling homicidal indigenes has a way of enhancing my sprinting ability." His tone darkened. "Of course, if you hadn't shot our *ride . . .*"

Kirk shook his head. "Can't hear you, Bones. Volcano noise."

"Volcano noise, my—!"

Computer-augmented stability controls notwithstanding, Hikaru Sulu had to fight to hold the shuttle steady. As the interior of a fast-rising volcanic plume and its accompanying blasts of acidic gases was not the most salubrious location for a hovering shuttlecraft, it required Sulu's full attention to keep the compact craft from being knocked ass-over-teakettle. Or worse, cast on an out-of-control vector toward the unforgiving ground below.

There was nothing wrong with audio reception, however. Kirk's voice filled the cockpit.

"Copy that, Captain!" A glance rearward showed that while well under way, preparations for the final aspect of their questionable intervention were not yet complete. Shorn of anything resembling spare time, Sulu made his concern known in no uncertain terms.

"We have to do this *now,* people! If we sit in this murk much longer, the acids in the offgassing are going to start impacting our systems. All we have to do is lose one thruster and we risk going down!"

His warning was acknowledged with a hand wave. It was not half-hearted, but half-human. Turning back to Nyota Uhura, Spock stood stoically as she continued sealing him into the exosuit. Designed for heavy-duty work under the most extreme conditions, the brilliantly metallic, copper-colored suit was far less flexible than its standard-issue cousins. It could protect its wearer from nearly anything, but it could not make Spock comfortable. The latter did not concern the Vulcan. Survival did. Tilting his head slightly to one side, he spoke toward the suit's pickup.

"Captain, did any representatives of the indigenous intelligence see you? At the risk of repeating the obvious and despite the difficulties inherent in our current effort, I must repeat that the Prime Directive clearly states that there can be no perceived external interference with the internal development of an alien civiliza—"

Despite the shuttle's increasingly violent rocking, Kirk's response came through clearly.

"No, Mr. Spock, they did not! I know what it says! I might have missed a few details here and there in certain classes . . ." The admirable clarity of the surface-to-shuttle transmission was confirmed as Kirk's communicator picked up the nearby McCoy's unmistakable sarcastic snicker. *". . . but I didn't miss that one. We're not supposed to be here at all. It's* because *of the Prime Directive that we're having to do this the hard way. Now, drop off your super ice cube and let's get out of here! Kirk out!"*

The science officer would have argued further with his captain save for two reasons: The time to do so had long since expired, and arguing with James T. Kirk frequently generated far more frustration than satisfaction. Filing the details of their brief conversation for future discussion, Spock returned his focus to the business at hand.

As Uhura stepped back, Spock knelt and opened a clamshell metallic case. In addition to the brace of simple unifying electronics that turned the contents of the container from an assortment of seemingly unrelated materials and components into a device of uncommon power and unusual purpose, it was first and foremost a basic but well-made timing unit. After entering final critical information into it, he watched and waited a moment longer to ensure himself that the apparatus had been properly activated. Only when he was certain of this did he stand, maintaining his balance as, despite its stabilizers, the shuttle was rocked by increasingly violent atmospheric forces.

Slipping on the suit's helmet, Spock locked it in place. After clipping the safety line to his chest plate, Uhura moved to ensure that it was solidly affixed to the shuttle's cargo winch. Spock then picked up the case and secured it to the equipment bracket on his side.

Uhura stared at him through the helmet's industrial-strength visor. "Sure you don't want me to go?" Requesting a response was one way of making certain his suit's comm unit was functioning. Her query provoked exactly the sort of reply she expected.

"That would be illogical," Spock responded calmly, "as I am already outfitted in the requisite gas- and heat-resistant equip—"

Stepping forward, she placed an open palm on either side of the heavy helmet. When she next spoke, her tone was utterly different. Soft, affectionate, and full of that meaning that went beyond words.

"Spock. I was kidding." Rising on her toes, she placed a quick kiss on the transparent front of his protective helmet.

"However transitory, even minimal visual distortion is not helpful," he muttered.

"It'll dissipate fast." She stepped back. "Hopefully the attendant meaning won't. You've got this, Spock."

Their eyes locked. The moment, if not the visual distortion, was broken by the anxious voice of Sulu calling back to them from the cockpit forward.

"If we're gonna do this, we've got to do it now! Or we'll lose the shuttle as well as the moment!" Erupting gases jolted the shuttle, sending it rocking dangerously from side to side. Constantly changing atmospheric pressure threatened to knock it into surrounding walls or send it plunging into the fiery lava lake not far below.

It would have been far easier if Spock could simply beam in and out with the ship's transporter. But while they could beam him into the volcano, it would be impossible to set him down on a safe, solid location. To do that would have required a preliminary visual fix: one they had neither the time nor the precise means to obtain. Sometimes, despite the availability of the most advanced tech, nothing worked better than a pair of experienced eyes . . . and being directly on site.

Uhura's hand patted the science officer on the side of his helmet. "I'll see you in a few minutes. Keep cool."

"It is my intention to ensure that everything keeps cool." Spock turned toward the rear of the shuttle's cargo bay.

"Spock!" Sulu yelled from the violently rocking cockpit. "You've got to go now!"

Uhura laid a last look on the science officer, then turned and joined Sulu in the cockpit. Airlock doors shut tightly behind her as she settled into the seat beside the helmsman. Sulu was now sweating as heavily as if he were floating outside in the volcanic flow. Uhura spared a final thought for the science officer rather than for what he was about to do, and then, taking a deep breath, she initiated the drop.

Safely encased in the exosuit, Spock was able to swallow once before the doors parted beneath his feet, sending him on a controlled plunge into the intense heat, towering flames, and swirling mix of gases below. Behind him, the shuttle bay doors immediately slammed shut. The cool transparency of the atmosphere inside the shuttle was replaced by angry yellows and reds as he embarked on a high-speed descent into hell.

Explosive emissions of dark gases, corrosive as well as poisonous, made visual monitoring of his immediate surrounds difficult but not impossible. The heat rendered standard infrared worse than useless. Only focused life-form imaging made it possible for those on board the shuttle to track the science officer's descent, and that only intermittently, what with the continual eruptions of large masses of hot magmatic material. One such discharge the size of a small personal vehicle barely missed Spock as he dropped. The shockwave from its passing rocked him, sending him spinning on the descent cable until he could correct for the atmospheric distortion and steady himself once more. He imagined himself a spider on a silken thread, hunting for the one stable perch above a vat of boiling oil.

Picked out by the shuttle's hasty surface scan, the landing site was right where it was supposed to be. Its spear of metamorphic stability thrust comfortingly above the lava that geysered around it. Though recognition of it was gratifying, securing the visual did not make touching down on it any easier. All around him, huge jets of molten rock the color of the sun fountained upward, threatening to collapse atop his precarious perch and drown him. Air currents rippling with heat made it difficult to maintain position, and despite the best efforts of Sulu and the shuttle's optimizing stability system, perfect immobility was impossible to achieve in the hissing throat of the volcano. The overwhelmed helmsman finally had to admit as much. His voice filled the increasingly warm interior of the exosuit's helmet.

"I can't hold us here! Activity is becoming more violent, and the

stabilizers' algorithms aren't designed to cope with this combination of heat and atmospheric distortion. Spock, we have to pull you back up!"

The Vulcan proffered a reply that was as characteristic as it was in startling contrast to his present surroundings. "Negative, Mr. Sulu. This will be our only chance to save this entire species. If this volcano erupts, this planet dies. I would be remiss in my duties as a science officer were I to terminate this mission now."

Then the cable, stressed by heat and circumstances with which it had never been designed to cope, snapped.

It was not a long fall, but the landing was hard enough. Spock winced as contact was made with the unyielding rocky surface. Jolted from his grasp, the case and its precious contents tumbled toward the molten rock that surrounded the solid stone on which he had landed. As he rolled and struggled to stabilize his position, he fumbled for the Rankine nullifier. Ignoring the pain in his back and ribs, he scrambled to recover it before it was lost to the seething lava. High overhead, the lower length of the broken cable had vanished into the roiling, toxic haze.

To a stunned Uhura, the unprogrammed rapidity of the cable's ascent could mean only one thing. "The line . . . there's no weight on it." Though equally distressed, Sulu had no time to comfort her. As individual components shut down or went offline, the shuttle's performance was being swiftly degraded. Frantically by-passing damaged elements and engaging emergency backups, he was fully occupied in striving to keep them from following the science officer into the volcano's blistering, molten depths.

Rocked by a tremendous blast of superheated air, the shuttle was blown upward several dozen meters before Sulu could regain control. Despite the danger of being knocked to the deck or thrown against the roof, Uhura began to unfasten her seat's safety harness.

"We have to get him back. There's another specialty exosuit in the cargo bay. I can suit up, go down, and pick him up."

With no time to spare for discussion, a grim-faced Sulu kept his attention focused on the controls. Too many readouts had turned a monotonously lethal red, too many more were shifting threateningly from green to yellow. In his left ear, a nearly invisible transmitter relayed a streaming updated info dump, none of it reassuring. Their situation was bad and growing worse.

"Given the ongoing degradation of the shuttle's functions, at this point I'll be lucky if I can get *us* back to the ship."

Her voice cracked; her eyes pleaded. "We can't just leave him!"

Sulu outranked her. At that moment, he wished he didn't. Wishing, however, had no place in the chain of command. "We don't have a choice! We barely have maneuverability, we've been in here too long, and if we stay a moment longer, I can't guarantee that we'll go anywhere but down."

No time, no time. Uncertain even if he could still hear her, Uhura addressed the console pickup. "Spock, we're going to try and get back to the *Enterprise*."

Their discussion was rendered moot as, at that moment, a sizeable chunk of solidifying, red-hot basalt slammed into the underside of the shuttle, sending it spinning wildly upward. Alarms screamed. Fighting to retain control, Sulu entered a navigation sequence, hoping that the shuttle retained enough aerodynamic functionality to comply. If he spent any more time at the manual controls, he wouldn't be ready when the time came to abandon the sturdy but beleaguered craft. Unsealing his flight suit revealed thinner material beneath. It gleamed silver in the uneven glare, incredibly lightweight yet impermeable, simultaneously smooth and scaled while possessed of operational characteristics that had nothing to do with the daily needs of a Starfleet officer. To his right, a visibly shaken Uhura was reluctantly shedding her outer attire to expose a similar undergarment that flashed crimson in the increasingly uneven light inside the shuttle. For the last time, the helmsman addressed the comm pickup.

"Captain, we're pulling out while we still can. Even so, I don't know if we'll be able to make it back to the designated drop location for the ship. I'm ditching the shuttle. You've got to make it to the *Enterprise* on your own."

"*Wonderful,*" came the response from the open comm. There might have been additional commentary, Sulu reflected, but if so, it was lost in a wash of interference. Like every other system on the shuttle, its communications were failing. Knowing the captain as well as he did by now, the helmsman wasn't sure he needed to hear any additional opinions Kirk might have had on the subject of his transport's failure anyway. He could just as easily imagine them.

Despite the damage it had suffered, the shuttle succeeded in exiting the volcano. Though the autopilot managed to put it on course, the rest of the crippled craft was rapidly failing system by system. It was evident to both officers that they weren't going to make it all the way back—though a dazed Uhura wasn't sure she cared if they did or not. Conditioning, not determination, forced her through the necessary motions.

As despair and indifference threatened to overwhelm Uhura's training, Sulu could see the danger. "Uhura—ready to swim?"

Struggling to keep her balance inside the increasingly unstable shuttle, she nodded tersely. "I know you did everything you could.

I'm ready." Her voice strengthened, her professionalism carrying her forward despite what she was feeling inside.

Her thoughts, not to mention her emotions, were elsewhere. If necessary, Sulu resolved to push her out should they have to go down. They'd already been forced to leave Spock behind.

He was damned if he was going to leave Uhura as well.

Kirk was about done. Though fresher than the captain, so was McCoy. The majority of the doctor's limited athletic capability lay in his hands. From the start of their flight, his legs had protested at the unnatural demands being placed on them. As a physician, he was intimately familiar with the physiological indicators of looming physical failure, and he heartily disliked having to apply them to himself. If only Kirk hadn't impetuously stunned the domesticated animal McCoy had obtained for them to ride. *If only a lot of things,* the increasingly exhausted doctor mused. Not that he was surprised. Saddened, was more like it. The entire operation had struck him as a fool's errand from the moment it had first been proposed. Present circumstances had, regrettably, only confirmed that initial opinion.

Nor did their current circumstances suggest that things were going to get any better, he told himself as he shouted at Kirk.

"Jim—Jim, the beach is that way!"

Something sharp and potentially lethal whizzed past the captain's head. A glance back showed that the mob of Nibirans was continuing to close the gap. At the two officers' present rate of retreat, it was only a matter of moments before the next flung knife, or spear, or simple rounded stone brought him and the captain to the ground.

Kirk might be brave, even at times recklessly so, but he was not blind to the reality of their limitations. Besides, they had accomplished his intent—drawing the natives away from the dangerous proximity to the temple. Barely slowing to a stop, Kirk proceeded to drape the parchment over a nearby tree branch. As he released it, the scroll unfurled all the way to the ground, revealing a host of markings and symbols that must have taken some Nibiran scribe untold hours of labor to render so precisely and clearly.

"Jim!" McCoy was nearly out of breath. "This is neither the time nor the place to make a dramatic presentation!" A glance showed that the bellowing Nibirans were nearly on top of them. "Besides which, I don't think your intended audience is in the mood to listen to anything you have to say!"

Kirk yelled without looking back at him. "Doesn't matter— we're not going to the beach!"

"No." Realizing the import of Kirk's words, McCoy's eyes widened. "No no no!"

Whatever the inscribed contents of the scroll, it caused the Nibirans to break off their furious pursuit of the sacrilegious strangers. Spying the cherished document dangling from the branch, they immediately came to a halt and dropped to their knees before it in profound supplication. With hands extended in front of them, they commenced a steady, reverent chanting: eyes closed, heads bobbing. The scripture of the gods had been recovered, and they were giving thanks.

A number of them, however, had more than passive veneration on their minds. For them, there remained the small matter of revenge. To the group of warrior/defenders who continued the pursuit, prayer could wait until those who had desecrated their most holy site had been suitably dealt with. If the gods so willed it, that reckoning would take place very soon now.

Struggling to keep up with Kirk, McCoy still put one foot in front of the other. He was simply not used to moving so fast. Having to do so now did nothing to improve his mood. He was not so fatigued that he failed to recognize the surroundings they had studied prior to the drop, however. He pointed to his left.

"Jim, this is all wrong! The pickup beach is *that* way!"

Kirk looked over at him, each word now interrupted by a short, hasty breath. "We won't *make it* to the beach!"

McCoy knew for certain what was coming now, and he did not look forward to it.

There was not a lot of red forest left in front of them. Unfortunately, its absence didn't translate into the presence of safe ground. It didn't, in fact, translate into any ground at all.

Directly ahead of them the forest disappeared, giving way to a line of blue-green and cloud-pocked sky above. The nearer they drew to the edge of the forest, the more the view ahead was replaced by sky and, soon, by sea. The alien ocean lay too far below, the line at the bottom of the sheer cliff they were approaching marked by gravel and wave-washed boulders. Not that they could have survived such a fall had the rocks been replaced by the softest sand.

They could stop and try to confront the howling locals who were drawing closer every second—or . . .

There was no time for analysis. Without breaking stride, the two men hurled themselves over the edge. As he plunged over the cliff, arms flailing and legs kicking, McCoy barely had time to hear what Kirk yelled as side by side they accelerated toward the waves far below.

It was a sentiment he echoed at the top of his lungs as rocks and water rushed toward them.

★   ★   ★

Slightly more salty than any of Earth's oceans, the water through which Kirk and McCoy now found themselves swimming was murky but unpolluted. Clouds of brightly hued local aquatic life-forms swam past and around them. For the most part, the two humans were ignored. On a couple of occasions, multi-finned predators flashing impressive cutlery approached for a closer look. Both times they circled the swimmers once or twice before twisting sinuously away, having decided that the peculiar shapes did not conform to anything recognizable as their natural prey. Or perhaps it was the suddenly wide eyes of a certain sub-merged doctor that caused them to depart.

Reaching up, McCoy tugged at the sleeve of his silvery, form-fitting suit. The advanced diveskins he and Kirk had worn be-neath their native kaftans now kept him warm in the cool alien depths. Extracted from inner pockets, goggles equipped with at-tached recycling breathers allowed both men to breathe comfort-ably underwater. The emergency devices would last only thirty minutes at most. That would be more than enough for McCoy. He had no intention of remaining in the alien sea even that long.

Despite knowing the location of their destination, it took a while for the two swimmers to orient themselves in their unfa-miliar surroundings. From time to time, they would exchange looks and hand signals before deciding to move onward.

Only when the outlines of a massive, familiar shape began to emerge from their watery surroundings did they begin to relax. Ahead lay something huge and foreign to the world of Nibiru: the submerged bulk of the *Starship Enterprise*. It loomed before them like some great shining inhabitant of the deep as schools of alien water dwellers flashed and darted around it.

The small personnel airlock through which they entered had been designed to deal with the airlessness of space, not an influx of seawater. It still served its function, however, and the minor mess caused by the damp entry of the two officers would not take long to clean up. The few flopping ocean dwellers that had been unlucky enough to be caught in the hasty entrance would profitably find their way into the ship's science labs.

Having removed goggles and inhalers, both men were still catching their breaths when the inner portal cycled to reveal the characteristically disgruntled figure of the ship's chief engineer, Montgomery Scott. The nearby continental supervolcano was not the only thing emitting an excess of heat. Scott's annoyed gaze flicked from one sodden officer to the other.

"D'you lot 'ave any idea how ridiculous it is to hide a starship on the bottom of a bleedin' ocean? Just so the locals won't get a regulation-breakin' gander at us? We've been down 'ere since last night, and my people are sick of 'avin' to—"

Head inclined to his left, a wincing McCoy was struggling to drain the last drops of water from his ear. "Believe me, Mr. Scott, no one regrets our inability to utilize the transporter under these conditions more than I."

Their recent close escape already forgotten, Kirk had no time for might-have-beens. His full attention was focused on the engineer.

"Mr. Scott—*where's Spock?*"

The chief's attitude immediately changed from irritation to worry, reflecting the captain's concern. "Still in the volcano, sir. We picked up Uhura and Sulu not long ago, and they say that's where they left 'im."

Kirk's expression tightened. "*Left* him?"

Scott rushed to explain. "Sulu said he was losing the

shuttle and they had no choice but to pull back. Apparently they were in the process of dropping him when . . . the lift cable broke."

"Broke . . . ?" Kirk was unable to finish the thought. As he fought to extricate himself from the diveskin, it seemed as if every snug twist and wrinkle in the fabric was conspiring to hold him back.

Being quite familiar from his studies with the ancient human concept of Hades, a part of Spock noted and filed for future examination its remarkable similarity to his present surroundings. He had no time for additional philosophical rumination, since the red-hot magma surrounding him was bubbling and heaving steadily higher, even as he worked with increasing speed to activate the device he had brought with him.

He was relieved to see that it had suffered nothing more serious than cosmetic damage. The assorted dents and scratches were of no consequence. Spock did not relax entirely, however, until his entry of a final series of numbers and commands triggered a rapidly decreasing numerical sequence on the nullifier's multiple readouts. On the right-hand side, a fist-sized hollow began to glow an intense bright white.

Rising to his feet, he gazed down at his completed handiwork with a considerable degree of satisfaction: so much so that he was able to ignore the rift that appeared in the volcano's flank. It provided a temporary respite from dying as the lava lake that had been building around him eagerly sought the new egress.

★　　★　　★

Acquiring speed thanks to gravity, the magma tsunami swept down a portion of the volcano's exterior slope, incinerating everything in its path. A tremendous blast sent volcanic bombs the size of shuttlecraft flying ahead of the lava. The first structure to be demolished was the largest native temple on the planet's main continent, crushed by one such plunging mass of rapidly cooling rock. Ordinarily the indigenous structure would have been packed wall-to-wall with worshippers and priests and genuflecting attendants. Uncharacteristically, it was completely empty—those who would normally have been praying and working within having been distracted and drawn away by the theft of an irreplaceable holy scroll. Captain Kirk's actions had saved their lives.

On the bridge, Pavel Chekov swiveled in the command chair. The look on his face was one of relief as he spotted Kirk among those stepping out of the elevator. Throughout the wide, curving room that was the heart of the *Enterprise,* officers and ensigns barely glanced up from the multitude of multihued flashing readouts and monitors that marked their respective stations.

"Keptin on the bridge!" Having formally announced the obvious, Chekov vacated the command seat and gratefully returned to his navigator's station.

Resuming full command as rapidly as he did his chair, Kirk directed his concern toward Communications. It had occurred to him that circumstances might have prevented Lieutenant Uhura from being present, and while Kirk was fully prepared to deal with her absence, he was gratified as well as impressed to see her seated at her assigned station. Those same circumstances prevented him from extending any immediate sympathy, though; there was no time.

"Lieutenant, do we have a channel open to Mr. Spock? Any channel, however limited."

Her reply was patently more taut than usual. "Extreme heat distortion is interfering with his equipment, but we've still got contact. I'll push it as much as we have to."

Struck by the underlying emotion in her voice, he considered commenting on it, and decided otherwise. The need for Uhura to carry out her duties would help to distract her from personal concerns. Right now, he needed everyone on the bridge functioning at a hundred percent efficiency.

How fortunate, he mused dryly, that *he* never overreacted in situations laden with emotion.

"Spock . . . report!"

With the lava lake beginning to rise around him once more, despite having found an exit in the volcano's flank, Spock concluded the final bit of necessary programming to the Rankine nullifier. Straightening, he stepped back from the case. Its dimensions were modest, its capabilities awe-inspiring. *If it works,* he reminded himself.

"I have activated the device, Captain. When the countdown is complete, the consequent geochemical reaction should render the volcano inert, thereby eliminating the volatile tectonic trigger that our calculations indicated would set off catastrophic seismic disturbances throughout the crust of Nibiru."

★   ★   ★

"Yeah, and that's gonna render *him* inert," McCoy put in tersely.

Kirk's mind raced as he growled something decidedly non-regulation under his breath. "Can we use our transporter to pull him out yet?"

At his station again, Sulu shook his head. "Negative, Captain. No more than we could use them from the start, when it was decided to carry out the operation utilizing one of our shuttlecraft. The unstable nature of the magnetic and other fields within the throat of the volcano are such that the usual immutable transporter reach and positioning systematics could be knocked off by as much as several millimeters—which, of course, would be fatal to anyone traveling via beam. I regret to say that the situation has not changed. If anything, it has grown worse."

Chekov chimed in with unnecessary emphasis. "A Mr. Spock retrieved several millimeters out of proper entanglement would not be a Mr. Spock as we know him, Keptin. Or likely one who would appear alive."

Neither of his officers was telling Kirk anything he did not already know. Still . . .

"There *has* to be a work-around, Mr. Chekov. Something we can do to make it function effectively. *We need to beam Spock back onto the ship*. If there's no *perfect* way to do it, then give me the *next* best way."

There was nothing the youthful Chekov liked better than a challenge—though he preferred those that did not involve putting at risk the life of another shipmate. His thoughts whirled, colliding and reforming even as he ventured some of them aloud.

"Maybe if we could manage a direct line of sight? One as close as possible. If we could get right above him, the interference would not be eliminated—but it would be greatly mini-mized. There's no guarantee it would work, Keptin, but it's the best option I can think of."

Scott would have been remiss in his duty had he not chosen to speak up. "Hold position above an active supervolcano on the verge of a cataclysmic explosion? Sir, this ship is designed to hold a position in interstellar space, or in orbit. It was not built to cope with radical in-atmospheric distortions. She maneuvers better at warp speed than on thruster power."

Looking back, Kirk smiled thinly at his chief engineer. "Seems to be doing okay right now, Mr. Scott."

The chief engineer didn't back down. "Because the surroundin' atmosphere is *relatively* stable, sir. I am willing to predict that if we are hoverin' directly above the volcano and it blows, conditions will be more than slightly altered—and not for the better."

"I believe Mr. Scott is correct, sir." Sulu spoke without look-ing up from his instrumentation. "If we were to be caught in a sufficiently violent eruption, I don't think I could maintain altitude. Especially taking into account how close we would be to the surface. There would be essentially no room in which to attempt emergency maneuvering."

A furiously cogitating Kirk contemplated his choices. None of them appealed to him. In any event, he had no chance to reach a conclusion before a voice over the comm interrupted his thoughts. Distortion fractured the message, but the voice was, once again, unmistakable. It also evinced a good deal of exasperation.

"That is unacceptable, Mr. Chekov. In the course of our ap-proach, the shuttle we employed was concealed within the ash cloud and subsequently within the volcano itself, but the Enterprise *is too large to employ such methods. If utilized in a rescue effort, it would invariably be revealed to the indigenous species."*

"More referencing of the Prime Directive," McCoy muttered. "To hell with the Prime Directive."

Fully aware that such an observation would be utterly ignored by his science officer, Kirk tried a more logical tack. "Spock, nobody knows rules better than you. So you must know that depending on the circumstances, there has to be variance allowed. There must be some exception to—"

Through heat, distance, and looming apocalypse, Spock cut him off.

"There are none, Captain. Not in this instance. Revealing the superior technology represented by the Enterprise *would constitute an action that unequivocally violates the Prime Directive."*

So much for logic and reason. Kirk knew there was no time to indulge in the kind of elaborate debate favored by his science officer. "Spock, we're talking about your *life*."

The response was calm and unrelenting. *"The rule cannot be broken under any circumsttssssss . . ."*

Kirk did not have to hear the rest to know that his plea had no more effect than his argument. But he *wanted* to hear the rest of his science officer's words, if only because as long as the Vulcan's voice echoed through the bridge, he knew that his friend was still alive.

"Spock?" Whirling, he addressed his chief communications officer. "Try to get him back online."

There was no one on the *Enterprise* who desired that more than Nyota Uhura. No one who would have given more to hear the familiar measured, assured tones of the ship's science officer. So when she turned to shake her head once, slowly, the full measure of the loss struck everyone on the bridge.

Speaking with difficulty, Chekov looked up from his readouts and broke the silence. "Ninety seconds until detonation, sir."

Kirk stared ahead, gazing at something that lay somewhere beyond the now-imageless forward screen. "If Spock was here, and I was down there, what would he do?"

When no one offered an immediate reply, he turned to once again eye Uhura. She started to speak, paused, said nothing. Her anguished expression told him what she wanted him to do, but as a Starfleet officer she could not say it, and the contradiction threatened to tear her apart.

In the end, it is always physicians who seem to address such questions. The doctor did not consciously seek to imitate the science officer's manner, but Spock would surely have approved.

"He'd let you die," McCoy said without hesitation.

McCoy's words, Uhura's expression. There are times when being captain of a noble ship is grand, times when it is confusing, times when it is troublesome.

At that moment in time, for James T. Kirk, it was hell.

Though very real, the fear left Spock quickly enough. He had been trained to deal with it. Fear was, after all, nothing more than another emotion. Possibly it was not really "fear" he had been experiencing at all. More of a disquiet at the certainty of approaching immolation and the subsequent lapsing of consciousness. That, and a looming sense of loss. Of things as yet undone, of experiences unfulfilled, of a certain relationship left unfinalized . . .

In its wake, there was peace.

It came to him with surprising ease, as much due to who he was as to any formal teaching he had received. Regrets cast aside, he readied himself for the ending. Spreading his arms in a gesture any Vulcan would have recognized, he closed his eyes, tilted back his head, and prepared to embrace emptiness.

They had vanquished the interlopers who had stolen the sacred scroll. The gods would be pleased. Some of those who had participated in the successful recovery ululated ecstatically before the recovered relic. That the gods were happy with their subjects was given additional proof when the temple was destroyed, for providentially, none had been trapped within when the molten rock had come downslope. The loss of the temple itself was not important. What mattered were the scroll and the words inscribed thereon. When queried about the destruction of the temple compound, the priests had avowed that it was the only way the gods could convince their subjects that it was time to raise a new temple, one grander and more impressive than its predecessor. This the people would surely do.

Further proof of the gods' satisfaction soon manifested itself in an entirely unprecedented fashion—one for which even the most loquacious priest had no explanation.

It was as if the air itself had become an instrument. Steady and throbbing, the strange high whine made itself known even above the consistent roar and rumble of the volcano. Then the god appeared before them, in shape unforeseen, in majesty mind-blowing.

Seawater falling from its central deck and nacelles, native aquatic arthropods scrambling to abandon their suddenly motile surface, the sleek bulk of the *Enterprise* rose from the water below the cliff face. It continued to rise above ocean, cliff, and open-mouthed indigenous bipeds until it could turn toward the erupting volcano in the distance. As it accelerated steadily, water from its sides spilled onto the dumbfounded onlookers below. Moaning and writhing, they willingly drenched themselves in liquid that could only be most holy.

00:15 . . . 00:14 . . .

It was genuinely astonishing, the kneeling Spock mused, how much longer a second seemed to take to pass when one had only a few of them left. Around him, the lava lake continued its inexorable rise. At least when the Rankine nullifier, which had cost him so much difficulty and now ultimately his life, finally went off, he would feel no pain. It was better than burning to death, though for a limited time, his exosuit would keep him alive even if submerged in lava before its systems finally failed or its integrity was compromised.

So bright and intense now was the expanse of molten rock that it started to affect his vision even with the photosensitive visor set to maximum dark. The diffused orange glow became pure white and seemed to tug at his optic nerves, taunting his eyes. No matter. If he was destined to go blind, it was a condition he would not be required to suffer for long. His natural curiosity chafed at the thought of being unable to observe the final moment preceding his passing.

There was a moment of disorientation. For the onset of death, it felt oddly familiar. Almost as if . . .

His vision began to clear. Responding to the decrease in the surrounding illumination, his visor now allowed him a more expansive field of sight. The heat that had begun to overwhelm the exosuit's advanced cooling systems did not simply begin to fade; it vanished.

He could see shapes coming toward him that were neither molten nor rock. He recognized his surroundings. He was alive. He was not pleased.

Kirk was first into the transporter room, with McCoy close behind. Reflecting his excitement, the doctor was breathing hard. He had been forced to do entirely too much running this morning. Halting near the entrance to the transporter room, he rested one hand on the doorway as members of one of the ship's relief and rescue teams rushed past him.

An anxious Kirk immediately focused on the figure in the center of the transporter platform. The smoke and steam that rose from the exosuit encasing the science officer made it impossible to tell if it was intact, just as it prevented Kirk from ascertaining the condition of the individual within. Even if the Vulcan was still alive, he might be burned beyond recognition: his skin peeling away, his lungs seared, his . . .

"Spock—you all right?" Unable to help and desperately wishing to do so, Kirk could only gaze worriedly, as the suit was still too hot to embrace.

For a terrible moment there was no reaction from the armored shape. Then the first officer of the *Enterprise* stood. Scanning the team that had assembled in the transporter room, he finally focused his attention on Kirk. When he spoke, his tone was disbelieving.

"Captain, you let them see our ship."

Standing next to Kirk, McCoy raised a hand and allowed himself to relax. "He's fine."

Ignoring both his science officer's admonition and his chief physician's sarcasm, an immensely relieved Kirk flashed a wide smile. "Good to have you back." He would have continued, but for an interruption from the room's speakers.

"Bridge to Captain Kirk."

Uhura's voice. Kirk kept his tone wholly professional. "Yes, Lieutenant?"

"Monitors indicate transporter function is complete. Is . . . Commander Spock on board, sir?"

"Safely and soundly," Kirk reported. Then he added, "The commander's principal concern of the moment is not for himself, but for the possibility that our ship may have been observed by the natives."

"'Observed,' indeed," Chekov murmured to no one in particular. "We passed right over a bunch of them."

Uhura responded to Kirk in an equally cool, professional voice.

"Please notify Commander Spock that his device has successfully detonated." Emotionally overwhelmed, she terminated the communication from the bridge.

His attention still on the safely returned Vulcan, Kirk did not dwell on the abruptness evident in his communication officer's response. "Congratulations, Spock. You just saved the world."

"Captain. You violated the Prime Directive."

"So they saw us." The commanding officer of the *Enterprise* shrugged. "Big deal."

Before the science officer could respond further, Kirk signaled to the members of the emergency response team. Any further deprecating comments disappeared beneath a whoosh of coolant gas and sprayed decontaminant.

In a way it was a miniature, if technologically far less sophisticated, version of what at that moment took place within the fracturing supervolcano. As the separate elements within the Rankine case Spock had delivered to the mountain's throat merged, the resultant physiochemical reaction sent a wave of blue energy blasting in all directions. The case and its physical contents disintegrated, but they were no longer necessary. The self-propagating reaction they had initiated spread and expanded, sending waves of force not only throughout the volcano but down into the rapidly expanding magma chamber far below. The effect was to slow molecular motion within the molten rock. In other words, to cool, with remarkable speed and extraordinary efficacy.

Around the rocky pinnacle where Spock had prepared to meet his demise, the lava solidified. Racing down into the depths, the reaction continued to work its magic. The throat of the volcano turned to solid basalt while the vast magma chamber below ceased to boil. Its energy stilled, its anger calmed, the violent eruption that had been building within the supervolcano was aborted. Still farther below, the three continental plates that had been on the verge of shifting catastrophically continued to grind away slowly against one another. The danger of a major quake devastating this portion of the planet and casting its rapidly maturing indigenous intelligence back into the darkness of the primitive hunter-gatherer receded. It might be hundreds of years, thousands, before such a danger to the planet's rising intelligence raised its threatening white-hot head again.

In the jungle outside, the already overawed natives looked on in astonishment as the sacred mountain belched forth not fire and fury, not flame and destruction, but a mile-high blast of rapidly cooling and perfectly harmless steam. Nor was this to be the last miracle, for truly the surprises of the gods were forever forthcoming. This final marvel was no less startling than the suppression of the looming volcanic eruption or the appearance of the enormous airborne deity. It was something even the simplest villager could reach out and touch.

Around the villagers, on their buildings and children and vegetable gardens and bemused domesticated animals, it had begun to snow.

II

Like the clock itself, the muted cry of the alarm verged on the antique. The ancient digits on its primitive face read 5:00.

The beeping woke a tired man who had long since ceased to be concerned about the latest, the newest, the most technologically advanced version of anything material. His entire world, his entire existence, had collapsed around him.

Unconcerned by such considerations and now equally awake, the dog clambered joyfully over him and the woman who had been sleeping next to him. Dark-haired, dark-skinned, she was more beautiful than the day they had married. She watched as he rose quickly. They did not speak. Speaking would invariably lead to the subject that concerned them most, that had all too swiftly come to dominate their lives: a shared heartbreak they could scarcely handle.

The pain that shone in his eyes did not arise from his back or any other part of his body. The ache that circumscribed his existence came from elsewhere. It could not be assuaged by medicine old or new, by physical manipulation traditional or unconventional. He only knew that he could not live with it. There had to be a fix. There *had* to be. Otherwise he knew that while his body might live on, his spirit would die.

Under normal circumstances, the silence that now filled the bedroom would have been comforting. That was no longer the case, and had not been so for some time now. Only one thing would now comfort the man. Maddeningly, that one thing was completely outside his control. He was a spectator to the slow, agonizing demise of his own soul, and could do nothing about it.

The knowledge of his own helplessness in the face of the tragedy that loomed over him tore at his gut every waking hour of every day.

Turning, he found himself gazing into the face of his wife, his life partner. They had been through everything together. Despite the anguish that now consumed them, their love held strong. If love could fix the present situation, all would have been well and done with months ago. But what they faced could not be healed by love.

It's all in the hands of others, he thought morosely.

Where his eyes flashed impotent rage, hers revealed a lack of sleep. Plainly she had been awake much of the night. Watching him, perhaps. Or staring off into the distance, hoping to see a savior and finding instead only four walls on which was painted nothing but desperation.

He shambled slowly to the bathroom. Like the rest of the apartment, it was modern yet comfortable, clean of line without being stark. He performed the usual ablutions. He treated his teeth. In the mirror, a half-dead man stared back at him.

Have to do better than this, he told himself. *For her, if not for yourself. Appearances. Morale. Pull it together, man.*

He splashed water on his face, and the cold shock helped. So did the attentive presence of the dog that watched and wondered and, by his casual canine indifference, helped to remind his master that the world outside had concerns that went beyond his own.

A glance through the window restated the dog's assertion. The towers of London soared skyward in the soft light of early morning. Some were of recent vintage, reflecting advances in building materials as well as shifts in architectural taste. Others lingered from earlier eras, refurbished to contemporary standards or preserved as structures of historical importance. Aircars both public and private soared between the towers. The Celts would not have recognized the skyline, nor would the Romans or the Vikings or any of their successors. London was every bit as much an eternal city as Athens or Rome. Bustling with triumphs and tragedies, it would go on no matter what.

As he headed back to the bedroom and to his waiting, silent wife, the man was not at all sure the same could be said of himself.

The rural thoroughfare down which the sleek silver hovercar hummed was not equipped with a guide strip embedded in the surface, thus forcing the man to do his own driving. The effect of the lush English countryside through which he and his wife were speeding did everything to try and improve their mood, and failed. Actually there were three passengers, if one counted the plush bunny that reposed in his wife's lap. The gentle permanent smile on its fuzzy face was not replicated on the visages of the two human passengers. In the distance behind them, loops of suburban London sprawl curled across the green hillsides.

By now the turnoff among the trees was all too familiar to them, as was the sign they whipped past: ROYAL CHILDREN'S HOSPITAL.

The original Victorian estate was well preserved and the extensive modern additions indistinguishable from their architecturally important predecessor. After parking underground, the couple made their way up to a corridor with which they had also become far too familiar. Alerted to their arrival, Dr. Ainsworth was waiting for them. He glanced at the bunny that the woman clutched to her chest like a plate of medieval armor, and began to speak. Softly, knowingly, but not reassuringly. He desperately wanted there to be a surrogate for the truth. That was something all physicians had wished for since the beginning of time. For this couple, he had none. No substitutes for a harsh and uncaring reality.

As he spoke, air gurneys driven by hospital attendants drifted quietly past them while nurses moved from room to room. His calm but unyielding words were, unfortunately, nothing new to both of them. Occasionally they nodded without comment as they listened, long since numbed to what had become a sorrowful, unyielding litany. No change. No improvement. There being nothing more he could do, the doctor left them to their grief. There is a point in medicine when more words become not only useless, but counterproductive. Experienced as he was, the doctor knew that point had been reached.

★   ★   ★

The girl on the bed was eight years old. Cocooned by the most up-to-date equipment at the disposal of modern medicine, she lay motionless, breathing slowly and evenly, her eyes closed. Her skin was soft and the color of fine cocoa. What remained of her long black hair was combed neatly away from her face. The disease that was devouring the raven strands along with the rest of her body had rendered her even more slender than usual. She was barely clinging to life. She would not see her ninth birthday.

Her mother lifted the little girl's too-thin arm and slipped the bunny underneath it, willing herself to believe that her daughter could feel the touch of synthetic softness. She looked for a smile, a twitch, a reaction of any kind. There was none—only the soft hum and occasional beep of the attentive but emotionless devices that were keeping her daughter alive. Bending, she gently stroked the girl's left cheek and kissed her lightly on the forehead while with her left hand she tightly grasped the delicate fingers of the girl's right hand. As always, there was no response. Having held back as long as she could, the mother began to cry. Outside the hospital room window, a country breeze stirred the leaves in trees that kept watch.

Unable to keep it together any longer, her grief-stricken father turned and fled the room.

It was peaceful on the old stone deck outside the hospital. In the distance, the towers of Greater London pierced the horizon. Here and there, patients sat alone in chairs, enjoying the fresh air. Nurses and attendants wordlessly pushed less mobile patients from place to place across the carefully landscaped yard, sliding them among rows of flowers and shrubs like ships between green waves. Birds called—against all odds, wild birds still dwelled in the English countryside. Even that cheerful chorus could do nothing to impact the man's misery. Complete, utter, and overwhelming, his despair was matched only by his sense of powerlessness. His daughter was being taken from him, her life draining away as surely and steadily as liquid from a punctured bottle, and there was nothing he could do about it. Nothing.

"I can save her."

Startled and uncomfortable at having been observed in such a vulnerable position, the young man turned.

"What did you say?"

The stranger who had spoken looked to be about the same age as the distraught father, though it was difficult to tell for certain. His hair was neatly combed, his body beneath the unremarkable clothing svelte and solid. His face was narrow, his eyes remarkably penetrating. Grief-stricken father and enigmatic visitor stood eyeing one another. At the moment, there was no one within earshot—they were alone with the grounds, the hospital, and each other.

"Your daughter. I can save her."

There had been no hesitation in the stranger's voice, no uncertainty. It hinted at an unshakable confidence that would extend to everything upon which it might choose to comment. The stranger had been stating a fact, one his tone suggested was incontrovertible.

A ridiculous claim, Tom Harewood knew. All the best doctors had been consulted. International specialist sites had been queried. There was nothing more that could be done for his daughter. And yet . . . and yet . . . there was something about the oddly imposing stranger that deserved, if not confidence, at least a question.

"Who are you . . . ?"

He broke off. The stranger's expression was one of silent, un-spoken presumption. Harewood struggled to focus on it, but it was difficult to see anything save the face of his wife, and of an eight-year-old girl whose condition had degenerated beyond anything resembling encouraging.

Those faces and not the words of the stranger kept Harewood from simply turning and walking away.

Like many finely crafted antiques, San Francisco's Golden Gate Bridge only grew more beautiful with age. Indifferent to humans and their steadily advancing technology, fog still rolled in from the cold Pacific. Easily pierced by modern communications and perceptors, it remained as lazy and soft in appearance as when its climatic magic had first been encountered by wandering sailors whose most advanced tech back then consisted of discs of ground glass slapped together inside a metal tube.

Constructed farther inland, the section of Starfleet Headquarters whose grounds two officers were presently traversing was contrastingly bathed in warm sunshine. Attired in gray dress uniforms, the pair drew appreciative glances from lower-ranking personnel and civilian visitors. James Kirk expanded under the admiring stares while his companion stolidly ignored them. Vanity, Spock reflected as he noted his friend's reaction to the sometimes envious looks, was among humankind's least estimable characteristics. Having pointed this out to his friend on more than one occasion and receiving only laughter in return, the science officer had ceased to comment on the widespread cultural defect.

"This is it," Kirk said confidently. "I can feel it."

"Your 'feeling' aside," the Vulcan responded sardonically, "I consider it highly unlikely that we will be selected for the new program."

Kirk feigned hurt. "Why else would Pike want to see us? Forget about seniority—this isn't about procedure. It all adds up. Consider: They gave us the newest ship in the fleet. Who else are they gonna send out? Who's better prepared or better equipped?"

The science officer did not hesitate. "I can think of numerous possibilities."

Undeterred, his fellow officer looked meaningfully skyward. "A five-year mission. Five years! Just think what that would be like. No proscribed patrol responsibilities, no spending months and months on standard maneuvers. Five years doing nothing but exploring deep space. An extended mission devoted to science and discovery. We could really get *out* there." He lowered his gaze. "As a science officer, I can't imagine anything that would be more appealing to you."

"In that opinion, I most heartily concur. However, I estimate the odds of our being chosen for the project at less than three-point-two percent."

Eyeing his companion, Kirk could only shake his head in wonder. Spock was his friend, but sometimes . . .

"So you're saying that our odds of being chosen are *more* than three-point-one percent?"

As usual, the captain's carefully crafted sarcasm was utterly wasted on his first officer. "Obviously."

"Where do you even *get* those numbers? We are for certain getting chosen. Why wouldn't we? Don't be such a pessimist, Spock."

The science officer looked over at him as they turned a corner on the open quad. "Realistic and considered analysis of a given situation is not pessimism. It is reality. My life is firmly grounded in reality. Something of which I believe yours could do with a more frequent injection."

For a second time, Kirk shook his head sadly. "Shoot me if I prefer excitement and happiness over stability."

One eyebrow rose. "I find more than adequate happiness in a firm appreciation of reality. As for excitement, in my capacity as your science officer, I experience a surfeit of that particular quality without having to seek it out. I would venture to go so far as to say that I experience it to excess."

"Ah, yes," Kirk murmured. "Moderation in all things. How typically Vulcan."

"It would not hurt you to try it," Spock shot back. "It might even benefit your captaincy."

Kirk drew himself up, suddenly stiff and formal. "All right, I will."

His first officer evinced genuine surprise. "You will?"

"Absolutely." He gestured ahead. "We're here. When Pike tells us we've been selected for the mission, I promise to exercise moderation by saying 'I told you so' only one time. Per day. For no more than several weeks, whose absolute number shall remain indeterminate until you express contrition."

As they started up the stairs, Spock did not comment. Knowing Kirk as he did, he realized there was nothing to be gained by prolonging the discussion—least of all, a sensible, mature reaction. It was not so very long ago that attempting to discuss similar matters had resulted in a physical altercation between the two men, not to mention a raft of violent arguments. All had eventually been resolved, and without hard feelings. But the memories certainly remained—as did their often radically different ways of approaching a problem.

For a long minute after being admitted to the admiral's office, the two younger officers encountered no reaction at all. Having not been instructed to seat themselves, they were left standing to ponder in silence as Pike stood staring out the window behind his desk, his back to them. The view of the city beyond was impressive and, on this especially beautiful day, engrossing. But not so much as to engender the continuing silence, Spock thought. Exchanging a glance with Kirk, he saw the same bemusement in his friend's expression.

After what was entirely too much time to qualify as reassuring, the senior officer finally spoke.

"Uneventful."

Though Kirk had to strain to hear it, the single word was perfectly intelligible. As to what it signified, he had not a clue. "Admiral? Sir?"

Reluctantly abandoning the view, Pike pivoted and seated himself at his desk. The silver-headed walking cane he set aside was smooth and functional, engraved. A new one, Kirk noted with interest. The admiral had amassed an impressive collection. Waving a hand, Pike activated the readout before him and spent a moment studying it. Eventually his gaze rose to meet Kirk's.

"That's how you described, in your captain's log, your survey of the world its inhabitants call Nibiru. Uneventful."

His attention on the admiral, Kirk missed the look cast in his direction by his science officer. It was as close to an expression of pure astonishment as a Vulcan could muster. With barely a shrug, Kirk indicated the readout.

"You know me, sir. I like my reports to be concise. Senior officers are confronted with so much information these days that I'd be the last to overload a captain's log with excessive detail. I didn't want to waste anyone's time going over—"

Pike interrupted the younger officer's amiable disquisition. "That's all right, Captain. I'm not put off by detail. I tend to find much of it more enlightening than excessive. Some of it proves to be quite interesting, in fact." He waved a forefinger at the readout. "Take the report's subsection on planetary geology, for example. Tell me more about this supervolcano. Supervolcanoes are very interesting structures. According to the data, this one was situated directly above a conjoining of three continental plates, a unique geologic nexus that was further destabilized by a number of proximate major earthquake faults. A very unstable tectonic situation; one might even say volatile. Sufficiently volatile, one could conclude, that if the volcano were to advance to a highly eruptive state, it might set off a series of quakes that in turn could severely jostle the relevant trio of continental plates. The resulting catastrophe could wipe out all life on that part of the planet. Certainly all higher life." His gaze narrowed. "*If* it were to erupt."

Kirk smiled understandingly. "Let's hope it doesn't, sir."

The admiral did not smile back. "Something tells me it won't."

"Well, sir," Kirk demurred, "'volatile' is a relative term. Far from scientifically specific. Anything is possible in such a situation. Maybe our data was off. We weren't at Nibiru long. Under such circumstances, a lot of data has to be gathered as quickly as possible and refined later. Information needs to be adjusted in light of additional study. Even data relating to a supervolcano that might at first glance appear to be on the verge of a violent eruption."

Pike nodded slowly, pausing a long moment before responding. "Or—maybe it won't erupt because Mr. Spock detonated a meticulously crafted and custom-designed counterthermal Rankine wave device inside it right before a civilization that's barely discovered the concept of the *wheel* happened to see a *starship* rising out of their ocean." His gaze shifted to the science officer. "My apologies for the somewhat condensed summary of your report, but that *is* the way you describe it, is it not?"

Sudden understanding hit Kirk like a chunk of falling meteorite as he whirled on his first officer. "You . . . filed a *report*?"

"Following exploration of a new or lightly contacted world, all individual starship sections are required to file a full report." He favored the familiar figure seated beside him with an unblinking stare. "Why would you assume Science would not do the same?"

"I thought you would, of course, but I assumed you'd run it by me first. Why didn't you *tell* me?"

His voice flatter and more machine-like than usual, the science officer responded in a tone that only slightly mimicked the voice pattern of his friend.

"I incorrectly assumed you would tell the truth in your report."

Kirk's expression tightened. "I *would* have if not for the inconvenient exception I had to make in order to *save your life.*

Or did you decide to omit that from your report because you considered it an 'excessive detail'?"

"On the contrary," the science officer responded, "I took care to include it along with all related information. It is something for which, on subsequent reflection, I am immeasurably grateful, and the very reason why I felt it necessary to take responsibility—"

Kirk would have none of it. "And that would be *so* noble," he broke in, "if *I* wasn't the one getting thrown under the bus, Pointy!"

Both eyebrows rose. "'Pointy'? Is that an attempt at a derogatory reference to my—?"

"*Gentlemen.*" The admiral's legs might not work as well as they once had, but there was nothing wrong with his voice. Both younger officers went silent as the senior officer rose from the seat behind his desk, utilizing his cane for support. "As you've clearly forgotten, please allow me to remind you: Starfleet's mandate is to explore and observe, and if necessary, to defend. Not to *interfere*. The Prime Directive is the first thing new cadets memorize—not the last. No matter how stressful the circumstances, I find it difficult to believe it could be forgotten. Or worse, overlooked." He eyed them meaningfully. "The Prime Directive supersedes *everything*, gentlemen. Even initiative."

Spock responded. "Had the mission that we set ourselves gone as planned, Admiral, the indigenous sentient species of Nibiru would never have become aware of our interference. Or our presence. The operation was designed from the outset to preserve every aspect of the Prime Directive."

"That's a technicality." Pike was plainly displeased by the science officer's response.

"I am Vulcan, sir. We embrace technicality."

"Sir, if I can be allowed to explain—" Kirk hurriedly injected.

Not hurriedly enough, as Pike glared hard at the Vulcan. "Kirk, shut up. Are you giving me *attitude*, Spock?"

Unfazed, the science officer continued. "I am expressing multiple attitudes simultaneously, sir, each one of which can be differently parsed. To which are you referring?"

Sitting back in his chair, the admiral began tapping the fingers of one hand on the desktop. "Logic should serve to illuminate, not complicate. Your attempt to substitute ambiguity for clarity is misguided. Out. You're dismissed, Commander."

Spock hesitated, cast an indecipherable look at his friend and superior officer who had not been summarily dismissed, and wordlessly departed. Behind him, he left a quietly furious Kirk and a thoroughly exasperated admiral of the fleet.

Pike started to say something, paused, chose to reload with different ammunition. "Do you have any idea what a pain in the ass you are?"

Kirk kept his reply as even as possible. "I think so, sir."

The admiral nodded slowly. "Good. That's progress, I suppose. Now, tell me what you did wrong. What's the lesson to be learned here?"

Without glancing back at the doorway or cracking a smile, Kirk replied stone-faced. "Never trust a Vulcan?"

Pike's frustration as well as his irritation came through plainly in his reply. "You can't even answer the question without injecting impertinence. Despite what it says on your record, I have to keep reminding myself that you're actually a starship captain. If not for your last-minute heroics in saving Earth from . . ." His voice trailed away, momentarily lost in memory of a recent near-catastrophe. Then he straightened in the chair. "What it boils down to is that you *lied*. You lied, Kirk, on an official report."

The younger man's reply was impassioned. "The intent was to observe the relevant rules to the letter, sir. Which we did. Had we not proceeded with the designed mission, it is highly likely a developing intelligent species would have been wiped out. Or at least had their maturation set back hundreds, perhaps thousands of years. Even worse, there was a distinct possibility that if we had held back, there would have been no interference with the Prime Directive, because you can't interfere with a species that's been rendered extinct. The decision to chance revealing our presence was wholly mine. Mr. Spock disagreed, and was ready to disagree to the death." His expression twisted. "My saving his life caused him no end of anguish, or the Vulcan equivalent thereof. Though I believe he has since come to terms with still being alive. With a Vulcan, one can never be sure of such things."

Pike was not appeased. "You think the rules don't apply to you because you disagree with them."

"With all due respect, sir." Kirk spoke deferentially, all trace of snarkiness gone. "I thought that's why you talked me into signing up in the first place. Why you took a personal interest in my progress. Why you gave me your ship."

The admiral sighed. Only when he spoke again did his fingers cease drumming on the desk. "No, I gave you my ship because I saw greatness in you." He hesitated. "And now I see you haven't got an ounce of humility."

Unwavering, Kirk met his mentor's gaze. "What was I supposed to do? Let Spock *die*?"

"You're missing the point."

The younger man's voice rose. "I don't think I am, sir. What would you have done?"

"I wouldn't have risked my first officer's life *in the first pla*ce. You were supposed to survey a planet—not alter its destiny. You violated a dozen Starfleet regulations and almost got everyone under your command killed!"

Kirk refused to back down. "Except I didn't. You know how many crewmembers I've lost since—"

"That's your problem," Pike harshly interrupted. "You think you're infallible. You think you can't make a mistake. There's a pattern with you, that rules are for other people."

"Some should be," Kirk muttered.

Pike ignored the comment as he continued. "And what's worse is using blind luck to justify your playing God."

Both men went silent for a moment before the admiral continued, more quietly. "Given the circumstances, this has been brought to Admiral Marcus's attention. He convened a special tribunal, to which I was not invited. You understand what Starfleet regulations mandate be done at this point."

Kirk did not, but as he pondered the alternatives open to such a tribunal, a terrible realization slowly began to dawn.

Pike confirmed it. "They've taken the *Enterprise* away from you. And they're sending you back to the Academy."

When he could finally speak again, Kirk tried to defend himself, even though deep inside he was beginning to realize that the decision, along now with everything else, was beyond his control. "Admiral, listen . . ."

"No." Pike was having none of it—frustrated, hurt, and angry, he seemed no longer inclined to listen to anything his disgraced protégé might have to say. "No, I'm not going to listen.

Why should I listen? You don't listen to anyone but yourself. No, I can't listen!" Realizing his efforts were futile, Kirk went silent.

"You don't comply with the rules," Pike continued more calmly. "You don't take responsibility for *anything*. And you. Don't. Respect. The chair. You know why?"

His next words fell on the already stunned Kirk like a hammer.

"Because you're not ready for it."

IV

It wasn't much of a room. More of an isolated loft. The imperfect accommodations did not matter to its sole occupant. With issues of much vaster import on his mind, he rarely paid attention to his surroundings. Any comfort he needed was found within himself. It had been intended that way from the beginning, though to look at him, no one could tell it was so. Off to one side, an antique music player was emitting the soothing sounds of a time gone by.

At the moment, he was engaged in drawing his own blood. Made to function painlessly, the extractor caused him no discomfort. It did not matter. He would have reacted with equal aplomb had it been necessary to hack off a finger and catch the resultant crimson flow in an ordinary glass. Such stoicism was his blessing. Such stoicism was his curse.

When a sufficient quantity of red liquid had been drawn, he

disengaged the extractor. As it left his flesh, the device automatically sealed the entry it had made, leaving the man's arm smooth and unmarred. From the extractor, he transferred the blood to a small glass vial. The man held it up to the light. There was nothing remarkable about its appearance . . . only its chemical composition.

Carefully, he slipped the vial inside a small rectangular box of polished wood. Into the opening beside the vial, he added a single ring of dull silvery metal. Though indicative of a division of Starfleet, the jewelry was not flashy or eye-catching. If anything, it was a bit on the bulky side, like the kind of rings that were commonly awarded for winning sports competitions. The owner of the vial and the ring smiled at his silent comparison. That there was no one present to see him smile did not trouble him at all. He knew the father of the sick little girl anxiously awaited the forthcoming gift. Expressions of mild amusement were for the benefit of the donor alone.

The bathroom was unchanged, but not its owner. The man staring into the mirror was scared. Tom Harewood had been terrified for a long time now, but for someone else. This was different. Not that it mattered. *The end justifies the means,* he kept telling himself over and over. Silly old trope. Nothing but a foolish juvenile meme. No less valid for all that, though.

The package had been delivered by private courier. He had half expected it never to arrive. In addition to a vial of blood, the dark-toned box contained a single ring. Harewood carefully switched it with the apparently identical silvery Starfleet Academy class ring he was already wearing. He was a bit surprised that the newly arrived metal loop fit perfectly. Given what he had managed to learn about the individual who had provided both vial and ring, he knew he should have expected nothing less.

A glance into the bedroom revealed the empty bed: its covers turned back, the spread rumpled. His wife was not there. She was at the hospital, keeping futile watch, waiting for a miracle without the slightest awareness that it was on its way. She would be expecting him, her daily relief in the ongoing tragedy that their lives had become, but not this early. He would surprise her.

Beyond the bedroom, a softly spoken word from the apartment's owner caused a closet door to slide open. Inside were neat rows of casual clothing, shoes designed for various outings, and shirts reflecting their owner's extensive travels. The far end was occupied by more formal wear. Each uniform was spotless and naturally sharp. Starfleet uniforms. Harewood selected the one he felt best reflected his mood and the deeds to be done.

In the final throes of her graveyard shift, the greeter at the hospital's front desk barely acknowledged Harewood's arrival. Like the rest of the hospital regulars, she now knew both him and his wife by sight. The fact that today he was clad in a Starfleet uniform as opposed to his usual civilian attire hardly registered on the sleepy attendant. She ran his ID without even looking at it, relying on the security processor to do its usual competent job.

Harewood found his wife sleeping in a chair not far from his daughter's bed. As usual, there was no movement from the bed itself. Careful not to wake his wife, he worked his way through the tangle of conduits that now were all that kept his little girl from expiring.

From a pocket, he removed the vial. Moving to one of the nearby medical instruments, he placed it in an open receptacle and watched as it began to drain. A proximate transparent container filled with liquid holding vital nutrients and salts now began to add medication of a different kind, as blood from the vial began to diffuse into the otherwise clear fluid. From there, it would flow into his daughter's body. Had a doctor or nurse been witness to the process, they would have been appalled and immediately sounded an alarm. But Harewood was alone in the room with his family, and had been assured the transfusion would work swiftly.

He had been here often enough and had asked the right questions to have a good idea what the numbers and readouts on the instrumentation surrounding the bed indicated. As he stared, they began to change. Indicators that he had not seen since before his daughter had been admitted to the hospital appeared and flashed. On the bed, a slight smile appeared on her face—a sign the pain that quietly racked her tiny body was fading. The stranger had kept his promise, Harewood realized.

His daughter would live.

That was it. Nothing more to be done.

No, that was not quite right. Bending over the girl, he kissed her softly on her smooth forehead. Much as he wanted to, he held back from repeating the gesture with his wife. However feathery, a kiss might wake her. Then there would be questions. Then she would wonder why he was not staying. Why today he could not take her place on watch.

The attendant at the front desk did not bother to sign him out as he hurried from the hospital.

Now, Harewood knew, it was time for him to keep his end of the bargain.

KELVIN MEMORIAL ARCHIVE

The sign above the imposing structure gave no indication of the importance of what was housed within.

Pausing on the rain-slicked sidewalk outside the entrance, something caused Harewood to turn. A flurry of vehicles soared past overhead, carrying early morning commuters to those jobs that required their actual physical presence as opposed to virtual. At that moment, Harewood desperately wished to be on one of them. Nothing would have pleased him more than to be on his way to a dull dead-end job, one wholly pedestrian and entirely without surprises.

Across the street stood the man with whom he had struck the bargain. The man who had somehow, in defiance of everything Harewood and his wife had been told, saved their daughter from a slow, certain death. He was watching. Quietly, calmly, without the slightest sign or suggestion of concern.

Harewood turned and entered the building. The arcade was old, perhaps eighteenth century. He was resigned now. At peace with himself. Renege on the agreement, and the miracle for which he was about to trade everything might evaporate, its promise never to be fulfilled. That was what he had been told, anyway, and he had no choice but to follow through on the last of his instructions. That was the warning Harewood had been given.

Can't back out now, he thought. It didn't matter. He had long since resolved to see the matter through to its end. It was not about him, anyway.

Would the frontline guard in the lobby notice anything

unusual about his latest visitor? No, the guard was interested only in verifying his visitor's ID as the light from the scanner traveled up and down Harewood's face and upper body. When the check was successfully completed, the guard waved him on and returned to monitoring his readouts.

Surely someone will notice something's not normal, Harewood thought. He fought to stay calm as he entered the thankfully empty elevator and thumbed a control. The lift started down, its descent uninterrupted. B-8, B-9, B- . . . A casual observer would have remarked on the unusual number of subterranean levels the elevator ticked off.

The real secret of the archive was that nothing was archived within. Few were curious enough to consider that in an age of multiple instant information backup, there was no need for such a facility to store anything that was not antique. The name was as much an artifice in reality as it was on the front of the building.

Emerging from the lift, Harewood entered a vast underground chamber. Working to maintain his poise, he paused to garner a glass of water from a dispenser. Around him, people and automatons were hard at work on shuttles and ship components, armaments, and modules that were intended for special operations in the cold reaches of deep space. Sparks flew, and in the distance, heavy machinery moved expensive equipment and components into position to be assembled by other robots. From time to time, he nodded in recognition to personnel as they passed.

An open work cubicle provided a semi-refuge from all the activity. Though he had barely been noticed, Harewood was still unaccountably nervous. Setting the water down on the small desk area, he made no attempt to mate a communicator, light player, or any other device to the cubicle's secure dock. Working quickly, he sent the brief transmission he had composed. Then he sat quietly, contemplating the glass of water.

When he had let as much time pass as he thought wise, he slipped off his finger the silver-hued ring dominated by the insignia of Starfleet. Holding it over the glass, he hesitated ever so briefly.

No going back, he told himself. *Not now.* For his wife's sake, for his daughter's sake, he dared not hesitate.

He dropped the ring into the water—a Starfleet Academy class ring that was something more than what it seemed. He might have murmured something under his breath. A name, a hope, a prayer. There sounded the mellifluous *plink* of something solid and metallic landing in liquid. It began to fizz. To tremble, then to bounce.

His wife . . .

He never finished the thought, or anything else.

Tom Harewood vanished, the first casualty of the shockwave that tore across the underground chamber, obliterating everything in its path. Metal was twisted and torn, ceramics shattered, high-tech materials shredded. In the fiery burning chaos, mere flesh simply disintegrated. There was scarcely enough time for those trapped to scream before they died.

Above ground, a section of London erupted in flame and smoke. Successive concussions continued to detonate for some time after the initial explosion, sending flames, earth, debris, and people many stories high.

As old blues and new conversation filled the bar behind him, an utterly miserable James Kirk stared at the liquid in the glass on the table in front of him. It was rich and golden—unlike the ruins of his career.

The woman a couple of seats to his right was beautiful, and she smiled pleasantly enough when he grinned at her. *Still have that, at least,* he told himself.

Without uttering a word, a charcoal-and-gray uniformed senior officer abruptly sat down between them. Staring morosely down at his half-empty glass, unable to meet the older man's gaze, Kirk could only sigh.

"How did you find me?"

"I know you better than you think I do." With a glance at the bartender, Admiral Pike ordered for himself. "The first time I found you was in a dive like this. Remember that? You got your ass handed to you."

"It wasn't like that," Kirk mumbled.

"It wasn't? It was an epic beating."

Kirk's voice was beginning to slur. "No, it wasn't."

"You had napkins hangin' out of your nose," a remorseless Pike reminded him. The image, if not the memory, forced Kirk to laugh softly. "A good fight," the admiral continued. After a pause, he added, "I think that's your problem right there."

Frowning, Kirk turned to regard his mentor.

"They gave her back to me," Pike told him. "The *Enterprise*."

Kirk took a moment to digest the news. He wanted to respond with something clever. Wanted to be brilliant, to be sharp. But all he could say was, "Congratulations." No, that wasn't enough. "Watch your back with that first officer, though."

Pike shook his head. "Spock's not going to be working with me. He's been transferred. *U.S.S. Bradbury.*" The admiral let that sink in before saying, utterly unexpectedly: "You're gonna be my First."

As Kirk gaped at him, Pike continued. "Yeah, Marcus took some convincing. But every now and then I can make a good case."

Stunned by a combination of alcohol and the unexpected revelation, Kirk could only mumble a reply. "What—what did you tell him?"

"The truth." Pike stared hard at the younger officer. "That I believe in you. That if anybody deserves a second chance, it's Jim Kirk."

Not a good place or time to lose it, Kirk told himself, fighting to keep a grip on his emotions. "I don't know what to say."

It prompted a gentle, knowing smile from Pike. "That *is* a first." Quietly he added, "It's gonna be okay, son."

He would have said more save for the beeping interruption of his communicator. Flipping it open, Pike regarded the information displayed, and frowned. "Emergency session, Daystrom. That's us."

"Yeah." Still overwhelmed by the sudden change in his situation, Kirk's reply was barely audible. Pike gave him a perfunctory rap on the arm.

"Suit up."

Kirk was securing an overlooked fastener on his uniform as he rounded a corner. Reflecting the lateness of the hour, the interior of Starfleet headquarters was bathed in light; perfectly adequate illumination that was less harsh than bright sunshine. Despite the urgency of the call to Admiral Pike, he was still surprised to note the presence of additional security within the complex itself. Incoming personnel were undergoing multiple scans. Something was surely amiss, or so many would not have been called in at this time of night. What in Holy Asimov's name was going on?

A figure appeared off to his right. Kirk increased his pace in hopes of avoiding any contact, to no avail. Recognizing him, the figure intercepted the captain long before he could hurry out of sight. Though caught, Kirk neither slowed down nor acknowledged the newcomer.

"Captain."

It was amazing, an irritated Kirk reflected, how much import the science officer could cram into a single word.

"Hey." Kirk kept on walking fast. This either did not offend the Vulcan or did not register with him as an indication of discontentment. Kirk's continued lack of response, however, did.

"I sense," Spock observed thoughtfully, "that you remain displeased."

Kirk did not turn to look at the slender officer who continued to parallel his progress. "As usual, your powers of observation and analysis remain unsurpassed."

"Sarcasm. You see, experience has taught me how to recognize it more accurately."

"Bully for you. Why don't you put your discovery in a report?"

"Linguistics are not my specialty. They are more the department of . . ." His voice faded away as if remembering something else. When he resumed, it was as it had been before. "Oh, I see. More sarcasm. Perhaps my sensitivity to that particular aspect of human speech is not as perfected as I thought."

This time Kirk did look at him. "What? Something about the redoubtable Mr. Spock is not perfect?"

"Please, Captain. I am trying to make general, nonspecific conversation. This will prove difficult if you respond with derision to everything I say."

Kirk's voice rose, though not so much as to draw attention from any of the other passing personnel—many of whom were wearing serious expressions and moving with unaccountable speed.

"What do you expect? They took the *Enterprise* away from me. From both of us."

If Spock was falsifying his reaction, it was superbly done. "Captain?"

Kirk shook his head sharply. "Not anymore. 'First Officer.'" No, the Vulcan was not faking: He was genuinely surprised. "I lost my ship, Spock. Demoted. And you were reassigned."

The science officer said nothing as they entered an elevator and Kirk snapped at the audio pickup. The door closed.

"It is fortunate the consequences were not more severe."

"What?" Kirk gaped at him. "Oh, come on! You gotta be kidding me! No, no—maybe you're right. I could've been kicked out of Starfleet altogether, right? Parsing the Prime Directive, that's a dismissal charge. Except that it resulted in saving a burgeoning civilization from being knocked back in development a couple of thousand years. Ordinarily that'd be reason for praise and promotion. It might've been, too, if the whole business had been left alone for a while. Things could have been mentioned through channels, revealed quietly a little bit at a time. Starting with the xenologists' news of the good that we did would have percolated gradually upward through Starfleet. Words would have led to papers, papers to discussion of an exception. But, oh, no, there's no room for patience in the mind of certain officers. It's all gotta be reported right away and by the book, or not at all."

Spock silently digested Kirk's rant before making an effort to respond supportively. "Captain, it was not my intention—"

A bitter Kirk cut him off. "*Not* Captain!" There was no

humor in his sardonic smile. "Let's keep the new ranks straight, shall we? By the book, as it were. I saved your life, Spock. I suppose I should be glad you mentioned *that*. Maybe that's why I'm still in Starfleet." He waved a dismissive hand as the lift door started to open. "It all boils down to one thing, Spock. You wrote a report, and as a result I lost my ship."

They encountered fewer personnel in the upper level walkway. Intent on their assignments, none paused in their grim-faced hurrying to acknowledge the arrival of the two other officers.

"I see now," Spock murmured, "that I should have alerted you about the report I submitted."

Taking a deep breath, Kirk tried to explain. "This isn't about the report! You just don't get it, do you?"

"Please enlighten me, Captain— Please show me where I am failing to 'get it.'" They turned a corner.

"Look," Kirk began, "what's done is done, okay? Nothing's going to change that. I made a decision to do certain things on Nibiru, and you made the decision to file a formal report. That's all over with, finished. I'm talking about afterwards. I'm talking about *now*. I respect your subsequent discipline or whatever it is, your decision to act but not to *feel* anything about the consequences of your action, but I can't react like that. So, yeah, I'm a little pissed off. What I'm trying to say is that it would be nice to see a little compassion for what's happened." Kirk changed his mind and rejected Spock with a wave. "Forget it. This is like trying to explain a kid's reaction on Christmas morning to a computer."

Spock was about to request a detailed explanation of this analogy when, probably fortunately, they were confronted by an approaching captain who chose to engage them. Or at least one of them. With a perfunctory nod at Kirk, the newcomer directed his attention to the science officer.

"Commander Spock. Captain Frank Abbott, *U.S.S. Bradbury*. Guess you're with me."

"Yes, Captain. I was only recently informed that I had been reassigned."

Continuing on the way the two other officers had come, the captain receded down the corridor. Both officers stood watching until Abbott had disappeared around the last corner. Kirk was still mad, but more than anything, he was unimaginably frustrated.

"The truth, Spock . . ." he mumbled under his breath. "I'm gonna miss you."

No response was forthcoming. There was only that mildly quizzical Vulcan stare. *Shouldn't expect him to understand,* Kirk thought. The science officer hadn't understood before: There was no reason why he should now. *Waste of time trying to make him see things from my point of view. From a* human *point of view.* Without another word, Kirk turned and resumed heading toward his destination.

Spock watched him go. His expression, as usual, was quite unreadable. After a moment's hesitation, he followed quietly.

He regretted very much that there must be appropriate words he did not know how to utilize in such situations.

V

Purposefully muted, the light in the conference room was dimmer than in the corridor outside, throwing the faces of the still-assembling group into sharp relief. Except for admirals Pike and Marcus, it consisted entirely of captains and their first officers. The absence of any lower ranks, even to monitor the meeting, signified the seriousness of the moment.

As Kirk sat down beside Pike, he noted those present. Some he recognized from personal encounters, others he knew from scanning records: at least two dozen in total. Whatever was going on must be more than a little significant to demand the presence of so many active Starfleet officers in person instead of virtually. Especially at this hour. So caught up was he in the gravity of the moment that he paid no attention to the fact that Spock had taken a seat beside Captain Abbott.

Whispered conversation ceased the instant Admiral Alexander Marcus began speaking. He launched into what he had to say before anyone could so much as salute or offer a greeting.

"Thank you for convening on such short notice. By now all of you have heard what happened in London. The target was a Starfleet 'data' archive. Now it's a damn hole in the ground and forty-two men and women are dead. One hour ago, I received a message from a Starfleet officer who confessed to carrying out this attack, and that he was being forced to do it by this man.

"Commander John Harrison," Marcus continued as the image of the individual in question appeared on each screen in front of the assembled officers. "And he was one of our own." Plainly, the admiral was struggling to repress the full strength of his feelings. "He is the man responsible for this act of savagery. For reasons unknown, John Harrison has just declared a one-man war against Starfleet."

This revelation prompted the expected murmurs of disbelief and uncertainty on the part of the assembled. There was nothing about the accused individual's appearance to suggest hidden homicidal tendencies, a proclivity for mass destruction, or for that matter repressed madness. If anything, he looked ordinary, younger than his actual age, both his face and bearing competent but undistinguished.

Kirk studied the image intently: registering the man's features, memorizing his physical details, intent on fixing in his mind a permanent image of who was ultimately responsible for the tragedy that had taken place in London. There was something about the aspect of this officer, though, something in his gaze that hinted at much more than a tendency to rebellion. Kirk couldn't identify it, but it was there.

Automatically he glanced across the table at Spock. The science officer was likewise locking away the appearance of the disaster's instigator for future reference, but otherwise the Vulcan betrayed no reaction.

A new image appeared before the assembled and now wholly absorbed group of officers. Kirk recognized it immediately as a still lifted from a security recording. Though taken from a distance, it had been magnified and enhanced so that the result looked as if it had been shot from an optimum angle. It showed the individual the admiral had identified as John Harrison in the process of entering a Starfleet jumpship. He carried no visible accoutrements other than a pair of duffel bags.

"Five minutes after the explosion in London, Harrison commandeered the jumpship that you see and made a run for it. Despite the confusion attendant upon the destruction, security was able to locate him only moments after his departure. We had him on our scanners until he entered orbit, then—"

"Any idea where he might be headed, sir?" inquired one of the assembled officers.

Marcus shook his head. "The natural assumption is that he's not operating alone. You are all aware that there are numerous entities human and otherwise who would be delighted to see Starfleet's operational capabilities impaired. Whether Harrison is doing this for reasons of his own or on behalf of as-yet-unknown forces, we have no way of knowing. Until individually eliminated, all possibilities must be considered. Bearing that in mind, under no circumstances are we to allow this man to escape Federation space." Harrison's image was now replaced by a dimensional map of the immediate stellar vicinity.

"You here tonight represent the senior command of all Starfleet vessels in the region, whether for R&R, refurbishment, or other reasons. As of now, your ships are recalled to full active duty. Those whose crews are presently aground will recall them immediately, and in the name of those we lost, you will run this bastard down. This is a manhunt, pure and simple, on a scale and of an importance unmatched in recent Starfleet history. So let's get to work. Captain Ford, you'll stand off and monitor Quadrant 11C. Captain Delcourt, *Yorktown*—you'll take Quadrant 12D. Captain Evans, *Vasquez*—you'll take . . ."

As Marcus continued doling out individual marching orders, Kirk examined the security still of the fleeing Harrison. The smaller but no less detailed image appeared directly in front of him, enigmatic and uninformative. Using the controls on the monitor in front of him, he was able to enhance it. His gaze traveled over specific sections of the image, seeking details that might not have been immediately apparent at first sight. Frowning, Kirk zoomed in further on the figure of Harrison, rotated it, turned it to and fro. What finally drew his attention was not the fleeing man, but the fact that he carried clean luggage that apparently had not been damaged in the extensive destruction. It suggested the two bags had been stored elsewhere. It also suggested forethought, preparation, and perhaps something more. He turned toward Pike.

"Wonder what's in the bags?" he murmured speculatively. "Where's he going?"

Pike quickly chided him. "Keep your mouth shut."

If the younger man's words escaped Marcus's notice, those of his commanding officer did not. "Chris? Everything okay there?"

Within the conference room, conversation suddenly ceased as all eyes turned toward the two men who had been whispering.

"Yes, sir," Pike responded. "Mr. Kirk is just acclimating himself to his new position as my first officer."

It wasn't enough for Marcus. "You got something to say, Kirk, say it. Tomorrow's too late."

Kirk swallowed. "I'm fine, sir. My apologies for the interruption. I was thinking out loud."

"Not loud enough, Kirk. I didn't hear you. Last chance to share your thoughts with the rest of us. Spit it out, son. Don't be shy. If you have something worthwhile to say, then say it. Speak up."

There was only one man in the room, perhaps on the planet, to whom Kirk would have deferred, and that man was seated next to him. He glanced questioningly at Pike. With a diffident wave of one hand, Pike peremptorily gave his protégé permission to bury himself. It was all Kirk needed to plunge onward. Looking on, a couple of the other officers shook their heads incredulously. But most were attentive, if dubious; curious to see what the recently demoted captain might have to say with regard to a complex situation that was painfully devoid of facts.

"I was just wondering," Kirk began, "why the archive? All that information is public record. If he really wanted to damage Starfleet, this could just be the beginning."

Marcus stared across the conference table at the younger officer. "The beginning of what, Kirk?"

"And then there's the question of what was in the bags he's carrying, sir. He obviously came prepared for the consequences of his actions. What really has me puzzled is, if he went to all the trouble of somehow convincing someone else to do the bombing *for* him, and if the bombing is then traceable back to him—which it obviously is, since you just told us as much—why would he be anywhere near London when the event occurred, much less on a Starfleet base, where his presence could be recorded? Couldn't he just as easily monitor its progress and 'success' from, say, Cape Town or Ushuaia, and then manage his getaway from there?"

Marcus didn't hesitate. "Maybe he suffers from an overriding urge to observe his handiwork in person. Maybe it's because he's a psychopath. Maybe it's because he—"

"If I might interject, Admiral . . ."

Attention swung from the byplay between Kirk and Marcus to the only Vulcan in the room. Next to him, his new commander struggled to keep himself under control as he admonished his recently assigned first officer. "*Mr. Spock,* first officers speak when spoken to, especially during a conference that is charged with—"

An irritated Marcus gestured impatiently. "It's all right, Captain Abbott. Let him speak." His tone was dry. "I'll resume when *everyone else* has had their say."

Whether or not the science officer discerned this most recent example of human sarcasm, it was impossible to tell, but in any event it did not dissuade him from continuing.

"It is curious that Harrison would commandeer a jumpship with no warp capability if his intention was to escape. Presuming the latter, one would expect him to try to reach a transporter-equipped orbiting station. I would think our efforts to interdict him would be better focused here rather than farther out, no matter whom he might count as possible allies. Unless, of course, his immediate intention is *not* to escape." At which point the science officer directed his gaze not at the listening admiral, but at Kirk.

His thoughts already accelerating down the same horrible, unavoidable path, his friend needed no prompting to voice his corollary feelings.

"Sir," Kirk said quickly to Marcus, "in the event of a terrestrial-based attack of the magnitude of the one London has just suffered, protocol mandates that if possible, senior command gather all available captains and first officers at Starfleet headquarters so that subsequent directives can be discussed and delivered in person. Right *here*. Right now. I'm of course familiar with security procedures for Starfleet in general, but at this moment I'm especially concerned about this one particular conference room." He glanced meaningfully at his immediate surroundings. "Is this area secure?"

The admiral's communicator beeped for attention. As he reached for it, Marcus nodded reassuringly at Kirk. "I'm well ahead of you. Standard perimeter automatics are on high alert and patrols with live personnel have been activated." He addressed the open communicator. "This is Marcus."

Having been caught up in Kirk's line of thought, Captain Abbott leaned toward his colleague. "So let's say that you're right and this renegade doesn't try to get off-world. Let's say that's just what he wants us to think he's going to do. But why? Why would he engage in an elaborate misdirection like that . . . ?" His eyes widened slightly. "You're suggesting this Harrison *wants* all of us here? While he's still on Earth?"

Kirk nodded vigorously. "Yes, sir, all of us, right here, right now."

"Kirk, you heard the admiral. We're completely secure here. Just because Harrison somehow managed to pull off one monstrous act of sabotage doesn't mean he'd be foolish enough to try and build on that by—"

"And this happened when . . . ?" an alarmed Marcus was saying into his communicator even as Abbott was finishing his thought.

First there was a whine, high-pitched and rising. Before it could be identified, it was accented by a blinding refulgence that flooded the conference room.

Kirk quickly got out of his chair and took a couple of steps toward the window that comprised one wall. Seconds later, he whirled and yelled:

"Clear the room!"

The conference room was located on the eightieth floor. Automated weapons systems mounted higher up normally would have targeted the intruder and let loose. Instead they remained inert, their internal programming having been interdicted . . . as the alarmed Marcus had just been informed. As if that were not enough, the intruding craft was now hovering so close to the tower's exterior, all but touching it, that the building's roof-mounted defensive weapons would have been unable to depress far enough to draw a line-of-sight on it even if their programming was suddenly restored.

Seated forward in the nearly transparent cockpit, John Harrison took note of the bipedal thermal images within the otherwise shielded conference room. He could have left the task of isolating them to the jumpship's automatic targeting software. It was not in his nature, however, to permit machines to intervene on his behalf. Not when he could take personal control of an action. There was no pleasure in flying an aircraft on autopilot, no satisfaction for a chef in cooking with a timer. For that matter, a few indiscriminate blasts from the jumpship's weaponry could quickly have destroyed the building's entire eightieth floor. But this was not London and he was not the pitiable, easily manipulated Thomas Harewood. This was much more intimate, much more personal. Where would be the terror for those impacted in perishing from a few quick, all-consuming bursts?

He found it much more satisfying to pick them off one by one, swinging the jumpship back and forth just outside the tower, unleashing its weaponry in a controlled, precise, and wholly enjoyable manner.

As the room around him disintegrated piecemeal, one violent explosion following close upon another, Kirk threw himself over a table and flattened himself against the floor. On the far side, Pike was talking rapidly into his communicator, sounding an alert and calling for help.

A cadre of security officers came pouring into the room, firing through gaps in the damaged walls at the jumpship hovering outside. The distraction forced the attacker to momentarily swing the jumpship out of range and then back again so he could deal with them, giving several of the senior officers in the room time to escape the flaming, blinding carnage.

Captain Abbott was pinned beneath a collapsed support beam, screaming in pain. Only Vulcan strength allowed Spock to free his commanding officer and drag him toward the door. Medical personnel who had accompanied the first rush of security brought the injured man down the corridor outside, toward the elevator and safety. No one would have said anything had Spock chosen to go with them. Instead, he hurried back into the room to try and help those who remained within.

The metallic gleam of a pulse rifle that had fallen from the hands of a dead security officer caught Kirk's eye. Snatching it up, he scrambled from the room. Unlike his colleagues who had successfully managed to flee, instead of racing for the elevator, Kirk turned and ran a short distance down the cross corridor.

Turning a corner, he pushed his way into an empty suite of offices. Through the transparent wall, he could see the raging jumpship hovering almost directly outside, still darting back and forth as it dodged defensive shots from the security officers inside the building. Its own armament continued to pour fire into the ruined conference room. Raising the rifle, Kirk let loose a single shot that brought down the thick safety glass in a shower of glistening shards. Rushing in from outside, a blast of cool moist air immediately struck him. Clutching the rifle tightly, Kirk took careful aim and began firing at the undamaged jumpship.

Rising, Pike made a break for the hallway. Damaged legs failed him and he didn't make it, taking a glancing blow from one of the dozens of bursts that were being unleashed by the jumpship. He went down hard, and tried to pull himself along the floor as the room continued to disintegrate around him.

Kirk soon saw that his shots were doing little if any harm, producing nothing but sparks on the flanks of the armored jumpship. Staring into the darkness, he could clearly make out the figure of the pilot seated in the cockpit. For a moment, John Harrison was staring directly at him. There was no anger in the man's expression, no unrestrained fury. For all the emotion he was showing as he continued raining mass murder on the interior of the tower, Harrison might as well have been a machine. In the brief instant he locked eyes with the desperate Kirk, there was no sign of strain, no indication of stress. No humanity.

Putting down the useless rifle, Kirk retreated into the building. There had to be something else he could use to put an end to the massacre. Something, anything. He looked around wildly. There was nothing in the offices he had entered that could be used to take down a flock of seagulls from the Farallons, much less a Federation jumpship. Desks, projection units, personal effects—he was about to give up and race back to check on Pike's condition when he spotted the fire panel in the far wall.

Fashioned of an unyielding carbon fiber designed to withstand the enormous pressure it had to contain, the thin fire hose coiled in the wall recess could fill a burning suite of offices with retardant in a matter of seconds, smothering an incipient blaze before it had a chance to spread. Unspooling it, Kirk frantically wrapped it around the rifle. That the weapon was still perfectly functional was evident when he used it to blow out the section of wall that framed the broken window.

Spock raced over to the severely wounded Admiral Pike; their eyes met in recognition an instant before yet another lethal burst from the jumpship struck both the floor of the room and the crawling Pike, sending him spinning to one side.

Marcus, to his credit, had not fled the room. Standing by the entrance to the hall, he fought to direct the activities of an increasing rush of personnel, waving and gesturing frantically. "Get those people out of here!"

As the jumpship was forced to dodge ever wider to evade the increasing stream of defensive fire from inside the building, Spock managed to reach Pike. Already in shock, mouth agape, the admiral now focused his gaze on something distant and unseen. Grabbing him under his arms, the science officer dragged his limp body out of immediate danger.

★　★　★

Rushing to the edge of the now-windowless gap and sliding to his knees, Kirk clutched the tied-off rifle. Eighty stories below, the main quad beckoned. Lights everywhere swept the sky as they tried to focus on the jumpship, whose weaponry continued to pour death and destruction into the tower. As ground-based defenses began to gather around the base of the tower, Harrison kept his craft bobbing and weaving like a prizefighter. He would dart upward, then down at a sharp angle, cut around one flank of the building before returning to let off another burst at the interior.

Forcing himself to bide his time, Kirk waited until the jumpship came closer. Then he rose and flung the pulse rifle as hard and far as he could in the direction of the deadly craft's starboard cylindrical air intake. One of the office desks would have served his purpose even better had he been able to tie it to the fire hose, but though strong, he was no Vulcan. The rifle would have to do.

Striking the jumpship's intake, the weapon was immediately sucked inside. Its arrival presented no difficulty to the craft's sophisticated propulsion system. Neither did the slender fire hose that remained fastened to the weapon. The considerable section of wall to which the sturdy end of the high-tech hose was secured, however, was a different matter entirely. As the massive chunk of free-pour polycrete and reinforcing metal mesh was ripped from its place, Kirk had to dive to one side to avoid it. Just missing taking off his head, the irregular mess whooshed past, ripping through office furniture as if it were made of cardboard.

Following the pulse rifle and the coil of hose, the heavy chunk of building slammed into the jumpship's critical intake. This was followed by an eruption of light, flames, and a thunderous explosion. Belching smoke, the fatally stricken ship shuddered, lost power, heeled to one side, and started to spin uncontrollably, picking up speed as it did so.

Rushing to the open edge of the building, Kirk looked out. A single figure was discernible through the transparent cockpit. For the second time, the two men locked eyes: one staring downward with satisfaction, the other peering upward through the transparent canopy and—unreadable.

Swirls of white light from the cockpit grew so intense that Kirk was forced to momentarily glance away. When he managed to look back, there was no sign of the jumpship's pilot. Kirk was still pondering that when the crippled craft smashed into the side of the building. Flames erupted from within. For an instant, he thought it might hang there, eighty stories above the ground. Then it broke free of its temporary perch to plunge to the paved quad far below. When it smashed into the ground, it sent up gouts of flame and debris that fell far short of reaching him. Clinging to dangling cables for support, Kirk gazed hard at the remnants of the ruined jumpship.

For a long moment there was no sound but the wind whipping in off the bay. That, and the distant cries of wounded officers and security personnel seeping out from the battered conference room nearby.

Within that scene of fire and destruction, an intent Spock gently laid a hand on Pike's face and commenced to do what he could. Too late. Not even a Vulcan meld could retrieve and heal that which was no longer present.

★   ★   ★

Returning to the scene of the attack, Kirk found Spock peering helplessly down at Pike's limp form. The admiral's eyes were still open. While there was no expression on the Vulcan's face, there was bereavement in his eyes as he removed his right hand from the dead admiral's head. Kirk put the tips of his fingers against Pike's throat. The gesture only confirmed what the science officer did not say. Both survivors—one fully human, the other only half—exchanged a wordless glance. As Spock looked on in silence, Kirk lowered his head and fought to stem the rush of emotion that surged within him.

Christopher Pike was dead. The man who had not only stimulated Kirk to enter Starfleet, but who had quietly mentored him, encouraged him, chastised him when necessary, and grudgingly praised him when possible, would no longer be there to provide advice, suggestions, consolation, and yes, discipline, when needed. Another father lost. Another of the very, very few with whom Kirk could reveal himself, with whom he could be open and straightforward and . . . innocent . . . was gone. Wordlessly, he rose, resting a hand on the science officer's shoulder for support. Spock did not object.

Relief and medical teams were pouring into the conference room. Hasty organization was taking the place of chaos. The injured were being evacuated, the dead placed to one side. Kirk might have assisted, but his heart wasn't in it. Given his present state of mind, it was more likely he would have simply been in the way.

That's what Pike would have told him.

Kirk did not get much sleep that night. His mind was filled with the sights and sounds of destruction and of men and women dying. Every time he would start to drift off, a face would catch his attention. It was that of John Harrison, shrinking away from him, trapped in the crippled jumpship, falling toward his death eighty floors below, and utterly, voicelessly, indifferent to his apparently imminent destruction. Falling—and vanishing, in spirals of white luminance. What had happened, there at that moment fraught with death and devastation? A brilliant flare, and then nothing. *Was* the man dead? Kirk doubted it. There had been too much purpose in that burst of luminosity—and in that preternaturally calm upward-gazing stare.

His communicator demanded attention, shattering his contemplation. "Yeah?" he said toward the unit.

The instant he heard who was on the other end, Kirk was fully attentive.

"Jim," Scotty was saying, "I searched the wreckage of the jumpship. You're not gonna believe what I found. You've got ta come, right away."

"D'you have any idea what we're dealin' with here, man?"

Belying the bedlam of the previous night, the day had dawned clear and sunny. Only the presence of crews working atop the headquarters' tower and around the crash scene at its base indicated that anything out of the ordinary had occurred. Repairs were being made to the eightieth floor, and the wreckage of the shattered jumpship was being hauled away. Not far from the damaged headquarters, oceangoing commerce on the bay moved normally.

Waiting for Kirk and Spock near the building's undamaged entrance, Montgomery Scott was cradling a piece of debris.

Kirk arrived out of breath. "Scotty. I got your message." He frowned at the mangled lump of metal, metallic glass, and synthetics. "Please tell me that you've got something that'll help us find who did this."

The *Enterprise*'s chief engineer hefted the mass of battered and fused material. Within its depths, like spots of color in a pointillist painting, could be seen individual components that were still recognizable. Most were shocked and scorched, but some stood out as nearly intact.

"This was recovered from the crashed jumpship." Turning, Scott nodded at where the salvage team was still picking apart the remaining wreckage. "Nobody was quite sure what it might be, so images were flashed around. As soon as I saw it, I came down and requested possession. Close inspection confirms that I saw what I thought I saw . . . I think."

Kirk cocked his head to one side. "So what is it you saw that you say you think you saw? Something worth saying?"

"I'll say." Scott turned serious. "If I'm right, and I'd bet 'alf the contents of the best back bar in Aberdeen that I am, this is the remains of a portable transwarp beamin' device. No wonder the scrap iron boys cuttin' apart that mess o' a jumpship didn't recognize it!"

Kirk stared hard at the engineer. "You know what happened here?"

The chief nodded somberly. "Makes no sense. Word is it might be some kind o' personal vendetta or somethin'."

"We'll learn the motivation when we find the perpetrator." Reaching out, Kirk tapped the ruined transporter. "Do you think there's enough math left in this thing's memory for you to trace where he went?"

"I already did, sir." Scott's tone was unusually grim. "And you're not gonna like it."

Though the device Scott cradled showed ample evidence of the damage it had suffered, one readout was intact. It showed only a simple number:

2314-3456

Kirk knew what it signified, and it only confirmed what the chief engineer had said.

He did not like it at all.

VI

The sheer number of security and administrative personnel packed into the office of Admiral Marcus made it difficult for anyone else to enter. Kirk and Spock lingered outside until the crowd had thinned considerably before deciding they could wait no longer. Ignoring frowns of disapproval and annoyed stares, they pushed their way forward until they stood in front and slightly to one side of Marcus's desk.

Though he spoke with resolve and clarity, the admiral had the look of a horse rode too long and put up wet. Kirk found himself sympathizing with the senior Starfleet officer. The higher up that one rose in the chain of command, the greater the pressure to perform. An emergency situation like the present one soon separated out those who could handle stress from those who crumpled beneath its weight.

". . . triple security details outside all major Federation facilities: Paris, Rome, Sydney. All automatics are to be activated, and I want anyone requesting access to a sensitive area to have to pass visual inspection based on the latest distributed data, as well as face-to-face querying from a live human being. Right now we can't trust security to mere machines. I want yellow alert imposed on—"

"Admiral." As Kirk rushed into the conference room, he spoke rapidly to get Marcus's attention. Before the senior officer could lay into him for interrupting the string of orders he was unspooling, Kirk charged forward. "There's no need for the enhanced security, sir. Not if your intention is to take him into custody. He's no longer on Earth." With the image of the dying Admiral Pike still at the forefront of his thoughts, it was all Kirk could do to maintain his composure. The fact that the ever-unshakable Spock was standing behind him helped. Aware that everyone including Marcus was now staring at him, Kirk breathlessly continued.

"He's on Qo'noS, sir."

Dead silence enveloped the room until Marcus spoke anew. "Gentlemen, ladies, others—give us a minute."

Casting curious glances at the two newly arrived officers, the security and administration personnel filed out of the office. The quiet that took the place of their absence was almost painful. Marcus did not allow it to last.

"Qo'noS?"

Kirk straightened. "Yes, sir."

"And you know this how?"

"Mr. Montgomery Scott, my—former—chief engineer, is an expert on many things, from the newest warp drive to the oldest scotch. Something in the widely disseminated visuals of the wreck of the jumpship Harrison used to attack Starfleet caught Mr. Scott's attention. At his request, this object was delivered to him. Upon more detailed examination and analysis, it was determined to be a portable transwarp beaming device. Externally it was a mess, but internally, much of it remained intact. By examining its innards and its inner records, Mr. Scott was able to divine the receive point from its last use." His gaze flicked upward. "Obviously no matter how advanced its tech, a unit small enough to fit on a jumpship wouldn't have the power to transport anyone much farther than orbit. Under Mr. Scott's probing, the device gave up a whole sequence of numbers and coordinates. Harrison transported to an automated cargo station. Before anyone on a nearby inhabited monitoring station could think to question what he was doing there, he had accessed its heavy-load transporter to continue on his way. According to Mr. Scott, *that* transporter was employed to relay him to an unmanned vessel in orbit around the moon. Subsequent inspection revealed that another unauthorized transwarp device had been placed on it and wired into the empty ship's engine. A device powerful enough, if its entire energy output was compiled and utilized for a single massive burst, to send someone willing to take the risk of attenuated physical dissemination and consequent serious injury to a single destination anywhere in this galactic region. The effort burned out the device, but a record of the attempt was retained." Kirk paused. "Mathematically, at least, it appears to have been successful."

"Very clever," Spock could not keep from commenting. "It would take an exceptionally robust human to survive such a radical transporting. Even a Vulcan would be stressed. But if successful, the perpetrator would be safe. Burning itself out with the effort, the transwarp device could not be used by anyone to follow."

Marcus listened carefully to both men, missing nothing, before nodding that he understood. "So Harrison's gone to the Klingon homeworld. Is he defecting? Or just defective?"

"There's no way to know for sure, sir," Kirk murmured, "without interviewing him for ourselves."

Marcus shook his head slowly. "Somehow I don't think John Harrison is going to sit still and answer questions, even if you could capture him alive. Which you cannot."

"That remains to be seen, sir," Spock pointed out. "The recordings preserved by the now-useless transwarp transporter were very precise. Not only can we tell that he transported to Qo'noS, we can resolve the transmitting to a specific corner of that world. It is apparent that he has taken refuge in the Ketha Province. His choice of Qo'noS as a refuge now makes sense. He likely believes that even if the Federation can determine where he went, it will not dare to follow. At the same time, he can hardly be certain of a welcome by the Klingons. So he transports to their homeworld, but chooses to materialize in a region that has been uninhabited for decades."

Marcus frowned. "How do we know this Ketha Province is uninhabited?"

The science officer continued. "The Klingons make no secret of its long-ago abandonment, sir. There was a plague in what was formerly a heavily developed region that their medical science could not counteract. The most ruthless methods were employed to finally stamp it out."

"I'd rather not ponder what passes for 'ruthless methods' among the Klingons. And this province has not been repopulated since?"

"No, Admiral. It is a well-known fact among those who are familiar with Klingon history and society. While the Klingon Empire has expanded to other worlds, this one province on their own homeworld remains deserted, rather like the obverse of a national park. Its extensive central conurbation and abandoned industrial facilities remain a place to be noted but shunned, not visited."

"He must be hiding there, sir." Kirk stepped up to the edge of the desk. "Spock's analysis is correct." Beside and slightly behind him, the science officer half raised an eyebrow but said nothing. "He knows if we even go *near* Klingon space, much less their homeworld, without a formal invitation, that would be all the excuse they'd need to ignite all-out war. They'd welcome it, I suspect. Starfleet can't go after him. Not formally. If we tell the Klingons there's a human refugee wanted on Earth for mass murder, they'd delight in giving him sanctuary just to spite us. That's if they haven't done so already. We both know that a formal Federation request for extradition sent through normal diplomatic channels would be laughed at. But if the *Enterprise* can get in close enough to insert a small landing party—say, one hoping to quietly study the lingering effects of the plague that ravaged the Ketha Province . . ."

Marcus let out a derisive snort. "And if the Klingons discover you . . . ?"

Kirk smiled. "We'll say that we just wanted to do a quick study and be gone. That much is true. We'll add that we did it without telling them because we know that if we'd asked they never would have given their permission. They'll appreciate that: It's in line with typical Klingon humor. They might still start shooting, but they'll appreciate it. Hopefully we won't have to employ that excuse. If we move fast enough, we can get in and out before they can detect our presence. We'll have surprise on our side. By the time they get over their shock at having their planetary defenses breached, we'll be warping out of the system, and no harm done. My guess is they'll be too embarrassed to raise a stink."

The admiral considered carefully. "What if you don't get out in time?"

Kirk shrugged. "Then we'll have to shoot back. I didn't say the plan was perfect." His grin this time was lopsided. "We'll tell 'em we experienced a severe navigational malfunction and got lost." The grin vanished. "Harrison is there, sir. He might not stay there for long, so we have to act fast. Starfleet can't formally go after him—but *I* can. Please, sir."

Spock stepped forward. "While I am unable to engage in nonrational pleading, Admiral, I would like to second Captain Kirk's suggestion."

"'Captain' Kirk?" Marcus's eyebrows rose. "You presume too much, gentlemen." Having said that, he studied both men carefully for a moment before continuing. "Mr. Kirk, Mr. Spock: I am going to share something with you that is not to be repeated outside this room." Both men stood expectantly, conscious of the seriousness in the admiral's tone and manner.

"All-out war with the Klingons is inevitable, Mr. Kirk. If you ask me, it's already begun." At his gesture, the room was filled with surveillance imagery: different types of Klingon warships, armed Klingon soldiers, worlds, statistics, and more. Eyeing the display, Marcus sniffed derisively. "'Diplomacy' and 'friendship' don't seem to have a place in the Klingon vocabulary. In fact, there's a whole section that might be labeled 'getting along with others' that seems to be missing from their culture.

"Since we first learned of their existence, the Klingon Empire has conquered and occupied two inhabited worlds that we know of: worlds populated by sentient species with no burning racial desire other than to be left alone. The Klingons don't like to leave other species alone. In their mind, pacificity is a sign of weakness, and weakness is something to be exploited. They've fired on our ships half a dozen times, always on the flimsiest of reasons. When we have the temerity to fire back, they withdraw, recalculate, and if necessary, offer up whatever excuses they think we'll accept. Our diplomats hem and haw but, being diplomats, end up coming to agreements." His tone hardened.

"Those 'agreements' will last only until the Klingons believe they've achieved an overwhelming superiority in firepower. Then there'll be another 'accident,' only this time there'll be no more agreements. They'll come straight at us, and they won't stop until they get to Earth itself. The galactic clock is ticking, gentlemen. They're coming our way, and I'll be damned if we're not gonna be ready for them." His gaze fixed on Spock. "We intend to see to it, Mr. Spock, that what happened to your world will never happen again, to Earth or anywhere else." He paused to let his breath catch up with his thoughts.

"London—that was not an 'archive.' It was the staging area for a top-secret branch of Starfleet research and development called 'Section 31'—as innocuous a designation as could be applied. The scientists, engineers, and military far-seers there were tasked with developing defensive technology as well as training operatives to gather intelligence on the Klingons and any other potential enemies who mean to do us harm."

As he spoke, images from the destroyed Section 31 facility appeared in the air above his desk. They were followed by a plethora of research material on the Klingon Empire: its ships, weapons, statistics, and much more.

"I'm sure you realize, gentlemen," Marcus continued, "that the galaxy is not an inherently benign place. In addition to dangerous natural phenomena, there are hostile intelligences out there who have reasons of their own for wishing to see the influence of the Federation reduced—or eliminated entirely. It is the task of Starfleet never to let down our guard against such entities."

"I thought our task was to seek out and explore," Spock injected pointedly.

Marcus nodded agreement. "Indeed it is, Mr. Spock. Also to be wary of what we find when we seek out and explore. Starfleet's approach has always been to extend the hand of greeting and friendship to whoever we may encounter—while keeping a fully charged phaser ready in our back pocket." Once again he shook his head dubiously. "Extend both hands to the Klingons, and they're likely to come back missing a finger or two. Plans are being made to defeat them, by any means necessary." Visual information on the Klingon Empire was abruptly replaced by a personnel file: that of Thomas Harewood.

"But Harrison somehow coerced a Section 31 officer to sacrifice his own life and detonate a device that destroyed the facility and killed innocent men and women. We don't know why Harrison turned against us." Marcus stared off into the distance, momentarily focusing his thoughts on another matter entirely before snapping back to his current surroundings. "He was one of our best agents. You cannot imagine how talented and valuable he was. One might almost say unique."

Kirk felt no sympathy. "Well, now he's a fugitive mass murderer, and I'd like your permission to take him out."

The admiral almost smiled. "'Take him out'? You are very young, Mr. Kirk. In fact, I would go so far as to say your response sounds a bit—Klingonish. Starfleet isn't about vendettas, sir."

"Maybe it should be," the younger man shot back. "Maybe if the Klingons thought we were more like them—instead of, say, the inhabitants of those two worlds they recently occupied—they'd show us a little more respect and stop shooting at our ships. I'm all for diplomacy, first and foremost, but there's a time for talk and a time for stalk."

"Straightforwardly put. I'd have expected nothing less. Pike always said you were one of our best and brightest. Also one of our most . . . impetuous? I think that's the word he used. You should have heard him defend you. He's the one who talked you into joining Starfleet, wasn't he?"

Kirk swallowed. "Yes, sir. If not for him . . ." His voice trailed away.

Marcus's tone softened. "Did he ever tell you who talked *him* into joining?"

The younger officer looked up sharply. Eyes met, understanding and emotion were exchanged in silence. Without anything more being said, an existing wall abruptly vanished. Looking on, Spock could analyze and comprehend what had just happened, even if he himself could not participate in the wordless exchange.

"His death is on me." Marcus spoke more softly than at any time since the two other officers had entered the room. "And yours can't be. I won't allow that. Harrison has cost Starfleet too many fine officers. I will not see your name added to that list. The Klingon homeworld—really, now. I'm not letting you get anywhere *near* that planet. Not even if the object is to 'take out' John Harrison." He started to turn away. "We'll deal with him through other means. There are less-known diplomatic channels that—"

"*Please,* sir," Kirk interrupted. "Diplomacy—if he declares his presence to the Klingons and tells them what he's done, they'll view him as an ally. He's just one rogue human, sure, but he's one who's accomplished something that would accrue considerable merit to any of them had they carried out such a stealthy attack. It would be just like them to grant him diplomatic immunity and parade him at a conference, or use him for general propaganda purposes. He has to be . . . excised . . . so that can't happen." He went quiet for a moment before adding, "'Vendetta' aside, there are practical reasons why he has to be dealt with as soon as possible."

Marcus thought it over. He had apparently made up his mind—but that didn't mean it could not be changed. His attention turned to the quiet science officer who had spoken little but heard everything.

"Mr. Spock, you said the city he's hiding in is uninhabited?"

"Affirmative, sir. And has been for quite some time. On the map of Qo'noS, it's an empty place: abandoned, deserted, and unvisited."

Marcus nodded to himself. "As part of our extended defensive strategy, Section 31 has developed a number of new, highly advanced weapons systems. One of these is a new kind of photon torpedo: long-range and undetectable. It's designed to be invisible to Klingon sensors."

"'Designed to be.'" Spock considered this. "Is it?"

Marcus didn't smile. "In all the computer simulations, it has functioned as intended. In a real combat situation—we have yet to find out." His gaze flicked from man to Vulcan. "You're going to have the opportunity to find out. Mr. Kirk, you will proceed to locate John Harrison. I don't want you hurt, but I want you to take him out. When you have conclusively established his position and, provided he remains isolated from his unknowing Klingon hosts, you lock onto his position, you fire, you kill him, then you haul ass."

Straightening, Kirk repressed a smile. "Yes, *sir*."

"Good."

Spock was noticeably less enthusiastic about this meeting of human minds. "Admiral, it is to be presupposed that the Klingons will look less than understandingly at the launching of photon torpedoes at their homeworld from a Federation vessel."

"As would we if the situation were reversed, Mr. Spock. However, if the torpedoes work as intended, no trace of their passage will be detectable. Klingon sensors *might* detect the presence of the *Enterprise*. They will have no way of connecting it with a detonation on an uninhabited portion of their planet. If all goes as hoped, the *Enterprise* will be in and away before they can even register its presence." He caught his breath before adding, "As you may know, Qo'noS has one major moon, Praxis, which is a center of energy production. There are also a number of smaller moonlets and planetoids. Too small to bother colonizing even with automatic stations; plenty large enough to conceal a single starship visually, electromagnetically, and gravitationally from sensors on both Qo'noS and Praxis. If you can emerge from warp space at appropriate predetermined coordinates behind one of these, the Klingons won't notice you. A patrol would eventually, but you should be in and out before that happens." His gaze shifted from Kirk to Spock. "Nobody suggests this is going to be easy. But it's possible. It's doable."

Kirk threw the Vulcan a look that said *See?* before turning back to Marcus. He was all business now. Very professional. Almost un-Kirk-like. "Permission to reinstate Mr. Spock as my first officer."

The object of this request regarded his former commander in obvious surprise. But he did not object.

"Granted," Marcus replied matter-of-factly. "Anything else?"

"No, sir. Thank you, sir."

"After you enter Klingon space, you may feel otherwise." Marcus paused. "No further questions, gentlemen? Then—good luck."

The massive shuttle hangar was a hive of activity: technicians going over final checkouts, shuttle crews preparing for departure, dozens of personnel comparing notes and assignments, supplies being prepared for loading. The hum and clank and whir of automatics combined with the buzz of conversation to create a symphony of expectancy: human and alien voices blending into a single chorus that subsumed any individual concerns. Haste was paramount and laggards not tolerated. If you didn't quickly find out where you were going and what you were supposed to do, you were liable to be left behind.

A man on a mission, James Kirk strode through the confusion, parting lesser ranks with a distinct lack of patience. Some of those he nudged aside started to protest, then recognized him and made way. His reputation preceded him.

Less impressed, one man fell in step alongside the newly reinstated captain. In place of awe, admiration, or just plain trepidation, the newcomer's face showed unrestrained annoyance.

"Jim. I waited and waited. Where the hell were you?"

"Waited? For what?" Kirk responded to Leonard McCoy's unconcealed irritation without slowing his stride.

"For the going-away banquet Starfleet's female contingent prepared in your honor." The doctor rolled his eyes. "For your pre-departure medical exam—what'd you think? You didn't show up." He didn't try to hide his dismay. "Jim, ten hours ago you were in a damn firefight. Subsequent to which you were never checked out. Now you're resuming command of the *Enterprise* without so much as having your blood pressure taken. What kind of ship's doctor do you think I am? It's my duty to—"

Kirk cut him off. "Bones, I'm fine."

Forgoing argument, McCoy reached out and brought Kirk to a stop by grabbing his arm. Concern replaced exasperation as he lowered his voice.

"The hell you are."

For just an instant, McCoy saw something unguarded and real in his friend's face. Sorrow, perhaps, or regret, or both. Then the instinctive cockiness returned full strength as Kirk shrugged indifferently.

"You wanna examine me? Examine me. But not until we're under way."

McCoy sighed heavily. "And the point of giving you a check-up when we're already halfway to who knows where would be what?" His frustration threatened to boil over. "I may do it anyway, just to satisfy myself."

Kirk had to grin. "Satisfy yourself about what? Whether I'm crazy or not?"

"No, I already know the answer to that one." He gestured. "C'mon, move, Captain. You're holding up the queue."

With a nod to one ensign and a word to another, Kirk checked himself onto the shuttle. McCoy was right behind him, but delayed in order to examine the first ensign's eyes, which struck the doctor as unnaturally dilated. While the two of them argued over what the ensign might have ingested or imbibed the previous night, Kirk wandered deeper into the compact vessel. He was not surprised to find his science officer already seated and ready for liftoff.

"Status report, Mr. Spock?"

"I am pleased to report that I am well, Captain, and that I have completed all appropriate pre-departure—"

"Not you," an exasperated Kirk muttered. "I can see your status well enough. I meant the ship." He slipped into the empty seat near the Vulcan.

"The *Enterprise* should be ready for departure by the time we arrive. I anticipate no delays in leaving orbit."

Kirk nodded approvingly and would have continued but was interrupted as McCoy arrived laden with a handful of medical instrumentation.

"Hey." Kirk leaned to one side in his seat as the doctor, utilizing a small scanner, commenced his examination. "I said you could do this once we were under way."

McCoy replied without lifting his eye from the device he was passing across Kirk's face. "Technically, as soon as the last door closes, we're officially under way. You want to lodge a complaint about my reasoning, file it with Starfleet Medical once we return." The device slid downward. "In the meantime, open your mouth and stick out your tongue so I can scan your teeth."

As a reluctant but defeated Kirk complied, Spock embraced the opportunity to convey something he had meant to say ever since they had left Marcus's office.

"Captain. I would be remiss were I not to thank you for requesting my reinstatement to the *Enterprise*. While I could as easily have remained with Captain Abbott's ship or requested assignment to another vessel, my preference is to serve aboard the *Enterprise* in the company of a crew with whom I am already familiar."

McCoy spoke without looking up from his work. "If you're going to say something about 'familiarity breeding contempt,' I may be forced to make a note in your official medical record."

"I would not think of doing such a thing, Doctor. The very notion leads me to suggest that after you are through examining the captain, you might consider examining yourself for symptoms of paranoia."

"It's not paranoia if the object of one's concern is omnipresent."

Ignoring this, Spock returned his attention to Kirk. "It would also be remiss of me if I did not now strongly object to our mission parameters."

Turning away from the new device that McCoy was pressing to his neck, Kirk glared at his science officer. "Of course it would," he said dryly. "Consider your objection so noted."

"There is more."

"And he thinks I'm paranoid," McCoy muttered, but under his breath.

"While I harbor only the ultimate disdain and contempt for the individual known as John Harrison, and desire strongly that he receive the punishment due him, I must point out that there is no Starfleet regulation that condemns a man to die without a trial—no matter how egregious his offenses. On a completely different matter of concern, I must say again that preemptively firing one or more torpedoes at the Klingon homeworld goes against every—"

McCoy removed the reading device and gaped at Kirk. "Wait a minute. I was told this was a priority operation, but—we're firing torpedoes at the *Klingons*?"

"No—technically, yes, but no. Because we're actually—look, Bones, it'll be explained in detail once we're at warp and clear of Earth's system." Angry at himself for having disclosed a portion of their still-secret mission, Kirk muttered an irritated response to his first officer. "Look, you yourself said the area's uninhabited. And there's only going to be one casualty. And in case you weren't listening, our orders have nothing to do with Starfleet regulations."

Spock was not to be dissuaded. "Regulations aside . . ."

Kirk looked sharply back at him. "'Regulations aside'? When did you ever put regulations aside, Spock—even for the sake of discussion?"

"What I mean to say, Captain, is that however justification for our mission may be rationalized, such an action is morally wrong."

Kirk barked a humorless laugh. "Regulations aside, pulling your ass out of a volcano on the verge of erupting was morally *right* and I didn't get any points for that either. As it seems that I'm wrong no matter what I do, I'd just as soon go with something that has a worthwhile purpose."

A glance at his main readout alarmed McCoy. "Jim, your vitals are spiking, and we're not even off the ground. Calm *down*."

Kirk whirled around to face the doctor. "I'm not gonna take ethics lessons from an emotionless robot who—"

"Reverting to childish name-calling suggests you are defensive," Spock observed calmly, "which suggests you therefore find my opinion valid—any ass-pulling-out-of notwithstanding."

At that moment, Kirk would have given a great deal to be waiting for liftoff on an entirely different shuttlecraft. "I didn't *ask* for your opinion." Reaching up, he swatted at the tricorder McCoy was passing across his field of view. "You think my vitals are up now? If you don't get that thing out of my face . . ."

Resigned, Spock concluded his polemic. "Captain, our mission is, by its very definition, immoral. Perhaps once we are on board and under way, you might find the requisite time to reach the same conclusion on your own, as it is amply apparent that you are not going to listen to me—or to anyone else."

Spock might have been finished, but Kirk was not. He had plenty more to say and would have done so enthusiastically—had not his line of sight suddenly been interrupted by something considerably more interesting than McCoy's instruments.

As the door was about to close prior to departure, a last, late arrival stepped aboard. After being cleared by the irritated ensign, the blond, blue-eyed newcomer made her way through the shuttle until she stood confronting the bemused Kirk. Trim and athletic, she smiled down at him.

"Captain Kirk? Science Officer Carol Wallace. I've been assigned to the *Enterprise* by Admiral Marcus."

Realizing he was expected to respond, Kirk kept his reply cool. "Isn't it a bit unusual, Wallace, for a senior ship's officer to be transferred aboard at essentially the last minute?"

"As you are aware, Captain, certain recent events have resulted in an atypical acceleration of asset application. It seems that I'm included."

Spock made an odd sound deep in his throat. "You requested an additional science officer, Captain?"

"I wish I had." Looking forward, a bemused but not displeased Kirk raised his voice. "I'm sure that's everyone for the *Enterprise,* Ensign. You can seal the door."

The officer hesitated only briefly before complying, thereby ensuring there would be no more surprises. This one, Kirk felt, was enough.

Moving closer, the newcomer passed her tablet to him. He skimmed the visible words silently until he came to one particular paragraph that caused him to comment aloud.

"Lieutenant Carol Wallace. Advanced doctorates in applied physics, astrophysics, materials science. Starfleet specialist in advanced weapons systems."

"Impressive credentials," Spock commented without rancor.

"Thank you," she told him.

"Though redundant now that I am back aboard the *Enterprise*," the Vulcan concluded.

Gesturing at the empty space between himself and his science officer, Kirk offered the new arrival a welcoming smile. "Have a seat, Doctor." Working her way across in front of the captain, Wallace settled herself into the restraints. Preoccupied with securing herself, she did not notice that the other science officer was eyeing her in a manner that, even for a notably dispassionate Vulcan, might have been construed as something less than welcoming.

As the shuttle rose skyward on its preprogrammed path, the sprawling metropolis of Greater San Francisco fell away below. Brown and green land gave way to the immense expanse of the deep blue Pacific, which in turn surrendered to the darkness of space and thousands of unwinking stars.

Pressed into his restraints, Kirk closed his eyes and inhaled. This was as near as he could come to breathing vacuum. Soon he would be on the *Enterprise* again and, hopefully not long thereafter, powering through deep space on warp drive. Once far from Earth and Starfleet headquarters, he would be at liberty to cope with the still-developing situation surrounding John Harrison as best he saw fit. There would be no one looking over his shoulder as he made necessary decisions on the spot. No admirals, no senior functionaries. He would be free.

Free from everything, he reminded himself pragmatically, except his responsibilities.

The source of those responsibilities appeared not long after the shuttle cleared the ionosphere: the immense orbiting facility that was Starfleet dock. As the shuttlecraft slowed on approach, Kirk was able to pick out his ship waiting in place. Like worker ants attending a queen, a swarm of small support craft darted silently around her, preparing and supplying her for imminent departure. A small smile creased his face. There were other ships in dock, but like anyone thoroughly smitten, he had eyes only for his beloved.

As far as James T. Kirk was concerned, there was only one ship in Starfleet, and her name was *Enterprise*.

VII

The *Enterprise* was being prepped for departure as per standard procedure, but on the sealed interior cargo deck near where the shuttle docked, there was turmoil. Like a whirlwind trapped in place, this rotated around the ship's chief engineer, who was railing loudly at a pair of patently unhappy but persistent security officers. The streamlined white-and-gray object of Scott's consternation rested on a hover palette floating beside the two immovable visitors.

"No. Absolutely not. I'm not signing anything!" Angrily he passed a transparent info tablet back to the nearer of the two officers. "I'm not puttin' me retina stamp on anything that's a blind delivery, especially on behalf of a load like this!" With a glance, he indicated the hovering palette. Following his gaze, Kirk decided that he could sympathize with the chief engineer's position.

The palette was stacked with gleaming photon torpedoes of a design and type unknown to him—the new weapon described by Admiral Marcus.

"Get those bloody things off my ship!" As Scott started to turn away from the unwanted cargo, he caught sight of the newly arrived Kirk. *"Captain!"*

Taking a deep breath and flanked by Spock, Kirk prepared to deal with the altercation.

"Mr. Scott," he said calmly. "Is there a problem?"

"You bet your . . . !" The chief engineer calmed himself with an effort. *"Aye,* sir—there's a 'problem.'" He gestured forcefully in the direction of the two security officers. "I was just attempting to explain"—he glanced at Spock—"in the most *calm* and *rational* way possible, that I cannot authorize additional weapons comin' aboard unless I know exactly what's *inside* them." He gestured at the palette and its coldly ominous load. "Especially when those weapons are of a new and unfamiliar type."

"Mr. Scott raises another concern," Spock began.

Kirk did not give the science officer an opportunity to elaborate. "Mr. Spock, report to the bridge. Now, *if you please.*"

"Yes, Captain."

While his expression betrayed no reaction, the Vulcan's body language indicated that he was unhappy with the summary dismissal. Nevertheless, he complied.

As soon as his first officer was out of earshot, Kirk turned back to his chief of engineering. "Mr. Scott, I understand your concerns, I sympathize with your position, and I admire your adherence to procedure—but we need those torpedoes on board."

Scott was openly puzzled. "Pardon me, Captain, but—why? The *Enterprise* is fully armed. There's not enough spare room in the weapons bay for a catapult, much less a load this size."

Kirk smiled. "I'm sure you can find space, Mr. Scott."

"It isn't even that, sir. Photon torpedoes run on their own miniaturized drives, each specific to a type an' model." Once more he gestured at the palette's heavy load. "But I kinna get a readin' on any o' these because their drive compartments are *shielded*. And the sections that are supposed to be open to inspection and repair are combination locked down. I could force one, but without knowin' the specifics of what's inside, I dinna think that's an especially good idea. Not while the device in question is aboard ship, anyway." He nodded at the nearest of the two security officers. "I asked to have the operational specs transferred over, and when I did"—the chief jerked a thumb at the man standing behind him—"he said—"

"It's classified," the officer finished for him.

"'That's classified,'" Scott echoed. "To which I said: No specs, no signature." His voice turned pleading. "You talk to them, Captain. Try to make them see reason from an engineering standpoint. Each of these little ship-busting packages has *its own* drive. If I don't know the specs on those drives, how am I supposed to be certain that when they're activated, they won't interfere with the *Enterprise*'s own drive, or some other critical component of the ship?"

"Come on, Scotty," Kirk urged him. "D'you really think Starfleet would put a new type of torpedo on one of its vessels without first testing to make sure it wouldn't cause any problems?"

"I'm sure they've tested it, Captain." The chief drew himself up. "And just maybe me refusal to blindly accept them is part o' that same testin'. I dinna know what tests Starfleet has run on them or with them, but I do know that none o' them 'ave been run on the *Enterprise,* and I'm not 'avin' those things on me ship unless I know what's inside them besides maybe gerbils runnin' nowhere inside little metal wheels!"

Sulu's voice sounded from above. *"Captain, the ship's ready for departure on your orders."*

"Thank you, Mr. Sulu! Scotty—"

The chief took a step backward. "If you'll excuse me, *Captain,* I've got a core to prime." Looking to his right, he barked at his first assistant. Checking storage instructions imprinted on its topside, the stubby Roylan was straddling one of the torpedoes. "What are you bloody gapin' at, Keenser? Get down!" Turning, he strode off toward Engineering with the silent alien ensign trailing behind and struggling to keep up. Thoughts churning, Kirk watched Scott in silence until he was interrupted by the senior of the two insistent security personnel.

"Captain? We need a decision regarding this cargo."

"I know what you need. I'm trying to decide what I need. Stand by."

Behind him, an unhappy McCoy looked up from his recorder. "Jim, these numbers aren't good."

Looking up the corridor, Kirk raised his voice. *"Scotty . . . dammit!"* When no response was forthcoming, he hurried off in the chief's wake, leaving a more than usually perturbed McCoy behind.

Kirk did not catch up to Scott until he reached Engineering itself, at which point he just did manage to intercept the chief before he disappeared among the *Enterprise*'s imposing drive components. Unable to flee openly, Ensign Keenser had to content himself with keeping as clear as possible of the two senior officers.

"Mr. Scott, I need you to approve those new weapons. They have special properties that may prove essential to the success of our mission. We can't leave without them, and as chief engineer, you're the only one who can authorize their loading. I can countersign for them. So could Mr. Spock. But Security won't relinquish them without your okay."

The two men regarded each other for a long moment. Then Scott turned and pointed with deliberation. "D'you know what that is, Captain?"

Kirk did not bother to look in the indicated direction. "No, Mr. Scott. As captain of a starship, how could I possibly be familiar with her propulsion system? Let me think a moment now. Could you be referring to the ship's food-processing facilities? Her hygienics systems? Or might you just possibly, just maybe, be indicating the warp core?" His tone hardened. "I don't have time for a lecture, Scotty, especially about aspects of ship technology with which I am more than marginally familiar. We have to—"

"It's not only the warp core, Captain: It's a matter-antimatter catastrophe waiting to happen. I dinna know what kind of mini-drive propels those new torpedoes, but 'tis reasonable to assume they would be more powerful than those they replace. Or differently configured. Otherwise they wouldn't be very 'new,' now would they?"

Kirk found himself hesitating. "Go on."

"More powerful drives implies the use of more powerful magnetic containment fields for the intermix. Dependin' on how they're utilized and the nature of the payload they're carryin', they could generate a greater magnetic field shift when they're activated than any earlier models. That could create an interaction with the main core's containment fields. Consider, Captain: In a combat situation where all weapons are armed, we'd be dealin' with *six dozen photon torpedoes of a new type* about whose individual drive containment fields I know nothing and to whose relevant specifications I am being denied access. If their activation interferes in any way with the core containment field, we could lose the ship."

Kirk fought for patience. "Mr. Scott, do you still think Starfleet would let new weapons on a vessel if they hadn't first been fully tested to ensure that such an event was impossible?"

"I guess I dinna 'ave your confidence in ground-based laboratory testin', Captain. This whole mission is a rush job. The crew were rushed back to the ship, the ship is being rushed out of orbit, and these bloody bang-sticks are bein' rushed on board." He shook his head. "Maybe it's a fault o' me trainin', but I've this congenital dislike o' bein' rushed. Especially when it involves new weapons systems and potential warp core breaches. Letting those things on the *Enterprise* is the last straw."

Kirk frowned. "I'm missing something, Mr. Scott. What was the first straw?"

"What was . . . ?" The chief engineer struggled to contain himself. "There are plenty of straws. A *middle* straw was Starfleet confiscatin' my transwarp equation and now some madman's using it to hop across the galaxy. Where do you think he got it?"

Kirk was running out of time as well as patience. "Put your personal issues with Starfleet aside, Scotty. As you yourself just pointed out, this is not a typical mission. We have our orders."

"That's what scares me. The more atypical a job, the less I trust it. This is clearly a military operation. Those torpedoes make it so. C'mon, Captain. I mean, *six dozen torpedoes*? Of an entirely new type? In addition to our standard compliment of weaponry? Is this what we are now? Because I thought we were explorers, I thought we boldly went where no man has g—"

Knowing his chief engineer as well as he did, Kirk also knew this unresolved debate could go on for hours. He did not have hours. He was charged with taking the *Enterprise* out *now*. Nor did he want to linger and perhaps give Starfleet Command the opportunity to countermand Marcus's directive. While he understood Scott's position and empathized with his concern, he would not give in to it. Like everyone else on board, the chief would simply have to find a way to cope with an unusual situation.

"Mr. Scott, I'm not interesting in arguing the matter any further. Sign for the torpedoes. That's an order."

"An order, sir? You're asking me to violate me own principles, t'go against me own judgment?"

"Don't make such a major issue out of it, Scotty. It's just a palette of new weaponry. Such deliveries are made all the time."

"I kinna sign for them." The chief folded his arms across his chest. "I'd be twa bubbles aff the center if I did."

Kirk was equally adamant. "You will sign for them, Mr. Scott. You have no choice in this matter."

"Is that so, Captain? You're right about one thing: I do have no choice. No choice but t'resign me duties."

It was the one response Kirk had not anticipated, and his surprise was evident. "Scotty. Come on, you can't be serious."

"As you say, you leave me no choice, Captain."

More frustrated than angry, Kirk consulted his own quietly beeping information tablet. It was filling up fast with queries, requests, and demands for decisions only the ship's captain could make. "You're not leaving *me* a choice. I don't have time—"

"D'you accept me resignation or not?"

Kirk tried one more time. "Will you as chief engineer sign for those torpedoes?"

"I will not."

"Then I accept your resignation. You are relieved of duty, Mr. Scott."

The chief looked shocked. This quickly gave way to a flush of anger, which he repressed, and finally to unabashed concern, which he did not.

"Jim—for the love a' God, whatever happens, *do not use those torpedoes.*"

With that, Scott handed over his work tablet, turned, and strode away without so much as a backward glance. He did, however, throw a murderous glare in the direction of Keenser. There being no need for additional explanation of the chief engineer's mood or meaning, Keenser likewise turned in his tablet and fell in beside his superior.

Kirk was left to wonder what he had just done. There wasn't a better chief engineer in Starfleet than Montgomery Scott, and he had just accepted the older man's resignation. Where was he going to find even a halfway suitable replacement? He had only moments in which to do so, not days or weeks. Even a competent chief would need time to familiarize himself with the *Enterprise*. Though platforms were unified across classes of ships, each vessel had its own peculiarities, its own modifications and upgrades that were specific to it. Furthermore, if he put in a request now, scarcely moments before scheduled departure, Starfleet was going to want to know why. Conflict between a captain and his chief engineer was unlikely to inspire confidence, and if word of Scott's resignation got out, it might jeopardize the entire mission.

What was it Marcus had recalled that Pike had said about James T. Kirk? That he was impetuous? Had he just demonstrated that particular flaw?

Time. Dammit, he had no *time*. Especially for nonsense like this. No matter the nature of a mission, insubordination could not be tolerated. Not even from Montgomery Scott. He had given his chief engineer a direct order, and it had been rebuffed. Despite what he believed, it was Scott who had been the one with choices. In contrast, Kirk had none.

Lieutenant Uhura fell in step alongside Kirk as he made his way toward the bridge. Around them, commotion was turning to order as more and more of the crew reached their stations and settled into departure mode.

"Captain, I'm so sorry about Admiral Pike." She was eyeing him intently. He did not return her stare.

"Thank you for your concern, Lieutenant. We all are."

"Are you okay?"

"Yeah. I'm fine, thank you, Lieutenant. Just a lot on my mind. The usual pre-departure concerns."

He increased his pace, and she had to walk faster to keep from being left behind as they stepped into the turbolift.

Once he was sequestered in the lift with his chief communications officer, something prompted Kirk to unburden himself.

"Actually, Scotty just quit. As if that wasn't bad enough, your boyfriend is second-guessing me every chance he gets." At the look on her face, he was sufficiently abashed to add, "I'm sorry, that was inappropriate. But he's so damn cold and removed and above it all. He's as affected as anyone else by what happens, but he doesn't bat an eye. Just occasionally raises a brow. Sometimes I just want to rip the bangs off his head. Sometimes I think our minds are on exactly the same track, and then when I look around, I'm heading one way and he's going the other. I can't have a first officer who's always second-guessing me."

"Isn't that part of his job? Isn't that the reason there *are* first officers? If all he has to do is say 'yes' to every one of your decisions, you don't need an intelligent second-in-command for that. A small machine with an endlessly repeating verbal loop will work just as well and won't argue with you."

"That's not what I mean," Kirk snapped. "What I mean is—oh hell, maybe it's not Spock at all. Maybe it's me. I'm still new at this. I mean, I doubt it's me, but maybe it's me."

"As long as it doesn't affect your usual unshakable confidence." When he didn't respond to her gentle dig, she added tiredly, "It's not you."

"It's not?" Her tone moved him to think of something besides himself. "Wait—are you guys in a fight?"

Turning away from him, she focused her attention on the turbolift wall. "I'd rather not talk about it."

"*Do* you guys fight? How does that work? Do you take a swing at him and he responds with five minutes of logical disquisition on why your primitive physical reaction was irrational and unproductive? Or do—?"

Before he could finish, the doors opened to reveal none other than the first officer of the *Enterprise*.

"Ears burning?" Kirk ventured pleasantly.

In response, the science officer eyed the captain uncertainly, but said nothing.

Time, Kirk told himself as he crossed the bridge to Chekov's station. He was always running out of *time*.

"Mr. Chekov. I know that you've made it a project of yours to shadow Mr. Scott and his work." He smiled encouragingly. "A genius like yourself gets bored easily."

The young navigator looked pleased, but a tad bewildered. "Uh, thank you, Keptin."

"Admiral Pike himself once called you a whiz kid." Kirk turned momentarily nostalgic. "I had to look up what that meant. Anyway," he continued brightly, "I gather that it means you're familiar with the engineering systems of this ship."

"Affirmative, sir." Chekov indicated his station and its abundance of readouts. "It's not that Navigation isn't fulfilling all by itself; it's only that in my spare time—"

"Your spare time has been put to good use. You're my new chief engineer. Go put on a red shirt."

Chekov hesitated. "Keptin, when I said that in my spare time I—"

"Are you reasonably familiar with the *Enterprise*'s engineering and drive systems or not?"

"Reasonably familiar." Chekov murmured something to himself, then rose. "I suppose I have to answer in the affirmative, Keptin. But before I move to Engineering, may I ask what happened to Mr. Sco—"

"No, you may not." Kirk's response was quick and unyielding. "Report to your new duty station, Mr. Chekov. If anyone in Engineering has any questions about your move, you may refer them directly to me."

"Aye, Keptin."

"And Mr. Chekov, one more thing." The ensign paused expectantly. "On your way to Engineering, I need you to stop in the cargo bay. There's a load of new torpedoes there that needs to be signed aboard. As acting chief engineer, you'll need to take care of that. Inform me as soon as this has been done and the delivery team has disembarked."

"Certainly, Keptin. I'll attend to it immediately."

Chekov was as good as his word. It was mere minutes later that Kirk received the notification for which he had been waiting and that had caused him so much grief. If only Scotty had . . . He put all thoughts of the disheartening confrontation out of his mind. Too much else demanded his attention. He turned to face the helm station.

"Retract all moorings, Mr. Sulu. Inform Dock Command that we're getting under way and transmit the usual exit information. We've been cleared for departure for over an hour, and we've spent enough time sitting here."

"Working, Captain," Sulu told him.

"Mr. Chekov, how are things looking down there?"

Chekov's reply was encouraging, if not entirely confident. *"All systems normal, Keptin."*

"Copy that."

"Warp available at your command," Chekov added.

"Thank you, Mr. Chekov." Kirk addressed his helmsman without looking at him. "All right, let's ride."

"Yes, sir," Sulu replied.

Instruments shunted commands. Monitors reported conditions. Matter was annihilated, and the *Enterprise* vanished from the vicinity of Earth.

Kirk continued dispensing commands. "Uhura, give me shipwide."

"Channel open, sir," she replied after complying.

Feeling much more confident now that he was dealing with straightforward matters of command instead of the far more complex business of interpersonal relations and individual introspection, Kirk leaned forward just enough for the command chair to recognize his voice and separate it from the rest of the softer-voiced conversation on the bridge.

"Attention, crew of the *Enterprise*. This is the captain speaking. As most of you know by now, through official channels or otherwise, Christopher Pike, the former captain of this ship and our friend, is dead." For those who had not yet heard, he paused a moment to let that sink in. "The man who killed him has fled our system and is hiding on the Klingon homeworld—somewhere he believes we are unwilling to go. We're on our way there now."

If some of the crew had been listening nonchalantly to the captain's departure address, to a man and woman and off-worlder, they now ceased what they were doing and turned their full attention to the words that seemed directed at each and every one of them individually.

"Per Admiral Marcus, it is essential that our presence go undetected," Kirk continued. "Tensions between the Federation and the Klingon Empire have been high from the time of first contact and have in no way subsided since. Any direct provocation could lead to all-out war. Each of us should strive to see that does not happen. We will carry out our mission in secret and as swiftly as possible, before our presence can be noted and our ship identified." He started to sit back, paused, and added, "These are our orders."

As he started to recline, he caught sight of Spock. From his position at the Science station, the first officer was eyeing him with as blatant a look of disapproval as a Vulcan could manage. Kirk's first instinct was to ignore it entirely. That was when some recent words of Uhura's came back to him. No harm, he told himself, in admitting to uncertainty—as long as the admission was made to oneself.

"All right. Let's go get this sonuvabitch."

Throughout the *Enterprise,* expressions hardened and activity quickened. There were even a few spontaneous cheers. Nothing of the kind emanated from sickbay, however, as McCoy finished running the last pre-departure checkouts of personnel and equipment.

"Great," he grumbled to no one in particular. "I'm told Qo'noS is delightful this time of year. And the Klingons are famous for their hospitality."

The biography Spock was perusing as he sat at his station was not especially long. This was understandable, given the age of its subject. Despite its brevity, it was impressive. Certain details he noted and committed to memory with particular interest. They were not, however, the ones that would normally have attracted the attention of the casual browser. With a slight frown, he dismissed the readout as soon as he had finished it, rose, and headed for the turbolift.

From the other side of the bridge, Uhura watched him leave. Ever since they had left Earth, the science officer had been more than usually preoccupied. Which for Spock meant that he was essentially noncommunicative. Whatever was on his mind was evidently not for sharing, since he hadn't mentioned the subject of his new preoccupation to her or, as far as she could tell, anyone else.

That included McCoy, who in passing Spock acknowledged with a cursory, "Doctor." He did not look up from whatever unknown held his attention, not even when McCoy responded curiously.

"Where are you running off to?" The older man gestured toward the now-unoccupied Science station. "We're hardly under way and . . ."

But the first officer was gone, swallowed up by the turbolift and whatever was preying upon his mind. McCoy stared after him. It wasn't like the Vulcan not to react to a direct query without at least a minimal reply, even if only an acerbic one. The doctor considered going after him, then shrugged. If it were something Spock wanted to talk about, he would broach the subject when it suited him. If it were something to be kept private, neither McCoy nor Kirk nor a small thermonuclear device would be able to pry it out of him.

No one questioned Spock's presence in the lower levels, where senior bridge officers were rarely encountered when a starship was in warp. A few glanced his way as he passed, but the Vulcan's stolid countenance was intimidating even to older crewmembers. If he needed help, they knew he would ask for it—even though Spock had never done so.

Having not yet been transferred to the weapons bay, the load of new torpedoes rested where they had been placed immediately following delivery. At present, they were being scanned by a science tricorder wielded by a lone officer. The expression on her face suggested that she was not comfortable with the uninformative readouts her instrument was generating. There was much here that required explanation, she had soon realized. She turned to leave. Proper inspection would require . . .

"Mr. Spock—you startled me!"

The Vulcan had come up quietly behind his counterpart. His gaze flicked tellingly from Carol Wallace to the load of torpedoes and back again, eventually settling on the device in her hand.

"What are you doing, Doctor?"

She mustered a reassuring smile. "Verifying that the new weapons' internal guidance systems are online and updated with the latest celestial mapping coordinates. That's critical if there's a chance they might be utilized in non-Federation space, be-cause—"

Spock cut her off. "I am quite familiar with the navigational properties and functions of all classes of photon torpedoes, Doctor. You misunderstand. What are *you* doing aboard this *ship*?"

She blinked at him, the smile fading. "You're right, Mr. Spock—I do misunderstand your question."

"Then I shall endeavor to elucidate. There is no record in the official personnel files of your being assigned to the *Enterprise*."

A half-laugh rose from her throat. "Of all the ridiculous . . . I believe there must be some sort of mistake."

Polite but relentless, her interrogator nodded in agreement. "My conclusion as well, Dr. *Marcus*. In addition, it would appear that you have lied about your identity. A serious charge, unless one discounts the source—and possibly as-yet-unrevealed reasons. *Wallace* is the surname of your mother. I have done some research, and I believe I can only assume that the admiral is your father."

Hand and identity caught in the proverbial cookie jar, she

dropped all pretense at deception. "I'd *heard* that you were the most persistent science officer in the fleet."

"My interests are not dissuaded by oblique attempts at flattery, if that is your intention. Aside from the fact of your assignment to this ship via other-than-normal channels, what is the point of this subterfuge?"

She shrugged, sounding tired. "I didn't want any special treatment."

"Ironic, considering you are receiving precisely that. Your mere presence on this ship smacks of special treatment. I still fail to understand why."

She opened up to him as much as she felt that she could. "Mr. Spock, my relationship with my father is . . . complicated. I know I have no right to ask this, especially since my presence here probably comprises a list of procedural violations as long as your arm, but please—he can't know I'm here."

An eyebrow lifted. "It was my assumption that he would have been the one to 'pull strings' in order to place you on the ship without going through the usual procedures. You are telling me that is not the case?"

"No. I—"

"Why *are* you here, Lieutenant?"

She started to explain and might have succeeded had the ship not slammed to a stop.

VIII

The *Enterprise* had not "stopped" in the usual sense, of course—it was not as if she had run into some vast interstellar wall or into anything else. She had simply performed a normal maneuver in a decidedly abnormal fashion . . . the physical effect of which had mimicked a body in motion coming to a complete halt. The actual physics were rather more complicated.

In contrast, Kirk's reaction was refreshingly simple.

"What the hell was that?"

No alarms were sounding, which was a relief not only to him but to everyone else on the bridge. In the alerts' absence, everyone hurriedly referenced their individual specialties in search of another possible explanation.

It was Sulu who was able to respond almost immediately:

"Engineering manually dropped us out of warp, sir." Unnecessarily, he added, "Without the usual interstitial planning."

"No kidding." Puzzled as well as angry, Kirk addressed the chair's pickup. "Mr. Chekov, did you break my ship?"

In Engineering, there was confusion but no panic. Something had definitely gone wrong, but insofar as any of the techs could tell, nothing was broken . . . at least, nothing that had produced any obviously deleterious side effects. Technicians scrambled to identify the problem and find a solution. As one of them hastily informed Chekov, finding the former might take as long as preparing the latter. It was with that unhelpful preliminary report in mind that the acting chief engineer rushed to respond to the query from the bridge.

"Sorry . . . sorry, sir! I don't know what happened! Nobody does . . . yet." He glanced over a shoulder. With a minimum of talk, the full engineering team was smothering the area with instruments and equipment. "There is . . . was . . . apparently a problem with the core. The usual fail-safes responded with an emergency shutdown—we don't know the cause yet. But we can't manually override the automatics—at least not until we identify the problem. Impulse only until then."

What James Kirk muttered under his breath would have gotten him thrown out of any formal Starfleet meeting of senior officers and a censure placed in his record to boot. However, the circumstances were anything but formal. Besides which, he was the senior officer present. Having verbally expressed his feelings in no uncertain terms, he rose from the command chair.

"Mr. Sulu, remaining time to our destination?"

The helmsman studied his readouts. "Twenty minutes, sir." His mien dead serious, he turned in his seat. "But that's twenty minutes in hostile space we weren't counting on, until we can settle in behind the moonlet we've chosen in our final coordinates. We're through the Neutral Zone and well inside the Klingon sphere of influence."

"All right, we'd better hop to it." A quick scan of the bridge revealed an unmanned Science station and its usual occupant missing. "Where's Spock?"

"I am here, Captain," the first officer announced as he stepped clear of the lift.

"You're coming with me to Qo'noS. Change of plans. We're gonna go down there and get him ourselves."

"Captain," Sulu began, "I feel it my duty to point out that depriving the ship of its two most senior officers while in hostile territory contravenes all recommended Starfleet and traditional military procedure going back to the beginning of warfare."

"And probably not for the last time, Mr. Sulu. In the absence of myself and Mr. Spock, you will be in command. Unless, of course, by making your observation you are indirectly disparaging your own competency?"

Taken aback, the helmsman sat a little straighter in his chair. "No, sir."

"I didn't think so." Looking across the bridge, Kirk next addressed his chief communications officer. "Lieutenant, how's your Klingon?"

"It's rusty, but it's good. *toHq, a' Niq?*" She smiled thinly. "That's colloquial. You want formal?"

Kirk nodded appreciatively. "If we have to deal with any Klingons in person, I don't think it'll be very formal. You're coming, too." A sudden thought made him pause. "That won't—be a problem, is it? You two, working together . . . ?'

"Absolutely not." Favoring Spock with a stern sideways glance, she headed for the turbolift. For his part, the science officer sounded mildly perplexed.

"Unclear."

Voice and expression exquisitely neutral, Kirk regarded his first officer. "What is unclear, Mr. Spock?"

The Vulcan started to reply, hesitated, got caught up in more than one interpretational conundrum, and finally responded. "A great deal, Captain."

"Then we are once again in full agreement, Mr. Spock. I'll meet you in the shuttle bay."

For a second time the science officer hesitated. Then he turned and, without further comment but carrying his confusion with him, followed Uhura into the lift. As Kirk moved to join them, he was approached by McCoy.

"Jim," the doctor murmured, "you're not actually going down there? As the old adage goes, you don't rob a bank when your getaway car has a flat tire."

For an instant, Kirk's thoughts seemed to wing elsewhere. "Last getaway car I was in I flattened the whole car, not just the tires, and I'm still here." He looked back at McCoy. "Engineering will have us patched up and ready to disappear by the time we get back." He raised his voice so the bridge sensors would detect and transmit his words clearly. "Isn't that right, Mr. Chekov?"

Down in Engineering the first warning sounds had begun to clamor for attention. Readouts were decidedly not cooperating, techs were starting to argue vociferously with one another, and there were too many red lights where a little green would have been far more encouraging. Through it all, Chekov managed the tersest possible response.

"Uh . . . yes, Keptin. I'll do my best."

Taking his chief engineer's hurried response for an acknowledgment rather than a question, Kirk looked once more to the helm station. "Mr. Sulu, you have the conn. Once we're en route to the surface, I want you to transmit a targeted comm burst at Harrison's general location. Keep it tight and narrow: It'll be on Starfleet frequency only; so between that, the fact that it's going into an expansive deserted area, and a little luck, the Klingons won't intercept it. They're not likely to be scanning for Starfleet messages right in their own backyard."

Sulu nodded his understanding. "Content of message, Captain?"

Kirk considered. "Tell him that we have a bunch of new, real big photon torpedoes pointed at his head and if he doesn't play nice, you're not afraid to use them." At the look of uncertainty that slipped over the helmsman's face, Kirk queried further. "Is that a problem?"

"No, sir," Sulu responded solemnly. "It's just that I've never sat in that chair before." He nodded toward the command position.

Kirk replied reassuringly. "You're gonna do great. Who knows—with good fortune you'll probably have a command of your own someday."

Following Kirk off the bridge, the ship's chief physician was considerably less sanguine. "You're sitting Mr. Sulu at a high-stakes poker game, having him take your seat and telling him to bluff with cards he can't use without running the risk of blowing up his fellow players." The doors to the lift opened, and the two men entered. "He's a good man and a fine officer," McCoy continued, "but he's not a *captain*."

"For the next two hours, he is. And stop talking in metaphors. That's an order."

"It's a southern North America thing." The doctor's explanation did not concede compliance.

Kirk made a face as the lift started down. "I'm not sure if that's a metaphor or not, but whatever it is, don't do it anymore. We're a long way from any of the Americas."

"Too damn bad about that," McCoy muttered.

On the bridge, Sulu changed seats, dropping into the captain's chair as a hastily called subordinate took his usual place at the helmsman's station. Though as a bridge officer, Sulu was perfectly familiar with the chair's instrumentation and functions, his posture was still tentative. It did not help that all eyes were on him.

Conscious that he was expected to do something besides simply occupy the chair physically, he addressed the comm. Identifying him via his physical profile, internal vitals, and voice, the chair's sensors responded obediently.

"Acting Captain Hikaru Sulu to Weapons Bay. Load and prepare for firing the torpedoes taken aboard just prior to Earth orbit departure. Coordinate targeting of new weapons via automatic geophysical positioning. Preliminary target should be the center of previously described deserted urban area within the Ketha Province on Qo'noS. Higher resolution of final target area yet to come. Landing team including the captain will be proceeding surfaceward, and I want those torpedoes locked in by the time he leaves the ship."

★ ★ ★

Clad in dark gray civilian attire and carrying a couple of bundles of clothing, the landing party of Kirk, Spock, and Uhura strode toward the hurriedly refurbished, compact K'Normian trading craft where it waited in Bay 12. As Kirk had requested, a pair of regular crew awaited them. They had been selected for their security training that, from a potential combat standpoint, put them a level up on their fellow crewmembers. Kirk recognized the bearded member of the pair immediately and smiled. There had been an earlier altercation on Earth, in a bar-cum-nightclub, prior to his promotion. Not a long time ago, but the details remained sharp in his mind. "Cupcake," he had called the man, with predictably insalubrious consequences.

Well, time and circumstance had changed things, most especially their relative positions within Starfleet. A lesser man might have made something of that, sought to impress his current superiority upon a former adversary. James T. Kirk had his faults, but carrying a meaningless grudge was not among them.

Besides, it could be argued that he had been as much if not more responsible for the fight that had ensued than his antagonists.

The crewmember in question barely glanced in his captain's direction. "Ready to deploy, sir."

Kirk gave no indication that anything other than a normal relationship existed between them as he passed out two bundles of civilian attire.

"Lieutenants, lose the red shirts—you're K'Normian arms dealers. Put these on."

"Sir?" Uneasily, the bigger of the two officers eyed the mass of wrinkled garments that had been handed to him.

"Look, if this thing goes south, if what we're about to attempt blows up figuratively instead of literally in our faces, there can be nothing tying us to Starfleet. If necessary, we have a complete and completely plausible story to tell the Klingons. Being more than a little interested in armaments and those who deal in them, they'll be intrigued by the details, and because of our stated profession, more than inclined to listen. If they encountered an unauthorized landing party that said it came in peace, the members of said party would be likely to end up in pieces. But one that sneaks in with the aim of buying or selling weapons—that they'll understand."

Uhura spoke up. "But sir, other than our personal side arms—illegally obtained from Starfleet sources, of course—we'll have no weapons to sell. What will we use to back up our cover story?"

Kirk nodded knowingly. "Not a problem. No K'Normian trader with half a brain would bring his inventory directly to a buyer where it might simply be confiscated." He indicated his communicator. "If it comes to it, we'll show them pictures of our 'goods.' On my 'stolen' Starfleet communicator, of course." He was brimming with confidence. "If nothing else, they'll be impressed that we managed to 'steal' so much Starfleet stuff. But if everything goes as planned, you won't have to speak a word of Klingon. We'll grab Harrison, slip back to the *Enterprise,* and warp out of here." He returned his attention to the two attentive officers.

"So—no matter what happens, *if* anything happens, and we do have to confront some Klingons, there can be no mention of any connection with Starfleet." He eyed his large, long-ago adversary. "Unless, of course, you want to start a war, Mr. Hendorff?"

"No, sir." The heavyset crewmember stared straight ahead. "Did that once, sir." He stared evenly back at Kirk as he recalled the incident in question. "Tried that once in your company, sir. Didn't work out well."

Betraying no emotion, Kirk nodded. "Good. I feel the same way." Reaching out, he patted the crewman on the arm: a gesture both men recalled from a previous meeting undertaken in more primitive circumstances. Both had changed since then, matured. That they still remembered the incident in no way impacted on their present captain-crew relationship.

With Kirk having made his intentions known, no one on the K'normian trader commented as it shot away from the *Enterprise*.

Coming in behind a cluster of ragged, sheltering moonlets expansive enough to cloud their small craft's drive signature, they dove toward the imposing, green-tinged planet rotating below. Uhura stared out one of the ports, her mind aswirl. "Qo'noS," she murmured gutturally to herself. Homeworld of the Klingons. A place she never expected to see outside of file recordings, much less visit in person. A glance showed Spock, seated forward beside the captain, similarly studying the planet they were approaching. What was going through his mind at this moment? What wondering, what anticipation of new sights and discoveries, what anticipation of possible marvels they might encounter?

Naw, she told herself. He's focusing on the task ahead. Always focusing on the task ahead. It was sometimes an—issue between them.

Not the time nor place to ponder it, she told herself firmly. In her mind, she was already reviewing basic Klingon greetings and responses in the event she would be required to employ them. The trick with speaking Klingon was not even the rough glottals or sometimes peculiar grammar. It was getting them to say anything at all before they tried to hit you with something large, heavy, and lethal.

It was several minutes before Spock finally felt confident enough in his reading of the K'Normian instrumentation to make a first report.

"I am detecting a single advanced sentient life sign in the Ketha Province. Given the information provided by Mr. Scott and the clear differentiation between this readout and what would be expected were it of Klingon origin, my conclusion is that it is most likely John Harrison."

Kirk nodded with satisfaction. "Then he's stayed in one place and hasn't tried to ingratiate himself with his unknowing hosts. That further confirms that he's hiding here and hasn't formally defected. If the latter was the case, then he'd be surrounded by Klingons or, more likely, not feel the need to sequester himself in an abandoned city. That makes our job a lot easier." He addressed himself to the secured, tight-beam comm.

"Mr. Sulu, I think we've found our man. Let him know we mean business."

"Aye, Captain."

Sulu fought to conceal his nervousness. It would help, he felt, if the ship's doctor would retire to his own department and quit hovering in the vicinity of the captain's chair. But ordering

McCoy away would betray an uncertainty Sulu much preferred to keep hidden.

This isn't how it's done, he told himself. Very un-bushido. Sitting up straight in the chair, he addressed Communications. The officer who was substituting for the absent Uhura was immediately attentive.

"Narrow beam, as previously programmed. Frequency as indicated. Pinpoint our broadcast to that exact location."

Uhura's replacement complied. "Channel is open and ready for transmission, sir."

With a terse nod, Sulu turned back in the chair and addressed the comm.

"Attention, John Harrison. This is Captain Hikaru Sulu of the *U.S.S. Enterprise.* We are aware of your present location and in position to bear on it from a distance. A group of highly trained officers is on its way to your location. If you do not prepare and agree to surrender yourself to them immediately upon their arrival, I am instructed to unleash an entire payload of advanced, long-range, undetectable torpedoes that is currently locked on your location. I must inform you that we are prepared to do this despite any possible diplomatic fallout or other reaction from the Klingon community." He paused, his voice tightening. *"If you test me, you will fail."*

There being nothing more to say, nothing he could think of to add, he sat back in the chair. Had he used the correct tone of voice? Could he have been simultaneously more forceful and more persuasive? A glance showed the doctor still standing nearby. Pursing his lips in a manner most familiar, McCoy peered down at him.

"Mr. Sulu. Remind me never to piss you off."

A quick nod and Sulu turned forward once more. The

smile that played across his face was slight, but full of meaning.

It was not a smooth descent. While the K'Normian controls were similar enough to be familiar, Kirk's experience at personally piloting a shuttle-size ship all the way to a surface touchdown was limited. Which was to say, he had never done it before except via simulations. Qo'noS's characteristically turbulent atmosphere did not make his task easier. The compact craft bucked and rocked in the rough air. Between the fact that he remembered a good deal from his studies and Spock forgot nothing, the two of them managed to wrestle the unsophisticated but sturdy craft past towering but abandoned structures that pierced the heavy cloud layer.

It wasn't long thereafter that they could make out individual structures on the ground. The dense complex of enormous, long-abandoned buildings extended as far as they could see. It must have been some plague, Kirk mused, to induce the Klingons to flee from so much costly infrastructure. It appeared that not a single building remained intact. Some had walls as well as windows blown out, though whether by weather or attempts by Klingon medical controllers to draw a physical line around the plague that had caused Ketha Province to be abandoned, he could not tell. If the latter, he would hardly be surprised. It was likely that Klingon plague control was as subtle as the rest of their cultural and scientific methodologies.

Easy enough to understand why Harrison had chosen this place as a potential refuge following his assault on Starfleet. Who would be foolish enough to try and run him to ground on the Klingon homeworld?

Spock was doing yeoman work, making use of the K'normian vessel's comparatively straightforward instrumentation, running it through his own tricorder and somehow obtaining useful results.

"We will arrive at Harrison's last verified location in three minutes, Captain." He looked over at Kirk. "It is unlikely he will come willingly. By way of contrast and with considerably more certainty, I calculate the odds of him attempting to kill us rather than surrendering at ninety-one-point-six percent."

Kirk's reply was dry as the empty avenues between the ruined buildings below. "Fantastic. I can always depend on you for encouragement in a difficult situation, Spock."

The science officer was not deterred. "You can always depend on me for an accurate appraisal of any situation, Captain. Most would consider that a more useful response."

"Unless they're Vulcan," Uhura suddenly put in from behind, "and they don't care about dying."

The object of her ire turned in his seat. "I am sorry, Lieutenant, but I am not certain that I could hear clearly what you said."

She raised her voice, more than was necessary. "I'd be happy to speak up on a wide assortment of subjects if you're ready to listen to me."

Fully engaged in piloting their craft, Kirk quite sensibly chose to say nothing in the hope the conversation would take another, more professional tack, or even better, die out completely.

It was in vain.

"Lieutenant," Spock replied firmly, "I would prefer to discuss this in private."

Uhura was not in the least dissuaded. "You'd prefer not to discuss it at all, is what you'd prefer."

Painfully aware they were very close to touchdown, Kirk felt he had no choice any longer but to intervene. "Whoa, guys, are you really gonna do this right now?"

"As our current circumstances require undivided focus," Spock put in, cutting off Kirk, "I suggest that—"

Now it was Uhura's turn to interrupt. "What doesn't seem to require 'undivided focus'—sorry about this, Captain . . ."

"That's okay," Kirk mumbled. "I can land this thing myself. No reason for you to be involved just because you're on board."

". . . is us," she went on, as if she hadn't heard a word he'd said. Or maybe she had heard everything, divined both his sarcasm and the implicit criticism, and had chosen to ignore both. "Two seconds, Captain. At that volcano, you didn't give a thought to us, did you? About what it would do to *me* if you died, Spock." She was fighting to keep her emotions out of her voice—and failing. "What I got out of it was that you didn't feel anything, you didn't *care*."

Try as he might, Kirk found that he couldn't focus wholly on the instruments. Knowing that this close to the surface, final touchdown would be handled largely by the ship's automatics anyway, he stared at his first officer. Normally that would have had no effect: Spock could outstare a cat. But whether it was Kirk's intensely thought but unvoiced *Say something to her, you idiot* or just something rarely utilized within Spock himself, the Vulcan finally responded.

"Your suggestion that I do not care about dying is incorrect. A sentient being's optimal chance of maximizing their utility is a long and prosperous life."

"Great," she muttered.

"In my particular instance, I hold an additional responsibility, given the small number of survivors of my kind. I therefore would greatly prefer to survive for as long as possible in order to be of use not only to Starfleet, but to the Vulcan diaspora." He paused. "But it is true that I cannot deny what you say regarding 'emotions.' In truth, as I faced my likely demise, I did *not* feel anything. This is not because I did not *wish* to do so—especially as regards to certain personal relationships. It was because it was the most personally efficacious course of action. I chose not to feel anything upon realizing that my life was about to end because it was the least disturbing course of action open to me."

Readouts were starting to flash and several to beep as instrumentation signaled they were on final approach to the designated landing site.

"To even consider the idea of one's death affecting a loved one would be so painful," the science officer continued, "that the only logical option in that moment would be to choose to feel nothing instead. This was recently confirmed for me as Admiral Pike was dying. As I tried to comfort him, I briefly joined with his consciousness. I experienced what *he* felt at the moment of his passing. There was a surprising dearth of pain. In its place there was anger. Confusion. Loneliness. Fear." Though he could not see Uhura, who was seated facing away from him, he looked back in her direction as he spoke. "Nyota, you misunderstand my choice not to feel at that moment as an indication of not caring, while I assure you the truth was exactly the opposite."

It made no sense. Uhura was more unsettled by his response than she would have cared to admit. No sense at all—unless, of course, you were a Vulcan. Seeing it from his perspective . . . How often had she tried to see things from *his* perspective? Where the first officer's thoughts were concerned, she was an outsider trying desperately to look in. Would it always be so? Could she surmount such a logical gulf? Or would it be possible, somehow, some way, for the two of them to meet in the emotive middle?

She was in the process of formulating a reply when an intense flash streaked across their bow, rocking them violently while briefly blinding everyone inside.

"What the hell was that?" Kirk blinked furiously, fighting to regain his vision.

There was equal confusion on the bridge of the *Enterprise* as contact with the K'normian trader was lost.

Sulu turned sharply toward Communications. "What happened? Where's the signal?"

"I don't know," responded the tech on station. "It cut out— I'm working to get them back."

Spock recovered his full vision faster than his companions. Elemental as they were, the trader's instruments were sufficient to identify the source of the warning blast. A rearward-facing scanner provided unwelcome visual confirmation: The craft that had fallen in behind them was winged, compact, and wholly lethal in appearance.

"A D4-class Klingon vessel, Captain."

Kirk muttered a curse, adding, "I thought this section of the planet was abandoned and unvisited!"

"It must be a random patrol," an anxious Uhura suggested. "Medical policing, maybe, to ensure nobody spends time in the plague region, where they could accidently pick up a latent virus and transport it back to a populated area."

"Hold on!" Wrenching on the manual controls, Kirk sent

the K'normian craft sideways and deeper into the clouds that masked the abandoned city below.

Farther back in the ship behind Uhura, a worried Hendorff leaned forward in his harness. "Can we get back to the *Enterprise*?"

"And lead them right to it?" she shot back. "Thus far the Klingons don't know there's a Federation ship in their immediate spatial vicinity. We can't even head in its general direction without committing to a revelatory vector."

Kirk didn't hear Uhura, but he didn't have to. The last thing they could do was try to return to the *Enterprise*. Aside from possibly igniting a war, it would mean the end of their mission to capture or kill John Harrison. With the image of a dying Christopher Pike still fresh in his mind, he had no intention of turning to run.

Beside him, Spock continued to monitor the instrumentation as Kirk took the K'Normian vessel through every basic evasive maneuver he could remember from his studies. But try as he might, he couldn't shake the pursuing Klingon patrol craft—in addition to being at least as maneuverable as the trading vessel, the Klingon crew had the advantage of operating in familiar territory.

Spock did not look up from the readouts in front of him. "May I remind you, Captain, that this ship has no offensive capabilities."

"Not necessary to remind me, Mr. Spock. I'm all too aware of it. We're simple merchants, that's all—though right now, I wish it wasn't that simple. Give me full power; everything down to emergency backup, all this ship's fuel cells."

Spock did not hesitate. "Aye, Captain."

The compact trading vessel banked abruptly. Intended for

basic shuttling between ground and orbit, it was not designed for high-speed atmospheric maneuvers, a fact Kirk seemed to overlook as he wrenched it over and sometimes through the towers of the abandoned cityscape. Repeated blasts from the pursuing ship just missed the fleeing trading craft. That was about the sum total of good luck they could expect, Kirk knew. The next shot would take out their engines or, if they were unlucky and the Klingon gunners especially accurate, the rear half of the evading vessel.

As she leaned forward, Uhura's attention was drawn to the main readout. "They're closing fast, bearing two eight five!"

"Dammit!" A glance through the dim daylight showed what Kirk presumed to be the center of the empty metropolis. The vast expanse of ruined towers, tangled metal, and demolished support structures were tightly packed against one another: some by design, others because they had collapsed. Such a concentration would have allowed pedestrians and small vehicles to travel easily between buildings. For a fleeing spacecraft, there was no such access. Unless . . .

Heart pumping wildly, Kirk nodded at the landscape ahead. "There! We can lose them there!"

The pursuing craft was clearly visible on the aft viewer. Though smaller than the D7 battle cruisers the Federation had encountered in deep space, this greenish gray "bird-of-prey" scout ship, with its arched "wings" and its angular markings, reflected its Klingon designers' penchant for engineering fighting ships that reflected arboreal predators. Numerous flanges, probably serving as cooling elements, festooned the aft portions of the fuselage. To human eyes, the Klingons' ships were a contrasting meld of elegant and efficient: They were ugly-functional.

Staring straight ahead, Spock spoke up softly but urgently.

"If you are suggesting we utilize what might or might not be a passage between the approaching structures, this ship will not fit between them."

"We'll fit." Kirk held tight to the manual controls as he started to angle them sideways.

"We will not." Spock's voice rose ever so slightly.

"We'll fit, we'll fit!" Kirk whipped the straining trading craft to the left so that it was now flying edge-on to the ground.

An increasingly alarmed Spock would have argued further, but there was no time. Inclining their ship to match the slender vertical opening just ahead, Kirk maintained full power as he aimed for the gap. At least, he thought, if he was wrong, he would not have to listen to the Vulcan chide him for a bad decision. As an additional benefit, there would be nothing left of the intruding ship or its occupants for the Klingons to conclusively identify.

Behind them, their pursuer broke off to gain altitude. By the time it would reconnect with its target, they would hopefully have slipped away to another part of the city. Kirk let out a yell as the outermost fringes of their ship scraped against one structure, then another, sending bits of the ancient buildings tumbling toward the ground. Sparks and smoke flew from the edge of the trading vessel, but unlike the structure it was impacting, nothing fell off. At least as far as Kirk could tell, nothing vital. He fought the controls to hold to a course that had mere centimeters to spare.

When they emerged on the other side of the cluster of tall buildings, the pursuing vessel was nowhere in sight. Keeping as low as possible, Kirk brought them around sharply. Using overarching structures for cover, he began to retrace their course, aiming to work their way back to Harrison's presumed location.

With luck, the Klingon patrol craft would assume they were still heading outward and would continue its search in a direction that would only increase the space between them. By the time those aboard realized their error, Kirk hoped to have Harrison in custody and be pushing for Qo'noS's ionosphere.

"I told you we'd fit," he noted, gasping for a long breath.

"I am not sure that qualifies." Utilizing multiple screens, Spock was analyzing the external damage the K'normian craft had suffered.

"You can put that opinion in your report." Kirk nodded at the instrument panel spread out before the science officer. "Any sign of 'em?"

"No. Which worries me."

"Relax." Kirk deftly guided them through a vast, now-empty staging area, further ensuring they would not be seen. Darkness momentarily enveloped the battered craft. "We lost 'em."

"Or they're jamming our scanners." Studying the walls that rose to form a curved roof above them, Uhura was not optimistic.

Kirk's voice rose slightly. "Or, we lost 'em."

As they emerged once more into open air, Spock nodded forward. "I suggest slowing to a hover here, Captain."

"Why?" It took Kirk another couple of seconds to focus on the source of the science officer's concern. "Oh. Damn." Muttering under his breath, he reluctantly brought the trading vessel to a halt.

Theirs was not the only craft hovering outside the vast but abandoned cargo facility. Another vessel had dropped down to position itself directly in front of them. There was also one to their right and a third directly overhead. As a technical battlefield englobement, it was lacking in thoroughness, but the presence of now three Klingon patrol vessels was more than sufficient to persuade even Kirk that any attempt to break free of the formation would result in annihilation.

"I thought we only had to deal with one of them," he growled.

"Your use of the past tense is unfortunately accurate, Captain." The first officer peered outward through the forward viewport. "I do not think we can escape from this formation."

Kirk snapped an angry response. "Tell me something I don't know, Mr. Spock."

A slight flush appeared on the Vulcan's forehead. Or more likely it was the fluctuating internal lighting. "Where would you like me to begin, Captain?"

Kirk's ready reply was cut off by a burst of consonants from the cabin's communication system. Even for a Klingon, he thought, the unseen speaker sounded more than usually irate.

It was left to Uhura to translate. "They're ordering us to land. They say any further attempt to flee will be met by immediate destruction." She looked forward. "Captain, they're going to want to know why we're here. We'll give them the story about being K'Normian munitions runners. They'll listen politely. Then they'll torture us, question us, and they're gonna kill us."

"Not a good list of options," Kirk murmured. "So we come out shooting."

Spock put out a hand to restrain him. "The fact that we are not wearing our uniforms does not release us from our obligations to—"

"Oh," Kirk interrupted him, "so we just go for the questioning, torture, and death?"

"There are specific procedures to be followed that can—"

Uhura inserted herself between them, if only verbally. "We're outnumbered and outgunned. Captain, with all due respect, there's no way we survive if we attack first."

"More wonderful options," Kirk muttered. "I'd be open to alternatives if there were any."

"There is one, sir." Surprised, both men turned to look at the determined communications officer. "You brought me here because I speak Klingon." She stared down at him. *"Then let me speak Klingon."*

IX

Two of the Klingon vessels paralleled the K'normian trading craft's descent while the third remained hovering overhead. Despite the threat of destruction, Kirk briefly contemplated throwing full power to the engines and making another run for it, but stopped himself.

Even if they were able to somehow get clear without heavy damage, their presence was now a recorded fact. A patrol vessel had chased them. Its commander had patently called for assistance, and two others had joined in the hunt. If the intruding vessel got away again, there was no telling how extensive an alarm might be raised on this corner of the planet.

Kirk was willing to play long odds, but not three to nothing.

★   ★   ★

Rocking slightly in the steady wind, the trading craft landed: no easy task among the tangled, collapsing ruins. Wings folding upward, the K'normian ship's descent was paralleled by the nearest of the Klingon patrol vessels. As soon as its drive shut down, a dozen armed Klingons in severe military attire emerged from it. Close-fitting helmets the color of bruised antimony covered everything above the neck save eyes, mouth, and nostrils, while multiple layers of faux leather that was tougher than anything gleaned from a dead animal protected muscular arms and torsos.

To the Klingons, the only mystery about the now-cornered and powered-down intruding vessel was where it had come from and what it was doing in the forsaken city. It had already demonstrated that, militarily, it was not a serious threat. One of the soldiers insisted to his companions that whatever it was, it was anything but a designated warcraft. Another remarked that he had seen more intimidating small vessels serving as funeral transports.

Conversation ceased among them as the airlock door opened in the grounded intruder's side. The Klingon soldiers did not even bother to draw weapons as a single figure emerged. Bipedal and rather small, it was clearly unarmed and wore no armor. Nor did it require the use of a special suit or supplemental atmospheric gases, indicating that wherever it hailed from, it breathed the same air as the soldiers themselves. Eyes concentrated on the physically unimpressive creature as it approached. It halted almost within arm's reach of several of the heavily armed troops, a cardinal mistake of combat on the part of the visitor that suggested either congenital stupidity or supreme confidence. When the newcomer spoke, there was a hint of command that hung in the air. By now, every one of the soldiers had identified the arrival as human. They were not half as shocked by this realization as they were by the visitor's consummate command of their language.

★　　★　　★

Within the K'normian ship, Kirk and his companions strove to make sense of the confrontation outside while keeping themselves concealed from possible view by the Klingon squad. An anxious Kirk regretted not paying more attention to his extrasolar speech studies. Along with several other specified languages, he had of course also tried Klingon, but the language had proven too much of a struggle for him. Speaking it made him feel as if he were going to sprain his larynx.

From what he could see, however, Uhura appeared to be making contact. Whether that would mean anything depended on . . . He sucked his teeth and whispered to Spock.

"This isn't going to work."

The science officer murmured a reply. "You don't know what she's doing."

"It doesn't matter," Kirk hissed. "Whatever it is, it isn't going to work."

"It may . . . whatever it is. And if you interrupt her now, you will not only incur the wrath of the Klingons, but that of Lieutenant Uhura as well."

"What if they just decide to shoot her?" It was maddening, Kirk felt, to only be able to *listen* to what was taking place outside, but he had no choice. If he, Spock, and the others showed themselves at the wrong moment, the Klingons might react instinctively. The first thing they would do is shoot the communications officer. On the other hand, if the four men charged the local patrol, she was likely to end up dead anyway.

As he scrambled to unpack their sidearms, he found he was not as much worried about the existence of a "wrong" moment as he was the absence of anything resembling a right one.

*   *   *

"I am here to help you. Who's in charge?" Uhura demanded in Klingon so guttural it hurt her throat. But it had the intended effect. Instead of immediately and wordlessly attacking, which would not have been out of keeping with local procedure, the officer who stepped forward challenged her only with speech.

"Silence, human!" declared the foremost of the armored, helmeted troops. *"You will answer my questions."*

She met his concealed gaze unflinchingly. Showing uncertainty now, or lack of resolve, could be fatal.

While the captain of the *Enterprise* was cogitating fruitlessly, his communications specialist continued to confront the Klingon officer. When the Klingon tried to propound a traditional intimidating posture by leaning over her, she simply took a step back and rose on her toes. Exasperated, the Klingon was compelled to resort once again to mere words.

"How do you know our language?"

Uhura replied immediately, without missing a beat. *"We K'normians are famous as traders. Knowing the language of others is my business."*

Decidedly un-martial looks were exchanged by the surrounding soldiers. One of them made a barely audible comment that generated unmistakable amusement among his immediate companions. At a withering glance from their commander, they went stone silent. He returned his gaze to the lone visitor, his tone slightly less inquisitorial than before.

"Your presence here is not authorized. What could possibly cause you to take the risk of making an unauthorized landing?"

Uhura's appropriately curt response was emphasized by a suitably severe accompanying gesture. *"With respect: There is a terrorist hiding in these ruins. He has killed many of our people. The reward for his capture is substantial: worth even the risk of landing on Qo'noS. We intend to collect it."*

The Klingon commander pondered her explanation. Slowly, he removed his helmet. It was then that she could see that he was smiling. When he spoke again, his tone was suspicious, his expression accusatory.

"Why should I care about humans killing humans? Why should any Klingon?"

Uhura didn't hesitate. *"Because you care about honor. And this man has none."*

From inside the grounded trading vessel, Kirk could only watch. *She can't keep playing this game forever,* he thought in frustration.

"You say you come to gain a reward," the Klingon commander spat back at Uhura. *"There is no honor in that, either."* Turning, he spoke to the nearest soldiers. *"We must find out how she came to be here. Her explanation may be truthful, but no matter how powerful the motivation, no human should be in this place."* Abruptly, he reached out with one hand and grabbed her face, his fingers digging deeply into the flesh. *"Reward or honor, it matters not. You should not be on our world."* With his right hand he reached down to draw a knife from his ankle sheath.

It was at that moment that a succession of killing blasts tore into the tightly packed squad of soldiers, dropping one after another. While Kirk couldn't see who or what had unleashed the surprise barrage, he was not one to look a gift phaser in the muzzle—besides which, the issue had now been forced. He charged out the ship's open portal while firing as fast as he could take aim.

Out of the crushed pillars and structural ruination off to his right came a hooded humanoid figure. It was firing two weapons: one a large handheld, the other—the other was designed to be mounted on a tripod and manipulated by two or more fighters. It was long and heavy and ought not to have been carried, much less operated, by one individual. Yet the new arrival wielded it as effortlessly as if it was a light pistol.

Uncertain where to train their fire first, the startled Klingons were forced to split their attention between the crew of the downed craft and the absurdly over-weaponized interloper. Lowering the muzzle of the impossibly large weapon he was wielding, the heavily garbed humanoid figure began to pick the Klingons off with extraordinary precision. The size of a small cannon and featuring a peculiar tooth-shaped muzzle, the heavy gun he held in his right hand continued to wreak havoc among the scattering soldiers.

Angling his oversized weapon upward, the stranger proceeded to hit one of the patrol ships precisely in its most vulnerable spot as it drew close and attempted to intervene. Gushing fire and racked by a succession of explosions, the craft veered sharply to one side before coming to ground in a gout of flame. Even as he took out the patrol craft, the newcomer was repeatedly firing the smaller weapon he gripped in his other hand, taking down one Klingon after another, no matter where they attempted to seek shelter.

In response to the downing of the patrol craft, a second brace of Klingons rappelled swiftly down from its companion vessels to join in the fight on the ground. As soon as they landed, they found themselves under fire from the intruder, who swiftly decimated their ranks, even swinging the enormous power rifle he was manipulating so that the heavy barrel took out the legs of the one Klingon who got near enough to threaten him.

Moving into narrower gaps among the ruins, the fight had quickly devolved into hand-to-hand combat. Narrowly avoiding a shot, Kirk took out his attacker in time to save Hendorff. He lived only another moment, however. Ducking around a debris-strewn corner, Hendorff all but ran into the lethal edge of a bat'leth that caught him square across his neck. Death came quickly.

Not only was this group of Klingons big, Kirk noted, but they were *fast*. Thanks to the intervention of the still-unknown stranger, however, their numbers were being rapidly reduced.

That did not prevent two of them from taking Kirk down. One quickly put a foot on his neck, preparatory to delivering a fatal blast. With astounding precision, a pair of carefully placed bursts from the intruder's hand weapon blew both of them off the prone captain. Seeing him go down, Uhura had rushed to his side.

Yet another direct hit from the stranger's larger weapon damaged the second hovering patrol craft so badly that it lost control. Careening to starboard, it spun wildly to one side before it slammed into the ground nearby and burst into flame.

Stunned, Kirk and his companions looked on as, by himself and without apparent strain, their savior proceeded to battle the remaining Klingon forces. It was a display of individual martial capability that seemed more appropriate for a war machine than a single, living individual.

And the intruder's identity, concealed behind the cowl and overcoat, was soon revealed as he pulled the protective wrappings away from his face.

Leaping from the crossbeam that had been his perch since the start of the fight, John Harrison took down the remaining Klingons in brief, efficient hand-to-hand combat, utilizing a combination of edged weapons and bare hands that seemed better suited to sport than to unregulated combat. Picking up a dropped rifle, he moved quickly to where Kirk lay flanked by his friends.

Aiming his own weapon at the rapidly approaching Harrison, Spock barked an order. "Stand down!"

Rifle still focused on Kirk, Harrison ignored the warning as well as the Vulcan who had spoken it. "How many of the new torpedoes are on board the *Enterprise*?"

"*Stand down!*" Spock repeated, more insistently this time.

Raising his weapon, Harrison fired with the same uncanny speed and skill he had already demonstrated to such devastating effect in the course of the preceding confrontation. The shot blew a startled Spock's weapon right out of his grasp.

While an equally stunned Kirk simply stared back at him, the renegade raised his smaller weapon to point it directly at the captain's face. "The torpedoes. The weapons you threatened me with in your message. *How many are there?*" His voice was insistent, demanding, and devoid of any indication that its owner had just participated in a lengthy battle so physically debilitating that he ought to have been fighting for breath instead of issuing calm demands.

Kirk found himself unable to reply. Not because he lacked the ability to do so, but because the rage that had now begun to build within him overwhelmed everything else. The last time he had seen the face now gazing earnestly back at him, it had been inside the transparent cockpit of a mortally crippled jumpship plunging to earth outside Starfleet headquarters in San Francisco.

Standing before him was the man who had slaughtered his surrogate father. Kirk lowered his gaze until it was focused on the gun that was pointed at him. Close to him now, Harrison smiled. The mass murderer looked none the worse for wear.

"I wouldn't, Captain Kirk. I assure you my feet can move faster than your hands." He gestured ever so slightly with the weapon that hung easily from one hand. "Not to mention a phaser blast. I'll ask one last time: How many torpedoes?"

Recognizing the possibility of a foolish move on the part of an increasingly angry Kirk, one that would inarguably lead to disaster, Spock quickly answered for the still-dazed captain.

"Six dozen—seventy-two in all, as I recall from my one encounter with the manifest."

Clearly the number meant something to Harrison. While noting the science officer's response, the renegade shifted his attention back to Kirk.

Harrison pondered Spock's reply for what seemed an excessive amount of time . . . at the conclusion of which he did something as extraordinary as anything that had come before. He dropped his weapon at Kirk's feet and lowered his voice.

"In that case, I surrender."

A dumbfounded Uhura looked over at Spock. If she was seeking enlightenment from the Vulcan, there was none to be found there, as the science officer was equally bewildered by Harrison's action in voluntarily disarming himself. That did not prevent Spock from recovering his weapon and training it once more—and with greater alertness—on the unexpected prisoner.

After a moment's hesitation, a glaring Kirk rose and moved forward, halting short of the man who had just put down his own weapon.

"On behalf of Christopher Pike," he said tightly, "I accept your surrender." Following which he struck out as hard as he could at their savior.

Blow after blow landed as adrenaline fueled a purging rage. Uhura tensed and Spock took a step forward, only to halt when it was apparent that the object of the captain's fury was not fighting back. Harrison did not even raise his hands to defend himself. Making no attempt to ward off Kirk's fury, Harrison occasionally stumbled once or twice, staggering backward under the repeated impact. Only when blood began to flow from his face did he reach up. Eyeing the red stain on his fingers, he smiled. His response was not contemptuous, not accusatory. More than anything, it smacked of the tone an exasperated adult might use with a child.

"Captain!" Uhura finally yelled.

It was his target's expression that finally caused a grimacing, winded Kirk to cease his assault. His own knuckles were red, though whether from his blood or Harrison's, he couldn't tell. They were as numb as the rest of him. For a long moment the two men stood regarding each other, the only sound that of Qo'noS's wind howling through the long-forsaken city.

Harrison eyed him pityingly, his voice soft. "Captain . . ."

Glancing down, Kirk considered the weapon Harrison had set aside. He could pick it up. One shot . . .

In the end, despite his personal grief and rage, James Kirk was still a Starfleet officer. His look, if not his response, was murderous as he glared back at Harrison. Turning, he headed in the direction of their waiting, empty ship.

"Cuff him," he muttered, turning to walk away and leaving that task to Spock and Uhura. Having already put his hands on the traitor, Kirk did not trust himself to do so again.

* * *

"Captain's Log, supplemental. For reasons unknown, our warp core has failed. We are stranded deep in enemy space. After an action on Qo'noS during which we lost a member of our crew, we now have in custody Commander John Harrison. This—man—has surrendered to us for reasons I don't understand. Knowing full well it was our intention to capture, if not kill him, still he saved our lives. I don't know why, but I intend to find out.

"Kirk out."

* * *

Standing on the bridge, staring out at stars and nebulae, Kirk spoke without turning toward the interior.

"Lieutenant Uhura, did you let Starfleet know we have Harrison in custody?"

"Yes, sir," she replied from the vicinity of the communications station. "No response yet."

McCoy strove to keep up with Kirk as they moved quickly down the corridor, with Spock following close behind.

"You don't look good, Jim," the doctor opined. "What's your concern?"

"I want you to run a full physio panel on our prisoner."

The doctor's tone was, as was frequently the case, querulous. "Why? Is he sick?"

"I don't know what he is, Bones, but I do know that he just took out an entire Klingon security team single-handedly. I want to know how—and don't tell me it's because he has a good shooting eye. There's something else going on here that's more than passing strange. I need you to help me substitute 'facts' for 'strange.'"

McCoy considered. "Sounds like we have a superman on board."

"You tell me." The captain looked over at Spock as the three men turned into another corridor. "It's evident that unless one of those three patrol craft managed to get off a warning, the Klingons continue to remain unaware of our presence. We can't continue to rely on that. I don't want to push our luck any longer than necessary."

His first officer nodded concurrence. "The sooner we depart this vicinity, the better, Captain. We have been fortunate not to have been detected by full planetary defenses thus far. Or it is possible orbital sensors have detected the *Enterprise*'s signature, but in the crush of daily processing have not yet identified it. If that is the case, I would not count on our ability to remain anonymous for much longer."

"Don't worry, Mr. Spock," Kirk assured him. "I have no intention of lingering here one nanosecond longer than we have to."

Indifferent to his stark-white, smooth-walled surroundings, John Harrison stood calmly on the far side of the brig. Studying the individual on the other side of the transparent floor-to-ceiling security barrier, the doctor was not especially impressed.

Standing nearby, Kirk and Spock looked on, the captain particularly anxious to get the procedure over with.

From the other side of the cell wall, McCoy considered the prisoner. Other than appearing preternaturally calm, there was nothing visually exceptional about him.

"Excellent posture, well-developed lean musculature, but I see nothing remarkable." Picking up a hand-held voider from a nearby table, McCoy placed it against the barrier. The irising device generated a slightly-larger-than-fist-sized hole in the transparency. Nodding at the individual on the other side, McCoy indicated the circular opening he had just created between them. "Put your arm through the hole, please." When Harrison just stared back at him, the doctor added, "I'm only going to take a small blood sample. Don't worry. It won't hurt."

The prisoner appeared to ponder the request. Then he approached the barrier and put his arm through the gap. McCoy placed the extractor against one of several prominent veins. When nothing happened, he frowned and pushed harder. Still nothing. The faintest hint of a smile creased the prisoner's face. In response to a third, harder shove, the device finally started to fill with red fluid. Harrison showed no reaction at all. Ignoring the flow of blood, he focused instead on Kirk.

"Why aren't we moving, Captain?" Harrison asked. When Kirk chose not to reply, not even to acknowledge the question, the prisoner freely elaborated. "Allow me to guess. An unexpected malfunction? Perhaps something to do with the warp core, conveniently stranding your ship on the edge of Klingon space?"

McCoy looked up from his work and gaped at the prisoner. "How the hell do you know th—?"

"Bones." Kirk cut him off before the doctor could finish the thought. Glad the captain had caught him before he inadvertently said anything else revealing, McCoy finished the blood draw. As soon as he removed the extractor, he nodded to its subject. The prisoner obligingly withdrew his arm; the opening through which it had protruded automatically closed behind his retreating fingers. Without bothering to inspect the site of the draw, Harrison calmly regarded his captors.

"I think you'd find my insights valuable, Captain. Don't you want to hear what I have to say?"

Ignoring him, Kirk turned to McCoy. "We good?" The doctor made a quick check of the extractor and its dark red contents before nodding. "Fine. Let me know what you find. As soon as you've got something."

"Assuming there's anything out of the ordinary to be got," McCoy responded. Kirk didn't hear him, having pivoted sharply to head back toward the bridge. Spock and McCoy fell in behind him.

But while he failed to overhear McCoy, Kirk could not help but hear the reverberant warning that rose behind him.

"Ignore me, and you will get everyone on this ship killed."

Kirk slowed to a halt. Steadying his breathing, he turned to his two companions. Spock was watching him closely, McCoy curiously.

"Give me a minute, Mr. Spock."

The first officer started to raise a hand. "Captain, I would not recommend engaging the prisoner further in . . ."

"Give us a minute."

Spock hesitated, started to say something else, then left without further comment. Only when he was sure his companions had departed did Kirk pivot and stride back to the containment cell.

Harrison was waiting for him, standing close to the transparent barrier between them. The only *physical* barrier. Meeting the other man's gaze, Kirk considered unleashing the rage he felt, giving in to the urge to lay into the prisoner with feelings held just below the surface. But he doubted it would do him any good or Harrison any harm. Besides, he had already vented his emotions physically, and that had been shown to have little effect on the prisoner either.

There had to be some way to get to him, Kirk thought tightly. Perhaps through what was obvious and inescapable. Spock would have approved. There had to be *something* capable of wiping that smirk off Harrison's face. Unless, of course, Harrison was completely mad and therefore unaffected by the sane world around him.

No, Kirk told himself. Harrison might be psychopathic, but he was not insane. Not in the clinical sense, at least. His crimes had involved too much planning, too much careful preparation. A crazy man might have sought refuge on Qo'noS, but he would not have survived there, not even for a short time. Something else drove the man on the other side of the containment barrier. Something besides madness.

Just possibly, if he proceeded carefully and calmly, Kirk felt he might be able to identify it. Barely keeping his anger under control, he addressed the cell's occupant.

"Let me explain what's happening here, in terms you can't possibly misconstrue. You're a *criminal*. I watched you murder innocent men and women, people who were doing nothing but going about their daily jobs. People with families. None of that mattered to you. I was authorized to *end you,* and the only reason you're still alive is because I am *allowing* it. If I had chosen to do so, I could have had Dr. McCoy slip a full measure of something suitably toxic into his extractor. He could have pulled your blood, concurrently fatally dosed you, and I'd be signing off on the orders for the disposal of your carcass instead of having this face-to-face right now. Think about that for a moment. So until *I* decide what to do with *you,* I recommend you shut . . . your . . . mouth."

Digesting this, Harrison studied Kirk quietly for a moment before replying. "Oh, Captain, are you going to punch me again? Over and over until your arms weaken and you can't raise them high enough to hit me anymore? Clearly you want to. You so *desperately* want to. So tell me—there is one thing I am very curious about. Why *did* you 'allow' me to live? Why do you continue to do so?"

It was a valid question, Kirk knew.

"We all make mistakes."

"No." Harrison looked away, thoughtful.

"Why did you surrender to me? You could have killed me. For that matter, you could have let the Klingons kill me and my companions and maintained your refuge on Qo'noS. At least, you could have until Mr. Sulu unleashed the waiting volley of torpedoes."

That observation generated an unexpected smile that did not last long, as Harrison grew serious once again. "I surrendered to you because, despite your attempt to convince me otherwise, you seem to have a conscience, Mr. Kirk." His tone became almost familiar. "If you did not, then it would be impossible for me to convince you of the truth. And it is imperative that I convince you of the truth."

Kirk hesitated. This was not the reaction he was expecting, this confession hinting at something akin to camaraderie. It simultaneously repulsed and intrigued him.

"What 'truth'? What are you babbling about?"

"23174611. Coordinates not far, spatially speaking, from Earth. If you want to know why I did what I did, if you can find room in your head and heart for more than just a primitive, animalistic desire for revenge, go and take a look." He smirked. "Such a search would not be out of keeping with your overall mission statement. There would be no repercussions from Starfleet."

Clever. The man facing him on the other side of the barrier was as adept mentally as he was physically. It was what Spock had warned him against. Kirk was wary of allowing himself to be drawn in even to something as seemingly harmless as a suggestion.

But Harrison was right. The *Enterprise* could scope out the indicated coordinates without the risk of being countermanded by Starfleet. Especially since said coordinates might somehow relate not only to the capture of Harrison but to the carnage that had taken place back home in San Francisco. Kirk wanted very badly to comply. Still he hesitated.

"Give me one reason why I should listen to you?"

Harrison leaned forward until his face was almost pressing against the barrier. "I can give you seventy-two. And they're on board your ship, Captain." His tone was relentless, matter-of-fact. "They have been all along." Gratified by Kirk's reaction, by the evident surprise on the captain's face, the prisoner stepped back from the transparent wall that separated them. "I suggest you open one up—and take a look."

X

Are you out of your corn-fed mind?"

Flanked by Spock, who hovered close, Leonard McCoy spoke as loud and as near to Kirk as he could without risking a charge of infringing on a commanding officer's personal space. Though McCoy's face was flushed and he bordered on the apoplectic, Spock made no move to intervene: a sign of how seriously the science officer viewed the doctor's opinion on the matter at hand.

"You're not actually going to listen to this guy? He killed Pike, among numerous others," McCoy continued vociferously. "He almost killed *you*. And now you think it might be a good idea to pop open a torpedo just because he essentially *dared* you to?"

Seated in the command chair, Kirk listened to his friend's words with half a mind while the other kept to its own counsel.

"He also saved our lives. Mine, Spock's, Uhura's. There's no disputing that. He could have killed me, killed all of us, with ease. Instead, he *surrendered*. I think it's important to know the reason why."

McCoy was not dissuaded. "That's what he *wants* you to think. Jim, someone like Harrison doesn't do things because they've suddenly experienced a change of heart. There's a reason behind everything they do, and it has nothing to do with a sudden penchant for philanthropy. If he saved your lives, he did so because he saw something in it for him. Something that would help advance *his* agenda—whatever that might be."

"The doctor does have a point, Captain," Spock added softly.

Looking away, an agitated McCoy muttered: "Don't agree with me, Spock. It makes me very uncomfortable."

Kirk swung around to face both men. "Scotty quit because of those torpedoes. He wouldn't stay on board without knowing what was inside them. I've decided that he was right, and not just because Harrison suggested it. We need to know."

Straightening, McCoy gestured in the general direction of the distant holding area. "Jim. That man in the brig is a homicidal maniac who wants us to blow ourselves up! Maybe that's why those 'new' torpedoes are on board. So he could maneuver you into poking through their guts. Maybe if anyone tries to open one, it's set to protect itself by self-destructing. He's hooked you with a challenge, don't you see that?"

Kirk spoke thoughtfully without looking up at the doctor. "No. No, that's too obvious a ploy, and whatever else Harrison is, he's not obvious. He's demonstrated that already. I think there's another reason he wanted to be brought aboard the *Enterprise*. We need to find out what that is."

"Maybe he wants to say all is forgiven so he can enlist." His tone acidic, McCoy was now beside himself. "I think he's gotten under your skin—he could be stalling for some reason. That would explain this challenge of his for us to go to these unvisited coordinates. He could be working with the Klingons!"

"Perhaps you, too, should learn to govern your emotions a little, Doctor," Spock broke in. "In this situation, logic dictates—"

"Logic!" McCoy sputtered. "My God, there's a maniac trying to make us blow up our own ship and you're—"

Having come to a decision, Kirk raised a hand to forestall the rest of the doctor's rant. "I don't know why he surrendered, but that's not it. We're gonna open one of the torpedoes. That's my decision. The question is, how." Having forcefully terminated one discussion, he energetically embarked on another. "What's the best way? The safest way?"

McCoy let out a snort of disdain. "I've heard the story behind the loading of those weapons. We have no schematics, no diagrams, no operating files. Without Mr. Scott on board, there's no one appropriately qualified to pop open a newly designed four-ton stick of dynamite. Even our weapons specialists won't attempt a break-in without explanatory software—or Mr. Scott's expertise."

"If I may offer a thought, Captain?"

Kirk eyed his science officer. "Always, Mr. Spock."

"It has come to my attention that the admiral's daughter also has an interest in the new torpedoes, and she *is* a weapons specialist. Perhaps she could be of some use."

Kirk whirled. Captain and physician gawked at the Vulcan. "What?!" Kirk stared hard at his first officer. "*What* admiral's daughter?"

"Carol Marcus," Spock explained blithely. "Your new science

officer concealed her true identity in order to be assigned to the *Enterprise*."

Kirk made no attempt to conceal his bewilderment. "When were you going to tell me that?"

"When it became relevant," a complacent Spock assured him. "As it just did."

"Are the torpedoes in the weapons bay?"

Carol Marcus spoke without looking at Kirk as the two of them strode swiftly down the corridor. Meanwhile, a hundred questions raced through Kirk's mind. Unfortunately, they were not neatly aligned, and the result was a jumble that prevented any one of them from coming to the fore in anything resembling a coherent fashion. It did not help that she plainly had an agenda of her own.

"Prepped and loaded for use in the weapons bay," he informed her. Somehow, he thought, everything that had happened since the slaughter at Starfleet Headquarters seemed to keep coming back to the new weapons system. But why? "*What* are they? What's so special about them other than that they're supposed to be undetectable when in flight?"

She looked over at him. "I don't know. That's why I manipulated a transfer onto your ship—to find out." Halting abruptly, she turned to face him, plainly embarrassed. "I do apologize for that, and I am sorry. I'm Carol Marcus."

Yeah, I know. He extended a hand. "James Kirk." Before he could add anything else, she whirled and resumed her rapid pace.

Fine, he thought. *She's apologized.* He could only hope she was planning to be honest with him from now on. So . . . if her serious interest was in the new torpedoes, why was she heading toward the shuttle bay? He could have stopped her and asked, but found it potentially more revealing to let her lead the way. She made no attempt to evade his attention or leave him behind.

"I don't understand," he finally pressed her. "You're investigating your own father? And how are you English?"

"He was stationed in London when I was born, but soon afterwards my parents split up. When I was old enough, I joined Starfleet to follow in his footsteps. I'm not particularly proud of using my connections, but it was the only way I could gain access to the diversity of programs he personally oversaw. He never seemed to mind. In fact, I think he encouraged my curiosity. We never kept things from each other. Not that I ever had much to conceal from him. Then"—she hesitated, uncertain how to proceed—"things . . . changed."

"How so?" Kirk prompted her.

"I learned he was working with programs intended to develop new weapons. When I started my usual poking around, my security clearance was revoked." She shook her head in disbelief, remembering. "There had never been a hint that I was doing anything wrong or that I was expressing an interest in something I shouldn't have been inquiring about. One minute I had access to anything and everything to which my father was connected; the next, to nothing. As far as security was concerned, Starfleet cut me off completely. But that wasn't the worst of it."

"Go on," he said gently. They were almost to the shuttle bay now.

"When I went to confront my father to find out what had happened, he wouldn't even see me." She made a small sound in her throat. "We'd been close, very close, my whole life, and suddenly he won't see me. Wouldn't talk via communicator, wouldn't even acknowledge receipt of a simple message. But it didn't stop me from trying to find out what had caused the rift. I suspected it might have something to do with his then-current project.

"I had to call in every favor I had ever earned. There were people, friends, who risked their careers to feed me information. I learned about the research on a new type of torpedo. Then, when I tried to dig a little deeper, what I found was that the very same torpedoes and everything related to their development had disappeared from official records. Hell, they'd disappeared from the *unofficial* records. Even rumors about them had been expunged from general discussion."

Realization had long since struck Kirk. "And then he gave them to me."

Standing on the steps leading into the nearest shuttle, she nodded and smiled back at him. "You're much cleverer than your reputation suggests, Captain Kirk."

Pleased to have the mood lightened, however indirectly, he responded in kind as he followed her into the shuttle. "I have a reputation?"

Without pausing or asking for authorization, she selected the nearest shuttle and started up the entryway. "Yes, you do. I'm a friend of Christine Chapel."

Something landed in the pit of Kirk's stomach that bore no relation to the remainder of his previous meal. "Oh. Christine. How is she?"

From the airlock opening Carol looked down at him. "She transferred to the outer frontier to be a nurse. She's much happier now."

"Well, that's good."

"You have no idea who I'm talking about, do you?"

"If you don't mind my asking, what exactly are we doing in here?"

"Would you please turn around?"

"Why?" He was genuinely baffled.

She eyed him evenly. "Just turn around."

He complied, and she continued talking.

"You said you wanted to crack one of those torpedoes. So we do, after all, have something in common. Since their explosive power is unknown, worst-case scenario is they're planet killers. Even if they're designed to do no more than their conventional counterparts and take out an enemy vessel, I don't think attempting to open one on this ship in the absence of so much as a snapshot of its guts would be very wise, do you?"

Aware that conversations were inevitably more efficacious when conducted face-to-face, Kirk turned. Inevitably, he did not make initial visual contact with her eyes.

Regulation Starfleet undergarments, he decided, had rarely looked quite so fetching.

"Turn around," she repeated.

"Yeah—right." For a second time he complied with the request. But the brief image he had glimpsed remained sharp in his memory.

"There's an uninhabited desert planetoid in range," she continued. "I can fly there—it lies within shuttle reach—but I cannot disarm a torpedo alone, especially in the absence of any relevant information regarding its insides. In lieu of such schematics, I'll need the assistance of your chief engineer."

Kirk coughed into a closed fist. "My chief, uh, quit."

As she continued to don the exosuit she had chosen, she looked over at him curiously. "Did he? Why?"

"I ordered him to sign off on delivery of the torpedoes." *The damn weapons really were at the center of everything,* he thought to himself. "He refused because he, uh, couldn't get any information as to their internal components and design."

She smiled thinly. "Well. What a coincidence. Not so clever after all."

If there was one thing Kirk never lacked, it was a smart retort to a direct criticism. Well, almost never.

The bar was sophisticated enough to be left alone by the authorities, yet sufficiently disreputable to be fun. Situated in a part of San Francisco that had been the location of such establishments since the founding of the city, it was a glittering farrago of flashing lights, obscure décor, and throbbing music. Its multilingual staff catered to the needs of every known species that enjoyed indulging in stimulants. While oxygen-breathers predominated, there was a separate room for methane suckers. Those who required gaseous supplements with different chemical compositions could put down a deposit and enjoy the use of the establishment's portable tanks and masks while paying only for what they inhaled.

Blasting loud and hard, music from several worlds overrode conversation, lover's quarrels, bad jokes, and the occasional San Francisco earthquake. The décor varied from antique North American southwest to outré samples of current technolo. Due to its location and the tolerant touch of its bouncers, the place was very popular with the personnel from the nearby Starfleet complex.

This extended to and included one Montgomery Scott. Having imbibed a considerable portion of the potion for which his

homeland was famed, the engineer exhibited in his present condition a decided inclination toward an unstable equilibrium.
Only the fact that he was presently seated in a booth opposite his
first assistant enabled him to remain upright. At least his upper
body remained upright. Other than that he could not be sure,
because he was having a hard time feeling anything below his
waist. Across from him the stone-faced non-human Keenser was
gazing morosely into his own drink out of wide black eyes, wondering why he had allowed his chief to talk him into resigning
along with him. As much as he respected Scott, the Roylan was
glad the table was wide enough to keep the chief from poking
him in the face as Scott punctuated each new sentence with a
challenging jab.

"You know what bothers me the most?" the chief was saying
for the third or fourth time. Keenser couldn't be sure, because
his own absorption of alcoholic liquids had rendered suspect his
usually infallible ability to crunch numbers. "The modifications
I made to standardized equipment. The enhancements I made.
And then just like that, I'm off the ship! Just for trying to do
what's right!"

Across the table the squat Roylan nodded solemnly, still
staring into his glass. Within its amber depths the lightly tinted
liquid held mysteries unknown, not to mention the shattered
fragments of his own aborted future.

Peering across the table, Scott bellowed accusingly. "And
what did you do, anyway? You just stood there like an oyster,
lookin' at me, ya wee sleekit cowerin' beastie!"

An insistent chirping interrupted the unfounded but nonetheless energetic harangue of his silently stoic assistant. What
was that damnable noise? Was the bloody universe itself now
intent on driving him mad? It had to be the focused emissions

of a dying pulsar, aimed with fiendish precision at the back of his head—or else someone was calling him. Unable to decide between the two or influence the first possibility, he opted to try his communicator. It required three fumbling tries to snap it open.

"What?" he shouted into the pickup.

The connection was not the best, suggesting that it was being bounced along via multiple relays.

"Scotty," came the static-distorted but now familiar voice, "it's Kirk."

"Oh, well now!" As he leaned against the back wall of the booth, an expression of enormous satisfaction spread across the engineer's face. "James *Tiberius* Kirk? Savior o' the galaxy and dismisser o' all rational thinking? Callin' *me*? A lowly an' self-disgraced engineer? To what do I owe the pleasure . . . *sir.*"

"Scotty, Uhura had to work a minor miracle to make this tight-beam transmission possible, not to mention secure." There was a pause, then Kirk's tone turned uncertain. "Is that technolo I hear in the background? Where are you?"

Scott dismissed the captain's question with an airy wave of his free hand while a morose Keenser dipped a thick forefinger in his drink and commenced stirring memories.

"At present, I'm somewhere between heaven an' hell, Captain. Otherwise known as San Francisco." The chief chuckled at his own humor.

Burdened with concerns of somewhat greater import, Kirk did not join in the amusement. "Are you drunk?"

"Is that an engineering question? Are you now questionin' me ability to handle liquids as well as me job? What I do in *me* spare time is entirely *me* business, Jimbo. And in case it has escaped your notice, I am no longer a member of your crew, and therefore no longer subject to your orders."

From a very long distance away, Kirk took a deep breath before resuming the conversation. "Scotty, I'm starting to have my doubts about those torpedoes."

Kirk's unexpected words managed to penetrate the alcoholic haze that had taken up residence in the chief engineer's cerebrum. "I will consider that an apology." Scott sat up a little straighter. Or at least that was the instruction he passed along to the muscles of his lower body. As he remained slumped, it was likely that the message got lost somewhere between his brain and his behind. "And I will *consider* that apology."

"Scotty, I need you to check something out for me. Will you take these coordinates down: 23, 17, 46, 11 . . . Are you recording?"

The chief glared at his communicator as if it were personally responsible for his current situation. "You think I kinna remember four miserable numbers . . . What was that third one again?"

"Forty-six. I need you to go there and report back. I don't know exactly what you're looking for, but I have a feeling you'll know it when you see it."

Communication concluded, Scott flipped the communicator shut and proceeded to exchange the device for the larger, rounder, and altogether more solid glass sitting on the table in front of him.

"Damn senior officers," he muttered as he downed a fresh shot.

By way of response, the stocky Roylan maintained his unblinking yet inquisitive stare.

Scott responded with a disturbing noise, not unlike the sound certain deeply installed components made in Engineering when the warp core was not functioning properly. "Self-pity will get you nowhere, man. Look at me. Am I pitying myself? Am I?"

Keenser pursed his lips as he regarded his superior. Though limited, his alien expression fully reflected what he was feeling.

"Can you believe his nerve?" Either Scott chose to ignore the junior engineer's observation or, more likely, he didn't hear it. "He lets me quit—resign—and then he *ignores* me. Not a hello, not a how-do-you-do, not so much as d'you happen to be alive, old friend, and now suddenly he *needs* me?"

When Keenser simply continued to gaze stolidly back at him, Scott's gaze narrowed as he glared across the table. "Don't judge me with those prunes you call eyes." Still Keenser did not move, did not blink. Just stared back at his superior.

Raising a hand, Scott tried to wave away something unseen. "No . . . *no!*"

Keenser kept staring. For a humanoid of modest resources, he could be remarkably determined. So much so that the chief finally couldn't take it anymore. Or maybe he couldn't take what was tugging at his guts, if not his heart.

"Oh fine, then, ya wrinkly little sonuvabitch!" Dazed and unhappy, he searched the table without finding what he was looking for. "I need a bloody refill."

Sulu reported to Kirk the instant the captain arrived back on the bridge. "Shuttle's almost in position, sir. Preparing to touch down."

His eyes fixed on the forward screen, Kirk slid into the command chair. "Any sign of activity from the Klingons? Any hint they've detected our presence here? Unusual ship movements, any indication that we've been scanned?"

"No, Captain," the helmsman replied. Kirk glanced back.

"Lieutenant Uhura: Any rise in local transmissions? Anything exceptional passing between Qo'noS and Praxis or the orbiting monitoring and defense stations?"

Looking over at him, she shook her head. "Nothing, sir. No unusual communications either in nature or volume. Chat-wise, everything's normal in this system."

He nodded with satisfaction. "Mr. Sulu: No indication of curious patrol vessels in our vicinity?"

"No, sir. It's all quiet out to a safe distance and beyond. Should there be anyone looking for us here?"

Kirk allowed himself a pleased smile. "Only if they find pieces of their colleagues lying around down on the surface and wonder what happened to them. There's no reason to connect what happened in Ketha Province with an off-world intervention, anyway. That's one thing we've got in our favor. Not only are Klingons noted for taking shots at other peoples, they're perfectly happy bashing up one another. Any local forensic follow-up will logically first assume that there was an altercation among the patrol members themselves that got out of hand. By the time anyone finds anything or suspects anything that might point to an intrusion from off Qo'noS, we'll be well away from here." He looked again to Communications. "Nice work putting together that relay so I could talk to Scotty, Lieutenant."

"Thank you, Captain. It was a bit of a project, tight-beaming all the way from here back to Earth and directly to Mr. Scott's personal communicator. But you know what the ancient philosopher Clarke said. 'Any sufficiently advanced technology is indistinguishable from magic.'"

Kirk nodded. "We could use a little of Mr. Scott's own brand of magic right now. Still no response from Starfleet regarding our capture of Harrison?"

"No, sir. No response yet."

Swinging back in the command chair, Kirk turned his attention to the pickup. "Mr. Chekov. Give me some good news."

The sounds of technicians busy with unseen equipment formed a counterpoint to Chekov's response. *"We've isolated the problem, sir, but there is some damage. We're working on it."*

Kirk pondered. "Any idea what caused it in the first place?"

"No, sir. It's very odd." The ensign sounded exhausted. *"But I take full responsibility. A ship should not just drop out of warp like that."*

"Something tells me it wasn't your fault, Chekov. Stay on it, and notify me the minute repairs are completed. No matter what else may be happening at the time. We're still undetected, but we can't sit here forever. Sooner or later a manned or automated craft is going to check this particular small section of emptiness and be surprised to find something. I don't want to be a surprise."

"Yes, sir. I'll let you know the instant that full warp drive capability has been restored."

Sulu wasted no time in passing along his own up-to-date information as soon as Kirk had finished with Chekov.

"Shuttle is standing by, Captain. They're in position on the planetoid."

"Any position's a good position so long as they weren't spotted," Kirk murmured. The forward viewscreen showed the shuttle's destination: a dusty, yellowish, uninhabited sphere. He keyed the chair's comm.

"Thanks for helping out, Bones. In lieu of Mr. Scott, Dr. Marcus asked for the steadiest hands on the ship. I know you didn't want anything to do with those torpedoes, much less be involved in trying to open them."

★   ★   ★

Within the shuttle, McCoy considered an appropriate response even as he continued to contemplate his present situation. Why *had* he agreed to something that, in his right mind, he ordinarily would have refused? Was it possible that when he accepted he hadn't been in his right mind? If that was the case, what was the appropriate medical explanation? He hesitated. He could be evasive, or he could be truthful—and he'd never been very good at being evasive. If he had, his divorce might have been less fiscally painful. Said divorce might also, however obliquely, have influenced his decision to agree to this insane subsidiary mission.

"You know," he replied glumly as he gathered his gear and headed for the shuttle's exit, "when I dreamt about being stuck on a deserted planet with a gorgeous woman, there was no torpedo involved."

As it sounded from the communicator Kirk's voice was mildly disapproving. *"Dr. McCoy, may I remind you that you're not there to flirt."*

"I know, I know." McCoy wasn't sure whether he was exasperated or simply regretting the circumstances in which he presently found himself.

Even for such a small world, the volcanic desert vista that surrounded them was strikingly barren. The black sinter plain underfoot was broken only by occasional towers and buttes of similar but harder material. McCoy might even have found it interesting if not for the potentially disruptive device lying on the surface near where the shuttle had set down.

Outside the *Enterprise*'s weapons bay, the torpedo appeared twice as massive and ten times as threatening. He checked the readouts on his instruments. A planetoid this small should have had light gravity, yet it was not much below *Enterprise* or terrestrial standards. Extra-dense core, he decided, somewhat surprised that the Klingons had not done any mining here. Idly, he wondered if he could stake a claim, then told himself that the locals were unlikely to honor it.

Carol Marcus had preceded him to the torpedo. At once ominous and innocuous, it rested on a support platform; a streamlined mass of metal, synthetics, and concealed electronics not much bigger than two people lying side by side. In the absence of accompanying schematics, its destructive potential remained unknown. After having carefully placed sensors along its length, she was now activating the monitoring device that linked them together.

McCoy nodded his understanding as he glanced at the readout on the monitor she was holding. It was not providing the hoped-for clear view of the torpedo's interior. There was too much protective shielding and intervening instrumentation for the small sensors to penetrate. He said as much and she gestured in agreement.

"In order to understand how powerful these weapons are and what's so special about them," Carol said, "we need to open the warhead. In order to do that, we need to access the drive compartment. Unfortunately for us, the warheads on these weapons are live. A lot of the talk was about the new drive system that renders the torpedo untrackable. So we go in that way, where the control system is supposed to be. However, since we have no way of knowing how our intrusion might affect the rest of the device, our first task is to disarm the warhead." She offered up a thin smile. "Our research won't go anywhere if the device goes off while we're poking around its innards. Sure you can handle this, Dr. McCoy?"

He shrugged diffidently as he lugged a heavy box of gear around the back of the resting torpedo. "Sweetheart, I once performed an emergency C-Section—or more properly, a G-section—on a pregnant Gorn. Don't ask about how I got talked into that one: It's not a pretty story. Neither was the operation. Octuplets. All healthy: alive, kicking slowly—and biting." His expression fell at the memory. "Boy, can those things *bite*. I think I can handle your torpedo."

"Right, then," she said without pressing him for further details. "Let us begin."

XI

Jupiter was beautiful this time of year, Montgomery Scott thought. But then, Jupiter was beautiful any time. Not that it was a suitable spot for a vacation. A bit on the breezy side, and the landscape—well, there was no landscape, only cloudscape, which would tear you and your ship apart if you dropped too close.

Hugging Io's surface, he soared toward the coordinates Kirk had given him. In an earlier age, its ferocious volcanoes and tormented sulfuric lakes would have drawn the attention of any passerby, but they were old news now. For every astronomical or geological marvel the solar system offered up, something twice as spectacular could be found in another system, circling another sun.

On the other hand, the massive block of blackness that abruptly appeared in the forward port and simultaneously on his shuttle's sensors was definitely something new.

It was enormous, enigmatic, drifting in an orbit all its own. What was it doing out here, so far from any established station or colony? Where did it come from?

Slowing his speed, Scott skimmed over the top of it. Evidence of long-term heavy construction was amply visible on all the structure's sides. For a structure it was unabashedly artificial, its construction representing a huge investment in time and resources. What equipment he could discern, he readily recognized. The immense orbiting edifice was terrestrial in origin then, and not some unfathomable alien intrusion.

Why build it way out here, so far from home? Yes, the location offered easier access to the resources of the asteroid belt, but surely those would be offset by placing the facility, whatever its purpose, so distant from Earth? Each question Scott asked himself only led to others, and he had answers for none of them.

As he contemplated making a try for a main entrance as its doors parted beneath him, his ship's receiver barked a query of its own.

"Shuttle on course 12-4-G. Identify yourself."

What the ladies from hell? That the insistent query came from the black rectangle was confirmed by his instruments. What was he going to do now? What was he *supposed* to do? As Scott's mind raced furiously, he was saved by an interjection from a second equally unfamiliar source.

"This is shuttle Hyperion, *inbound. We've got six pallets of dilithium cells. Awaiting vector."*

Wait a minute, he told himself. *They weren't talking to me.* Whoever *they* were. In fact, from the gist of what he had overheard, "they" weren't even aware of his presence. Not surprising. This close in to the gas giant's powerful magnetosphere, there was all kinds of distortion on the spectrum, and plenty of upper hybrid resonance instability. Communicating inside the Io plasma torus was difficult enough, and scanning more so. Subject to such powerful external influences, instruments didn't behave the way engineers wanted them to.

And speaking of scanning, Scott was free to do a little of his own.

A check of his instrumentation followed by a glance through an overhead port revealed the presence of a dozen supply shuttles, of varying class and capacity, traveling in a loose formation and heading directly toward the black rectangle. The conversation he had overheard was already being subsumed in a jumble of overlapping exchanges between the shuttle crews and their mysterious destination.

"*Shuttle* Kirby: *rations and personnel . . . This is the* Athena; *we've got storage pods . . .* Trimble *on approach, restoratives and boosters . . .*"

As each of the arriving craft gave their name and detailed their cargo, it occurred to Scott that he might just possibly be able to lose himself in the confusion. Bringing himself down and around, he slipped easily into the cargo fleet's scattered formation. There was plenty of room for Scott to maneuver among the other shuttlecraft. No one questioned his presence. After all, what would another single, small shuttlecraft be doing in Io's vicinity? All current scientific work was performed by automated spacecraft and instrumentation.

Then what the haggis, Scott mused wonderingly, was this enormous structure he was entering?

As the supply fleet moved inside, he was able to resolve the finer details of its construction. He did not need much to tell him that what he was entering was a product of Starfleet engineering and design.

Something else drew his attention. His eyes widened and his mouth opened as he stared upward through a viewport.

Whatever that unknown intangible might be, its physical manifestation was mighty impressive. His eyes widened as he caught his first glimpse of it through the shuttle's forward port. His whispered verbal reaction was as heartfelt as it was involuntary.

"Holy shit . . ."

Dr. McCoy stood by and watched as Carol Marcus used a specialized tool and monitor to open an outer protective panel, and then a second inner one. Carefully examining the interior of the weapon, she instructed him without taking her eyes from her work.

"There's a bundle of cables against the inner near casing." She studied the monitor. "You'll need to cut the twenty-third one down to eliminate contact between the internal controls and the detonator. I'll direct, you cut." She smiled. "Can't search-scan and cut at the same time; it's far too tricky and the internal instrumentation much too densely packed. Which is why I needed your help. Twenty-third wire," she repeated. "I'll guide you. Whatever you do, don't touch anything else. Do you understand?"

"Thought never crossed my mind," he replied tensely.

Since leaving the *Enterprise*, Carol Marcus had been all business. If anything, she now grew more serious than ever.

"Dr. McCoy, this is no joke. Touch *nothing else*. Nothing. The last thing we want is an automatic signal rerouting via accidental physical contact while you're interdicting the original linkage. Wait for my word."

Selecting a small precision cutter from the box of tools he had brought with him, McCoy sidled up close to the torpedo and peered down into the rectangular opening that had been created by the removal of the two panels. The interior was a daunting jumble of solid cables and optical state links. None of the links were glowing: They would not spring to life until and unless the torpedo's more mundane but nonetheless critical components were activated. Gripping the cutter as firmly as any surgical instrument, he gently pushed his hand and arm into the opening and slid it into position.

"Cut nothing until I say," she reminded him as her fingers danced over the monitor's contacts. "I'm rerouting as much of the internal programming as I'm able to access in the absence of the relevant coding."

With his arm plunged deep into the weapon, he looked over at her. "I don't entirely understand what that signifies, but I'm ready."

Her eyes never left the monitor she was now holding. "Okay, good luck. Here we go. On 'one.' You ready?"

"And rarin'." He sighed. The sooner this was over with and they had learned what they needed to about the weapon, the sooner he would be back on the ship.

"Three . . . two . . . one . . ." A forefinger flicked across a contact on the face of the monitor.

There was a curt metallic sound as the outer panel unexpectedly snapped shut, sliding sharply backward to pin McCoy's arm in place. He let out a yelp and tried to pull free. While the pressure on his upper arm was not cutting, it was plenty uncomfortable. Everything in the immediate area of contact began to throb as the main blood supply to his trapped limb was impaired. As if that wasn't bad enough, a soft, steady, and not at all reassuring beeping had commenced somewhere deep within the torpedo.

To Carol's horror, a sequence of numbers had now appeared on her monitor. All in red and linked to another section of the weapon, they had begun a steady countdown from sixty.

"What the hell just happened!?" McCoy grimaced in pain as he continued the futile struggle to free his arm.

"I—I don't . . ." Carol was staring at her monitor. She began to nudge contact points, to try and redirect specific links. What her sensors *could* tell her about what was happening inside the torpedo was alarming.

Since Carol's handheld was linked to its equivalent on the *Enterprise,* everyone on the bridge could see what was happening below in real time. It was a startled Sulu whose instrumentation confirmed what everyone feared.

"Sir, the torpedo just armed itself."

"Warhead is set to detonate in sixty seconds, sir," declared another crewmember tersely.

"Why would it do that?" Sulu wondered aloud. "Why wouldn't it wait for appropriate final instructions? Torpedoes aren't equipped with self-destruct programming."

Without bothering to say *This one is,* Kirk addressed the Science station. "Lock onto their positions. Beam them back aboard. *Right now.*"

Spock's response came even faster than usual. "With his arm

trapped inside it, the transporter is unable to differentiate between Dr. McCoy and the torpedo. We cannot beam one back without the other. Furthermore, there are additional concerns if using a transporter to beam a heavy weapon, which, of course, is why it was taken to the surface below by shuttlecraft in the first place. By the time I could get to the transporter room . . ."

Kirk was sure Spock had detailed explanations for many other matters related to the present situation. Unfortunately, there was no time to listen to them. He addressed himself to the images visible on the forward screen.

"Dr. Marcus, can you reverse the action that just took place within the torpedo? Can you disarm it?"

"I—I'm trying!"

On the planetoid below, Carol Marcus's fingers were flying over the monitor's front panel—to no apparent effect. Individual sections continued to appear in red, as did the numbers that maintained their inexorable countdown.

Wincing in pain, McCoy prodded her through clenched teeth. "I can't get my arm out!"

As a physician, he should have been analyzing the pain in his arm and speculating as to possible permanent damage. If they had a phaser between them, he would have considered having Carol cut off his arm so they could be beamed back to the ship. A missing limb he could deal with, later. He was healthy, and the prospects for full regeneration down to the neural level were acceptable. But, expecting no confrontation on the surface of the uninhabited planetoid, they had not brought any weapons with them. Except the torpedo, of course. In contrast, it might take as much as half a minute to amputate his arm with the use of a precision cutter. And, wonder of wonders, they had a precision cutter.

Unfortunately, McCoy was holding on to it with the hand that was trapped inside the torpedo.

Reaching a decision, Marcus abruptly moved to the side of the weapon. Using the same tool that she had employed to detach the first two outer panels, she began to remove the protective transparency that covered the torpedo's main visible readout. As she worked she kept muttering to herself, "I can do this . . . I can do this."

Watching her, McCoy came to a decision of his own.

Quietly, and without fanfare, he addressed his comm unit. "Jim, I'm . . . boned. No reason for both of us to be. Get her out of here. You can beam her back aboard without any problem."

Overhearing, Marcus snapped a response in his direction even as she continued to work on the weapon's innards. "No! You beam me back, he dies! *I can do this, dammit!* Trust me!"

"Standing by to transport Dr. Marcus on your command, sir." Sulu was not as emotionless as Spock, but in doing his job he was trying his best not to influence his captain's decision one way or the other.

Carol Marcus removed the outer panel and then the LCD readout within, exposing a mass of cabling and optical connections that now pulsed with intensity. Without hesitation, she began digging through them. As her arms interrupted the opticals, there were flashes of light and a few sparks. But she didn't retreat or remove her probing fingers.

"Twenty seconds," McCoy mumbled as he stared in horrified fascination at the remorseless readout. "Eighteen . . ." Full awareness of what she was doing interrupted his morbid count. "Hey, what are you doing over there? *I thought we weren't supposed to touch anything?!*"

"Like I'm going to make things worse by trying?" she responded. "Please be quiet."

Four . . . three . . .

So many cables, so many connections, so many unknowns.

"Shit!"

Grabbing a double handful of cables, Marcus leaned back and yanked as hard as she could.

From somewhere deep within the bowels of the torpedo there came a puff of vapor, neither toxic nor explosive. The steady beeping that had emanated from the weapon's depths since it had been armed gave way to a falling whine. The panel pinning McCoy's arm retracted, releasing him. As he fell to the ground, he clutched at his freed arm—it was deeply bruised, but it was still attached to his shoulder and, as near as he could tell, fully functional. Gritting his teeth against the painful tingling sensation as full blood flow resumed to his hand, he flung the now-unneeded cutter aside. Nearby, a relieved Carol Marcus slumped onto the gravel, still clutching both handfuls of cable.

On the bridge Spock turned and reported, calm as ever. "Deactivation successful, Captain."

Letting out a relieved breath, Kirk leaned forward and shut his eyes. Remembering McCoy's distress, he then half straightened and addressed the comm. "Dr. McCoy, are you all right? Report. Bones?"

McCoy wasn't listening, nor did Carol Marcus step in on the doctor's behalf to acknowledge the captain's query. Her action had done more than deactivate a supposed live warhead. It had also resulted in the protective paneling that shielded the special drive compartment opening, sliding backward, revealing . . .

McCoy stared downward. "Jim, you're gonna want to see this. Spock is gonna want to see this." He paused. "Everyone is going to want to see this, but I'm not sure everyone should. Not until we know more about what I'm looking at right now. A *lot* more."

Located between the supposedly secret advanced new drive and the control compartment that had threatened to cut off McCoy's arm, there was something else. A sizeable additional compartment. What it contained wasn't part of a drive system at all.

It was a human being—a man, to be exact. His skin was terribly pale. Which was not inappropriate, as he was as frozen solid as ice.

Though portions of the *Enterprise*'s sickbay were designed to, if need be, accommodate alien life-forms who bulked considerably larger than human, it still proved a difficult and awkward task to wrestle the disarmed torpedo all the way into one of the examination rooms. That was where Kirk and Spock found Carol Marcus hovering over the deactivated weapon, gazing down at the restful, pale-white face of the man lying within. His age was indeterminate. *His physical age,* Kirk reminded himself. There was no telling how long this man had lain in his present state. Seated on a nearby bed, McCoy acknowledged their arrival with a nod. Shirtless, he sat patiently while one of his nurses tended to his injured arm.

"What have you learned?" Kirk immediately asked Marcus.

"A little. Not nearly enough." She indicated the torpedo and its unlikely, unreasonable, and utterly inexplicable contents. "It's brilliant, actually. Somebody managed to shrink the drive unit to the point where they had room for an additional compartment and retrofitted the space that had been freed up to accommodate a cryogenic capsule. A portion of the onboard stored energy meant to maintain the weapon's electronics and related systems was redirected to sustain the capsule's functionality." Marcus shook her head at the wonder of it all. "A capsule like this requires only minimal power to sustain cold stasis for a considerable period of time."

Kirk's gaze shifted from her to the figure in the torpedo. There was no movement, of course, not even a rising and falling of the chest or a flexing of the nostrils. The man lying within was not breathing. Which, given his current frozen state, was not conclusive of anything.

"Is he alive?"

Standing on the other side of the torpedo, McCoy spoke up. "Yeah, he's alive. His vitals are minimal, barely detectable, but they're there. Slowed *waaayyy* down. To levels you'd want if you chose to take a long nap on the floor of the Antarctic Ocean."

Kirk pressed his chief physician. "Can he be revived?"

McCoy was plainly dubious. "Not without the proper equipment. You can't improvise this sort of thing. The same science that was used to put him in this state has to be used to bring him out of it. If we try to bring him back without the proper instrumentation, the attempt could kill him as soon as revive him. . . . This technology's beyond me."

"How advanced, Doctor?" an obviously intrigued Spock inquired.

"It's not advanced," Carol explained. "That cryotube is ancient."

"We haven't had to freeze anyone since the earliest days of deep space exploration," McCoy added. "The discovery and development of warp capability made this particular branch of biotech obsolete. An instant antique. And speaking of antiques, that's the most interesting thing about our friend here." He winced as pain flared in his injured arm.

"I did a quick scraping off his right shoulder. Less than a flea would take, nothing he'd notice even if he was awake. But enough to run some tests." McCoy nodded at the torpedo and its frozen occupant. "He's three hundred years old."

Kirk exchanged a meaningful glance with his science officer. Though neither man spoke a word, their thoughts were aligned.

The two armed security officers on duty at the entrance to the brig had to move swiftly to open it. As fast as Kirk was moving and as angry as he was, he might have gone right through the door. He wasted no time confronting the room's single prisoner.

"*Who are you?* Why is there a man in the torpedo we examined?"

Gazing back through the barrier at the intent Kirk, the prisoner sighed tiredly.

"There are men and women in all the torpedoes, Captain. And I put them there."

Once again captain and first officer exchanged looks. Kirk repeated himself.

"Who the hell are you?"

It was a question the prisoner had been asked too many times before; one which he had been forced to answer far more often than he wished. But no one had asked him in some time, he reminded himself. So despite how much it bored him to do so yet again, he deigned to explain himself.

"I am a remnant of a time long past. Genetically engineered to be superior so as to lead others to peace in a world at war." He looked away. "But I and my companions were condemned as criminals. Forced into exile. For centuries we slept, hoping that when we awoke, things would be . . . different. Always these vain hopes."

Spock interrupted. "You imply that you too were in cryostasis?"

The prisoner gifted Spock with a nod of approval and smiled at Kirk. "He's smart." Looking away from the captain, Harrison turned his attention to the science officer. "If your planet had not been annihilated, I would still be asleep. But as a result of the destruction of Vulcan, your Starfleet began to search distant quadrants of space more aggressively than before. They found my ship adrift. I alone was revived, after which I was able to learn about the destruction of Vulcan and . . . many other things."

Kirk listened to it all, the look on his face indicating that everything he was hearing might very well be the elaborate invention of a disturbed mind. Or a sheer fabrication being dispensed by a clear mind. Either way . . .

"I looked up John Harrison," Kirk told him. "Up until a year ago, he didn't exist."

It was the prisoner's turn to move close to the barrier. All that separated the two men now was a laminated layer of malleable corundum-silicate glass.

"'John Harrison' was a fiction created the moment I was awoken by your Admiral Marcus to help him advance his cause. A smoke screen, a nonexistent reality, an imagined self, all concocted to conceal my true identity. Because it would not have gone well for your admiral had my true name become known at the time of my revival. Some curious ensign might have decided, in a moment of boredom, to run a search on it. Then everything might have become . . . difficult." He paused, smiled, and went silent.

For a long moment, it was as if he were no longer present. As if his thoughts, if not his physical self, were focused on a time, place, and events long ago and far away. An impatient Kirk was about to comment anew when the prisoner finally came back to where he was, and to himself. He moved to stand directly opposite Kirk on the other side of the glass. For a long moment they regarded one another silently: captor and prisoner. Finally the man in the brig spoke once more.

"My name is . . . Khan."

"I'll accept that much as truth," Kirk replied carefully. "For now. Pardon my cynicism, but why would a Starfleet admiral need a three-hundred-year-old frozen man to help him do *anything*?"

The individual who had until now called himself Harrison gave an indifferent shrug. "Because I am . . . better. Better for your admiral's purpose than anything—than anyone—else."

"Better?" Kirk's expression contorted. "Better *at what*?"

"Everything." This was spoken not as a boast, but as a matter of fact by one who knew it to be so. "Alexander Marcus believed he needed to respond to an uncivilized threat in a civilized time, and for that, he needed someone less civilized. He needed a warrior's mind. A mind dedicated to combat, to winning, to surviving at all costs. He needed *my* mind. He needed . . . me."

The prisoner's story found Mister Spock at least as unconvinced as Kirk. "You are suggesting that the admiral violated every regulation he vowed to uphold simply because he wanted to exploit your intellect?"

Khan was not offended by the Vulcan's skepticism. After all, his was a truly remarkable tale. When presented to others, incredulity was to be expected. He could only hope to counter disbelief with truth. Whether others accepted it or not meant nothing in the end. The truth would remain in spite of their doubt.

"He wanted to exploit my savagery. Intellect alone is useless in a fight, Mr. Spock. As a Vulcan, you should know that."

Spock's expression did not change, but only Khan noticed the slight tensing of the science officer's hands. "I was well trained in the military arts, and I assure you that should the need arise, I am fully capable of handling myself in matters of physical combat—as was only recently the case."

"Mr. Spock, I'm not talking about *training*. I'm not talking about the application of learned skills. I'm certain if it came out of a book, that you're an expert on every chapter. I'm sure that if there is an accepted procedure for countering a blow, for firing a weapon, for maneuvering against an enemy in space, that you can both quote and direct every one of them to perfection." His tone darkened slightly. "I'm talking about what humans generally refer to as 'gut reaction.' Fighting *without* thinking. Battle in the absence of any procedure or rules. If you can't break a rule, how can you be expected to break bone?"

The science officer did not reply. It was evident their prisoner was, however mildly and in his own peculiar fashion, enjoying taunting him. It appeared that Spock would not give him the satisfaction of participating in such a meaningless exchange.

But his hands tightened just a little more.

Tiring of a game in which only he knew all the rules, Khan turned back to Kirk. "Your admiral used me to help design new weapons. To realize his vision of a heavily militarized Starfleet. That was the purpose of his precious, private Section 31. Starfleet was content to let him supervise one small, unimportant research project: After all, was he not an admiral of the fleet? Some minor improvements, some small advances, he allowed to be passed up along the research chain to show that his project was making progress and that it was deserving of continued funding. Other advances, particularly those in whose development I personally participated, he continued to shroud in 'necessary' secrecy until they were sufficiently 'perfected' for them to be revealed to Starfleet at large.

"And then? He sent *you* to use those weapons. To fire *my* torpedoes at an unsuspecting world. He purposefully saw to it that your ship would become crippled in enemy space, leading to one inevitable outcome."

He had their full attention now, he saw. It was all so easy.

"The Klingons would come searching for whoever was responsible for the intrusion and assault on their homeworld, and you would have no chance of escape. You would have no choice but to fight back. The Klingon Empire, quite reasonably, would be outraged. Marcus would finally have the war he talked about—the war he always said he *wanted*—all because of a renegade captain engaged in an unsanctioned mission of personal vengeance. Think now a moment, Captain: Where did your orders come from to sally forth to kill me? Directly from Marcus. Did you ever receive any complementary orders from anywhere else or anyone else in Starfleet? No. It was all Marcus, it was just Marcus, it was only Marcus. You were, you *are,* not engaged in a mission on behalf of Starfleet. You are engaged in a mission on behalf of Admiral Alexander Marcus." He paused a moment to let it all sink in.

"You are a *pawn,* Kirk. Advanced across the board to be sacrificed for the aims of your king."

The captain met Khan's gaze and did not waver. "No . . . no. Whether true or not, none of that changes the *known* fact that I watched you open fire on a room full of unarmed Starfleet officers and support personnel. You killed them in cold blood."

For the first time, Khan allowed a crack to appear in his hitherto-unvarying visage. A hint of pain, or perhaps a suggestion of loss, finally drove him to raise his voice.

"Marcus took my crew from me. While I alone was revived, they were kept in frozen stasis. My pleas to similarly revive them fell on deaf ears. Ears were numb to my need, to my pain. Help design new weapons, I was told, and eventually your crew will be restored to you. 'Eventually.'" The laugh that escaped his lips was short and bitter. "'Eventually' came and went, with no indication that even one of my crew would be revived. No matter how much I pleaded, no matter that I went down on my knees and begged, 'eventually' always kept receding into the future. It was plain that in the mind of Alexander Marcus, eventually actually meant never."

"You," Kirk countered sharply, "are a *murderer!*"

Racked with growing rage and emotion, Khan pretended not to hear him. "He used my own friends to control me. Realizing that he meant to keep me his vassal until I died, I tried to smuggle out my crew to safety by concealing them in the very weapons that I designed. But I was discovered. At that point, I knew Marcus would no longer risk my being alive, lest others in Starfleet discover what he had done. In attempting to save my crew, I had made myself more of a threat than a help. For my friends, as well as for myself, I had no choice but to escape—alone.

"Once that action had been forced upon me, I had every reason to believe Marcus would kill every single one of the people I hold most dear, letting them defrost and shrivel one at a time until or unless I turned myself in—for my own execution." He had now turned away from the two Starfleet officers, and they could not see the tear that ran down his right cheek. "So I made arrangements to have them moved before Marcus could begin to carry out his program of execution. As a privileged supervisor of Section 31, I had access to resources of my own, you see. The work was done quietly, without Marcus being aware of the move.

"But he found out . . . and had them transferred to your ship. To carry them to Qo'noS so you could fire them at me." His turned toward them, his expression twisted. "Very neat and tidy, isn't it? Kill me with my own people. Dispose of all of us in one move. But as I said, I had access to resources of my own." He leaned forward, so close that his face was almost pressing against the barrier.

"*Why do you think I surrendered to you, Kirk?* I learned that the 'special' torpedoes were on the *Enterprise*. My intent all along was to be reunited with my crew. I would never have let you fire them at Qo'noS." He stepped back from the barrier.

"To me, murder premeditated, Captain, is murder committed. I did what I did at Starfleet headquarters because I was responding in kind only to what I perceived to be Marcus's intentions." His gaze shifted to focus a moment on Spock before returning to Kirk. "Perhaps my action in attacking your colleagues was not entirely logical, but it arose out of emotion and conviction I could not repress. My crew is my *family*, Kirk." Tears now running down his face, he cast an imploring gaze through the barrier.

"Is there anything you would not do for *your* family?"

Before Kirk could manage a response, Sulu's voice sounded from the brig speaker.

"*Proximity alert, sir. There's a ship at warp heading right for us. It will intersect our coordinates in—*" There was a pause while the helmsman checked readouts. "*I don't have a specific time frame, sir. Soon. A matter of minutes.*"

"Klingons?" an anxious Kirk shot back.

It was Khan and not Sulu who responded immediately to the captain's query. "At warp? Any local ships coming for you would by now have dropped out of warp and would be proceeding on impulse power lest they overshoot your position. No, Kirk." His tone was almost pitying. "We both know who it is."

"*I don't think it's Klingons, sir,*" Sulu was saying. "*It's not coming at us from Qo'noS or Praxis or any of the known outlying monitoring stations.*"

That clinched it. Turning, Kirk spoke in clipped tones to the brig officer on duty. "Lieutenant, move Khan to sickbay and post six security officers on him. Full time, full rotation, full arms."

"Yes, Captain."

Following the captain with his eyes, the first officer of the *Enterprise* studied Kirk closely as both men exited the brig.

So did the room's only prisoner.

XII

As he entered the bridge, Kirk was snapping orders even before he reached the command chair.

"Mr. Sulu, do we have an ETA yet on the approaching ship?"

"Three seconds, sir."

Not much time, Kirk told himself as he sat down in the command chair. *Not much time to do anything.* Harrison's—*Khan's*—words continued to echo in his head, bumping up against long-held beliefs, knocking loose previously secure assumptions. No time for examining them, either. But "them" might prove critical in whatever was to come.

"Shields," he crisply ordered.

★   ★   ★

It slammed out of warp from the depths of the green nebula that had been the most prominent stellar feature ever since the *Enterprise* had been left drifting.

It dwarfed the *Enterprise*. Jet black, it was constructed along the general design of a Federation starship . . . but her lines were heavier, her entire appearance from greatly extended nacelles to bow more massive and armored. Weapons blisters were amply in evidence everywhere on the huge vessel. Every part of her had been reinforced, beefed up, and braced. A glance was sufficient to indicate that this was a ship that had been built not for exploration, but for battle.

Overwhelming in scope, it was so immense that it blocked out the entire view forward.

It was just so damn *big*.

No one here had ever seen anything like it. Hell, Kirk thought, he'd never even seen diagrammatics that were anything *close* to what they were now confronting in reality. In person and in images, he had noted or studied every type of vessel in Starfleet's arsenal, from tenders to the sister ships of the *Enterprise*.

This was the first Federation starship he had seen that looked . . . mean.

The shock of the new and unexpected stunned everyone on the bridge. The ship on the forward screen was nothing short of a raging belligerent's most extreme Starfleet fantasy come to life.

"Captain," Uhura announced, "they're hailing us, sir. Standard Starfleet intership communications frequency, short-range tight beam."

Further confirmation of the enormous vessel's origins, Kirk mused tensely. No point in trying to ignore it. "On screen. Broadcast shipwide, for the record. Everyone on board might as well bear witness to whatever transpires."

Any rapidly fading notions that the crew of the new ship might be non-human vanished with the appearance of a familiar figure on the forward screen. He was immediately recognizable, seated on a bridge that was at once more advanced and somehow leaner, colder, than that of the *Enterprise*.

"Captain Kirk." Admiral Alexander Marcus's tone was professionally cordial.

Kirk nodded, more to himself than in acknowledgment of the speaker's identity. "Admiral Marcus. I wasn't expecting you. That's some ship."

"And I wasn't expecting to get word that you'd taken Harrison into custody in violation of your orders. Or did you forget that you were directed to find him and take him out?" Marcus shook his head sadly. "Orders disobeyed are orders never forgotten; the more so when they're as simple and straightforward as the ones you were given." He leaned forward slightly in his dark command chair. "What happened, son? What went wrong?"

If Academy gaming had taught Kirk anything, it was that when you can't play for the win, you play for time. "The unexpected happened, sir. Not something to be dismissed lightly, when one considers our present location. We had to improvise when we experienced a warp core malfunction." He responded in what he hoped was a manner both engaging and innocent. "But you already knew that, didn't you, sir."

Marcus looked annoyed while sounding increasingly impatient. "I don't take your meaning."

"Well, that's why you're here, isn't it? To assist us with repairs? Why else would the head of Starfleet personally bring a ship to the edge of the Neutral Zone?"

From his position at the helm, Sulu murmured to Kirk. "Captain, they're scanning our ship."

"Did you hear that, Admiral? Having a quiet look around?" Kirk's smile tightened. "Something I can help you find, sir?"

Tiring of the game, Marcus leaned forward. "Where's your prisoner, Kirk? And don't tell me he's no longer on your ship. You know what he did. You'd never release him from custody and certainly not to send him back to Qo'noS. Tell me where you're holding Harrison, and drop your shields so we can beam him over. I'm superseding your authority as of now."

Kirk sat a little straighter in his own command chair. "No need for that, sir. As the captor of record, it's my duty and responsibility to maintain control of the prisoner until he can be turned over to the appropriate authorities." Though he put no additional emphasis on the word "authority," both men knew what he meant. "All as per Starfleet regulations. The fact that I'm familiar with his crimes changes nothing. I'm preparing to return Khan to Earth for trial, sir." He paused, and added, "I would hope we can proceed with your understanding. I assure you that the prisoner is being well looked after and is completely under our control." Pausing again, he then said, "We didn't even have to fire so much as a single one of the 'new' torpedoes at him."

Expecting an angry response, Kirk was surprised when the admiral scratched at his forehead, leaned back against his chair, and appeared to soften . . . but not relax.

"Well, shit. You talked to him." Marcus shook his head sadly. "This is exactly what I was hoping to spare you from."

"'Spare' me?" Kirk did not try to hide his bemusement.

"Listen to me, son." Marcus's tone turned benign, even avuncular. "I made a mistake. I'm not afraid to admit it. There'd be no point in not admitting it. Not when your prisoner has gone out of his way to provide ample proof of my error. I took a tactical risk waking that bastard up, thinking his super brain could help us protect ourselves from whatever came at us next."

Kirk supplied an answer. "The Klingon Empire."

Marcus nodded. "At the moment, yes. In the future, who knows? I was hoping to use this creature to give Starfleet a boost in combat knowledge, skills, and material development. At first, it seemed as if that was going to be exactly the result. I was elated at the progress made by Section 31, but I decided to hold back on releasing any results until I had something really spectacular to present to the general staff. My problem . . ." His voice trailed away, and it took him a moment to compose himself.

"My problem with your prisoner was that I didn't really know what he was—what he *really* was—and now the blood of everyone he killed is on my hands. That is something I will have to deal with separately, on my own. But not until this episode is resolved. I blame you for nothing, Kirk. Not even for failing to carry out your orders, now that I know you've spoken to him. Because I know what he's capable of. He fooled me; he's fooled you. There will be no reprisals against you or any of your crew. I'll see to that personally. In fact, if I can mange it, the entire incident will be expunged from the official records. Now I'm asking you: Give him to me so I can end what I started, and let's put all this behind us."

It all makes a good deal of sense, Kirk told himself. Not only did the admiral's words explain a great deal, they held out the promise of a full amnesty for him, Spock, and anyone else who had chosen to participate in taking Khan alive instead of killing him outright. Hadn't Spock warned him against listening to the prisoner? Certainly Khan was persuasive, but was Kirk to believe the words of a confessed murderer versus those of a venerable admiral of the Fleet? Besides, there was nothing for him to gain by refusing Marcus's demand. Hand over the prisoner, the man who had killed his mentor, Christopher Pike, and forget the entire incident. Go quietly back to exploring where no man . . .

Except for one thing. A small matter that could not be avoided. Something that Marcus had not even mentioned.

"And what would you like me to do with the rest of his crew, sir? Fire them at the Klingons? With their downsized internal drives, they'll travel far more slowly, but they'll still reach Qo'noS. You want me to murder seventy-two people in their sleep and start a war in the process?"

The admiral's brow furrowed. He did not sound like someone striving to propound an elaborate lie. If anything, he sounded more convincing now than at any time since he had first greeted Kirk on screen.

"War? Is that what he told you? That's why you were fishing around with all that nonsense about your damaged warp core? You think I sent you out here and hung you out to dry? The man is too clever by half, Kirk, capable of twisting words as easily as arms. Listen to him too long, and he'll have you believing anything. I know; he did it to me. Just consider for a moment." He shifted in his command chair.

"*He* put those people in those torpedoes. Or oversaw the process, at least. Nobody else did that. What was his real purpose? Did he have, did they have, no alternatives three hundred years ago? No other options than to commit themselves to cryostasis for an unknown length of time, without having a clue as to what the circumstances would be when—and if—they were thawed out and revived? I didn't want to burden you with knowing what was inside those tubes. Better to dispose of them without knowing. Without having to deal with the unnecessary and stressful ethical conundrum you just related to me." He was almost pleading now. "*Think*, Kirk. Step back and consider the situation objectively. If you managed to find this man and get him off Qo'noS successfully, then I suspect you've seen what he can do all by himself. He got himself to Qo'noS and, more significantly, managed to survive there. Alone, on a hostile, militaristic world, among a non-human species. One man. Can you imagine what would happen if we woke up the rest of his crew and they managed to get themselves *organized*? What else did he tell you? That he's a 'peacekeeper'? *He's playing you, son.* Don't you see that?"

Kirk tried to object. "He and his crew were misused, forced into cryosleep in order to escape the—"

Marcus cut him off. "Khan and his people were war criminals, condemned to death before they managed to get away! I thought I could make use of his knowledge and subsequently deal appropriately with the resulting fact of his revival. As I've told you, I was wrong, and for that bit of hubris, I will eventually have to answer. I seriously underestimated what I was dealing with. I suspect that has always been the case with this individual and his colleagues.

"Now it is our duty to carry out the original sentence that was passed on the prisoner and his cohorts before anyone else dies because of them. I intend to oversee that myself, as part penance for what I foolishly allowed to happen. So I'm asking you again. One last time, son. Lower your shields and tell me where he is."

Kirk tried one final ploy. "Assuming I'm correct in taking that as a threat, sir, are you saying that you feel so strongly about this that you're willing to fire on another Starfleet vessel?"

The admiral was remorseless. "It has nothing to do with 'feeling' anything, Captain Kirk. It has to do with removing a threat to the entire Federation. That must be balanced against the possible harm that might be done to a single vessel and her crew. For which I *will* hold you responsible, should further measures have to be taken to secure the appropriate disposition of the prisoner."

Kirk knew there was little more he could do. He was outranked and, more important, outgunned. Always a gambler, he preferred the odds to be in his favor, or at least even. Challenging the dreadnought visible on the *Enterprise*'s sensors was a chance he could not take. He took a deep breath.

"He's in Engineering, sir. Under heavy guard, awaiting continued questioning. But I'll have him moved to the transporter room right away."

Marcus was visibly relieved. While implying that he was prepared for a fight, it was clear he didn't want one, and was pleased that it had been avoided.

"Thank you, son. I'll take it from here."

The image of Marcus on the viewscreen was replaced with that of the enormous warship hanging in space.

The instant intership communication was terminated, Kirk looked to his helmsman. "Do not drop those shields, Mr. Sulu."

"Yes, sir," Sulu said. "Understood, sir."

A familiar voice insinuated itself from just behind Kirk. "Captain, bearing in mind that the reality is that Khan is in sickbay and not in Engineering leads me to believe that you are contriving a plan that conflicts with what you have just told the admiral."

"Can't fool you, Mr. Spock. My 'plan' consists of doing exactly what we said we were going to do. I told Marcus we were bringing a fugitive back to Earth to stand trial, and that's what we're going to do." He addressed his comm pickup. "Mr. Chekov, can we warp?"

"*Sir, we're working on it as hard as we can,*" came the reply from Engineering. "*There is some functionality, but if we engage it now, we risk further damaging the core.*"

"Can we do it or not?" Kirk snapped.

"*Technically, yes, but I would not adwise it, Keptin! The dangers are multiple and we risk undoing all the difficult repair work that has already been completed.*"

"Objections noted." Kirk turned to the helm. "Mr. Sulu, set course for Earth."

"Yes, *sir.*" It took the helmsman scarcely a moment to enter the necessary command. "Course laid in."

Having been privy to the entire conversation between Kirk and Admiral Marcus, those posted to the bridge could be forgiven for exchanging more than one uneasy look. But no one raised an objection. Previous experience had taught them to put their trust in their captain.

"*Punch it,*" Kirk ordered his helmsman.

One moment the gigantic black ship had loomed over the *Enterprise*; the next, it dominated only empty space and the uninhabited planetoid that had served to shield both ships from detection by the Klingons.

On board the fleeing starship, there was calm. Outwardly, at least, everyone was content to attend to their duties. There was no voiced uncertainty, no murmurings of dissatisfaction with the captain's decision. Only in Engineering were there signs of, if not discord, then imminent alarm.

Reports flooded in to Chekov almost faster than he could peruse them. This element overheating, that module teetering on the verge of meltdown, this containment component threatening to fail. As fast as the information came in, he strove to respond. There were no more questions on how to repair a failing bit of the ship's propulsion system—there was no time for that—but only on how to keep it functioning.

Somehow, between the frantic efforts of the nearly overwhelmed technicians and the orders of their chief engineer's replacement, things continued to work. The engines droned dangerously—but they functioned. The warp containment vessel deformed and flexed in ways that would have sent any sensible engineer rushing for the nearest escape pod—but it held. And the *Enterprise* powered through warp space and toward a distant Earth as fast as her damaged constituent parts could propel her.

Secure in sickbay and surrounded by guards who never took their eyes off him, Khan sat quietly, his expression blank, deep in thought and gazing at nothing in particular. Dr. McCoy studied the man. Peel back the layers of personality, of emotion, and what might one find? A murderous maniac or a man wronged by not one but two societies: his own of three centuries ago and today's as represented by Alexander Marcus?

"Well, at least we're moving again," McCoy pointed out conversationally as he passed a tricorder over the prisoner's face.

From where he was seated, Khan lifted his gaze to meet that of the doctor. "If you think you're cleanly away, if you think you're safe at warp—you're wrong."

McCoy just grunted at the prisoner's reply, but it touched something in Carol Marcus. Having taken a break from her research, her eyes now grew wide at the prisoner's remark. Before a curious McCoy could think to question her, she had bolted from the room.

Abnormal vibrations interspersed with the occasional atypical jolt were enough to let everyone on the bridge know that all was not right with the ship's engines. Despite that, every pertinent readout indicated that they were traveling at the specified speed. The *Enterprise* continued through warp space until indicators showed that they were approaching their destination.

"Lieutenant Uhura, contact Starfleet," Kirk said from the command chair. "Identify us and tell them we were pursued into the Neutral Zone by an unmarked Federation ship."

Uhura had to interrupt him. "Can't do any of that, sir. Comms are down. All ship auxiliary power's being diverted to warp."

That's a bit of information Chekov neglected to pass along, Kirk thought angrily. His temper dissipated as quickly as it had flared. Pressed into service in Scott's absence, the navigator had performed multiple miracles in just getting the ship moving again. That he had somehow held things together long enough to reach the solar system was a wonderment of the first order. Chekov's actions called for praise, not censure. Later, Kirk told himself, he *might* proffer a mild criticism or two. But they were not quite home, and he did not want to do or say anything that might interfere with the running of the ship.

He was almost relaxed when Carol Marcus came running out of the turbolift. "Permission to come on the bridge!" she exclaimed even as she was halfway to the command chair position. Her expression was frightened, her tone urgent. Kirk eyed her uncertainly. What did she want on the bridge?

"Dr. Marcus?"

"He's going to catch up with us, and when he does, the only thing that's going to stop him destroying this ship is me, so you have to let me talk to him."

Preoccupied as he was, he did his best to reassure her. "Carol, we're at warp. He can't catch up with us."

"Yes, he can." She was utterly positive, he noted. "He's been developing a ship that has Mark IV capabilities and—"

The sounding of the ship's proximity alarm interrupted her, its blare counterpointed by cries of surprise and astonishment from bridge personnel. Of these, Kirk focused his attention on his helmsman.

"Mr. Sulu, *what's going on?*"

Scarcely daring to look up from his instrumentation, Sulu found himself unable to avoid reporting the impossible. "Captain, I'm getting a reading I don't understand. There's a—distortion." He squinted at one particular readout. "A very big distortion. There's something in the warp tunnel behind us."

This time, Admiral Marcus did not bother with professional niceties. Closing fast on the *Enterprise,* his state-of-the-art warship unleashed an array of powerful, state-of-the-art weaponry. Already barely traveling at warp on a wing, a prayer, and an assortment of increasingly frantic Russian entreaties, the *Enterprise* was rocked, jolted, and finally knocked sideways by a succession of explosions.

Airtight barriers slid shut as a hole was ripped in the side of the *Enterprise*. Under the relentless pull of escaping air, desperate screaming crewmembers clung to beams, instruments . . . anything that remained fastened to a wall or the floor. One by one, they were sucked down corridors that were now exposed to remorseless space, perishing quickly in the unforgiving void.

In Engineering, overstressed elements let out inorganic shrieks of their own as, pushed beyond all reasonable design boundaries, they began to fail despite the best efforts of frantic techs to keep the intricate mechanisms functioning. Entire sections went dark. Illumination returned only because of luciferin-based lighting that was chemically integrated into the coatings that covered walls, ceilings, and deck.

Under such a sustained attack, not even Chekov and his dedicated team of technicians could keep the warp drive functioning. With a shudder and an electric crackling that sounded like sheet metal being torn, the core slipped out of alignment. Yelling instructions, Chekov saw to it that it was shut down and its containment compartment sealed off before it could further damage the ship.

Conditions were not much better on the bridge. Emergency lighting only served to illuminate the extent of the damage. As crewmembers stumbled about suppressing incipient fires and shutting down instrumentation that was likely to ignite in the closed atmosphere, Kirk steadied himself in the command chair. Like his ship, he was shaken but still functional.

"Sulu, damage report!" Mentally calculating the time they had spent in warp space gave him only a general idea of their possible position. An unprogrammed drop out of warp could have deposited them anywhere. Chronologically if not spatially, they should be close to home, but . . . "Where are we?"

"Shields are dropping, all weapons systems are offline!" Sulu reported promptly, ignoring the gash on his head. "We're twenty thousand kilometers from Luna."

"Almost home," Kirk muttered disconsolately. "So close."

"Captain," Spock announced, "Marcus's ship clearly has advanced warp and weapons capabilities proportionate to her size."

Another blast rocked the artificial gravity on the bridge. If they lost that, Kirk knew, they would be almost helpless. "Evasive maneuvers! Get us to Earth now! Full impulse! Once we cross the halfway point between home and the moon, we can—"

"Shields are gone, Captain," Sulu broke in. "Impulse power failing! We're losing the last of our powered forward momentum."

Having been thrown hard to the deck by an earlier concussion, Carol Marcus finally managed to pull herself up and totter over to where Kirk was standing. Protocol forgotten, she stepped so close in front of Kirk that he could not avoid her.

"*Please,* we are going to *die, all* of us, if I don't talk to him!"

Aware he was nearly out of options, Kirk now found himself contemplating a most unlikely one. "He won't listen to me. Not now. What makes you think he'll listen to you or anyone else?"

Her fingers tightened against him. "What have you got to lose by letting me try?!"

Kirk considered the badly damaged bridge, the fact that they were virtually defenseless against the warship's advanced weaponry, and the potentially mortal wounds to the rest of the *Enterprise*. As a captain from an earlier time would have said, they were essentially dead in the water. Inclining his head in the general direction of Communications, he nodded reluctantly.

"Lieutenant Uhura—hail them."

It required two workarounds on her part just to generate a functional link. "Channel's open—*go*."

Shifting to one side, Kirk nudged a single control and then nodded at the anxious young woman standing beside him. Leaning forward, she addressed herself to the command chair pickup.

"Sir—it's me, it's Carol. I'm here. *I'm on the* Enterprise."

No response, no reply. Two ships drifting in space: one crippled, the other looming nearby like some brooding vulture in armor. And no words passing between them.

On the silent bridge, Uhura checked her instrumentation and assured Kirk that as near as she could tell, a ship-to-ship link was open and operating. Carol tried once more. "Sir—can you hear me?"

The viewscreen forward activated, the image at first flickering and unstable. While reception remained sporadic, the likeness of Alexander Marcus was unmistakable. He acted concerned, looked pissed, and sounded confused.

"What are you doing on that ship?"

Father or no father, it was plain to see that she was scared of the man on the other end of the communication. She would have one opportunity to convince him.

"I heard what you said—Father. That you made a mistake and now you're doing everything you can to fix it. But, Dad—I don't believe that the man who raised me is capable of destroying a starship—a *Federation* starship—full of innocent people to fulfill your aims. And if I'm wrong about that—" She paused to ensure that he knew she meant full well what she was saying. "—then I guess you'll have to do it with me on board."

A moment of silence ensued as Admiral Marcus pondered his lone daughter's declaration of solidarity with the crew of the crippled ship. Reaching a decision, he leaned forward to peer intently into the vid pickup in front of his command chair. Unsettlingly, he did not sound particularly concerned.

"Actually, Carol—I won't." He glanced to his left.

Her eyes widened as the import of her father's words struck home. As an all-too-familiar set of lights began to swarm her, she turned helplessly toward Kirk.

"Can we intercept their transport signal?" he called out.

"No, sir!" a tech quickly responded.

Racing past him, Carol ran for the turbolift. While she couldn't hide from the other ship's probing transporter signal, if she could just confuse it for a while, if she could only escape its grasp long enough to . . .

Kirk started after her, knowing that interposing himself in the field that was reaching out for her might just possibly throw it off enough to render at least the first attempt a failure. He was too slow, and she was gone before he could reach her. As Kirk caught himself, the now utterly cold and implacable voice of the admiral sounded behind him.

"Captain James T. Kirk: Without authorization and in league with the fugitive known as John Harrison, you and your crew went rogue in enemy territory, leaving me no choice but to hunt you down and destroy you." He looked to his right. "Lock phasers."

"Wait, sir!" Raising a hand, Kirk ran toward the forward screen. "Wait, wait, *wait!*"

"I'll make this quick. Target all aft torpedoes on the renegade's bridge." Marcus turned away from his visual pickup.

"Wait!" Kirk shouted one last time. Now that he had no more choices, it was almost a relief. He did not have to think. He knew what he had to do. "Admiral, I take full responsibility for my

actions. But they were *my* actions, and mine alone. I'm sorry." He was pleading now. Though it was something at which he had little experience, he found it came naturally enough. In a sense, it was the exact opposite of how Spock would have responded. Whether it was sufficient to change anything, he would know in a moment.

"My crew was only following my orders. From my first officer . . ." Over at the Science station Spock raised an eyebrow. ". . . to the lowest-ranking new inductee into Starfleet, they acted only as instructed. Following a captain's orders should be reason for commendation, not termination. If I transmit Khan's exact location to you now, all that I ask is that you spare them." He stepped still closer to the screen and, by extension, the pickup that was transmitting his voice and image to the looming black ship.

"Please, sir," Kirk continued. "Let them live. I'll do anything you want, including and not restricted to turning myself over to you in concert with Khan. If, following that, it's your intention to pronounce and carry out summary judgment on me, then I'll accede to that without protest. There'll be no request for clemency; I give you my word."

Admiral Marcus processed Kirk's speech without interrupting. When the captain of the *Enterprise* had finished, the older man sighed approvingly.

"Well, Captain, I have to say . . . that's a hell of an apology. But if it's any consolation . . ." He paused meaningfully as he resumed his seat in the command chair. ". . . I was never going to spare your crew. Too many witnesses. Too many potentially awkward questions. My preference when dealing with a difficult situation was always to leave . . . a clean slate." This time he did not even bother to glance to his right. *"Fire."*

★　　★　　★

At the rear of the great warship, two banks of photon torpedoes that, in themselves, were larger than many Starfleet vessels unfolded like the devil's hands. Each held more torpedoes than several ships the size of the *Enterprise*. With Marcus having given the command, as soon as they locked in position, they would unleash enough destruction to destroy a large planetoid.

Having left his station to move to Uhura's, Spock now found his hand grasped tightly in hers. With seconds left in which to make their peace with eternity, other crewmembers both on and off the bridge composed final thoughts, embraced crewmates, or whispered words they had wanted to say but previously had not possessed the courage or wherewithal to do so.

As for James Kirk, he had done all he could. He turned toward his chief science and communications officers. At such a moment there was little to say.

"I'm sorry."

Closing his eyes, he silently awaited the inevitable.

XIII

The inevitable came—and went. On board the giant warship, the weapons officer unenthusiastically but professionally inputted the command. When nothing happened, he repeated the instruction not once but several times. Concurrently with his final attempt, a falling whine filled the ship's bridge—the sound of power dropping.

"Sir," he reported, at once alarmed and confused, "our weapons won't fire! Phasers and torpedoes alike are inoperative."

"Shields are down," came the startled counterpoint from the helm. "We're losing power!"

Meanwhile the chief science officer eyed the descending numbers of his multiple readouts and summed up the situation with an exclamation that would have been understood but not duplicated by his counterpart on the *Enterprise*.

"Admiral—what the hell, sir?"

"Someone in Engineering just manually reset every system on the ship, sir!" declared the weapons officer. "Not only can't we use our weapons—I can't even access the relevant instrumentation!"

"What do you mean 'someone'?" Marcus snarled. *"WHO?"*

On board the *Enterprise,* Sulu gazed in disbelief at his readouts. "Their weapons are powered down—sir."

Deep within the giant ship, a lone figure came tearing around a far corner and down an empty corridor, throwing furtive looks behind him. If he was not being actively pursued at the moment, he knew he soon would be. That he had accomplished what he set out to do was nothing less than a minor miracle. While well aware that his efforts could not pass unnoticed, he hoped that he himself might be able to at least survive. For a little while longer, anyway.

Fumbling with the communicator he had not dared to activate until now, Montgomery Scott stammered into it even as he continued fleeing from his deliberate acts of sabotage.

"Enterprise—*can ye hear me?!*"

On the bridge of the Federation starship that should by now have been reduced to a rapidly expanding sphere of ragged fragments above Earth's moon, Kirk's eyes snapped open at the sound of a familiar voice.

"Scotty . . . ?" He swallowed hard, not daring to believe what he had just heard.

The communications link was weak, but intelligible. Without waiting for a command from Kirk, Uhura was already working to isolate and enhance it. Meanwhile, Spock had hurried back to his station and was attempting to pinpoint the communication's location. Thanks to their combined efforts, the chief engineer's next words were far more audible.

"Guess what I found behind Jupiter, Captain?!"

A thoroughly dumbfounded Kirk could scarcely make sense of the question. "You're on that *ship?!*"

"I'm sure as Ifrinn not on the Enterprise, *Captain! An' seein' as how I've just committed an extensive act o' treason against a Starfleet admiral and sabotage on Starfleet's newest vessel, I'd bloody well like to get off this bloody ship—now beam me the hell out! You should 'ave me located by now—assumin' Mr. Spock's been doin' his job and not lollygaggin' about while I've been talking!"*

The *Enterprise's* science officer commented without looking up from his position. "Still fine-tuning for transfer, Captain. And," he added in his usual monotone, "I do not 'lollygag.'"

It was left to Kirk to respond to the frantic chief engineer. "Uh, we're a little low on power at the moment, Scotty. That includes power for the transporter, I'm afraid. Stand by, we're working on it . . ."

"You stand by!" Scott howled back. *"What happened to the* Enterprise? *If you don't get me . . ."*

Was that the tattoo of boots on metal he was hearing via the chief's communicator, Kirk wondered? He shouted a query, even though he knew that the ship's instrumentation would automatically moderate the volume of his response.

"Scotty? *Mr. Scott?!*"

"Call you back," was the last the captain heard from his ex–chief engineer.

"Scotty?"

There was no reply. Either the chief had been forced to run from pursuit, or else . . .

No. There could be no "or else." Not now. The *Enterprise* had been spared, though for how long it was impossible to know. Moving to the back of the bridge, he confronted his science officer.

"Spock, our ship—how is she? Suggestions for immediate operations."

"Our options remain very limited, Captain. We cannot fire and we cannot flee."

"There is one option." Kirk looked toward Communications. "Uhura, as soon as you can re-establish contact with Scotty, patch him through." His gaze returned to his first. "Mr. Spock, you have the conn." Turning away, he headed for the turbolift.

Without hesitating, Spock moved to follow. The Vulcan succeeded in entering the open lift before the doors could react to his presence. He was speaking anxiously even as the barrier closed behind him.

"Captain, I strongly object—"

Kirk didn't give his first officer time to finish the thought. "To *what?* I haven't said anything yet. I haven't proposed anything yet."

Spock was not so easily put off. "I believe I can make a reasonable attempt at divining your intentions based on the limited number of alternatives available to us. To prevent Admiral Marcus from resuming the attack that he launched and was only just prevented from concluding, we must somehow either permanently put his vessel out of action or take control of it. Since we cannot take the ship from without, the only way to do so is from within. And as a large boarding party would quickly be detected and met with appropriate counterforce, it is optimum for you to take as few crewmembers as possible.

"Since there is a good chance one is still likely to eventually encounter resistance, it stands to reason that any boarding party will require personnel with advanced hand-to-hand combat abilities. It also stands to reason that a boarding party would benefit immensely from the presence of someone with innate knowledge of the design and schematics of that ship. All of which would indicate that you plan to ally with Khan, the very individual we were sent to destroy and who we decided instead to capture."

Too perceptive by half, Spock was. Since the science officer had thought everything out so thoroughly, Kirk decided there was no point in trying to deny any of it.

"And we would've been destroyed if he hadn't saved our lives on Qo'noS. Or have you forgotten that a Klingon officer had his foot on my throat and his gun at my head?"

"The disturbing image remains regrettably fresh in my memory, Captain. That was then: This is now. Think, Jim. A man like Khan does nothing without a reason. He is a self-confessed warrior, bred to be a fighter. That means that in addition to knowing ground combat, weapons, and ship capabilities, he is also familiar with tactics and strategy. Faced with possible annihilation, someone like that focuses on survival. I do not for an instant doubt that his saving our lives was a means to an end." He straightened slightly. "If it is learned that it was done out of altruism, I will resign my commission."

Though he had already made up his mind, Kirk was willing to listen. Especially to the Vulcan. "A means to what end, Spock?"

"We do not yet know. But for all that he has not chosen to reveal it to us, I do not doubt that it exists and that its nature is not benign. Furthermore, Admiral Marcus's guilty actions do not in any way invalidate Khan's crimes."

"'The enemy of my enemy is my friend,'" Kirk recited as they stepped out of the turbolift and into a lower corridor.

Paralleling his superior as they made their way quickly across a catwalk, Spock was unsurprisingly ready with a rejoinder of his own. "An Arabic proverb attributed to a prince who was betrayed and decapitated by his own subjects."

"Still," Kirk mused as they rounded a corner, "it's a hell of a quote. My feeling is that time validates such sayings, and the longer they hang around, the more validity accrues to them."

Seeing he was unable to change his friend's mind, Spock resolved to try another tack. "Very well, then. If you are determined to do this, I will go with you."

Kirk shook his head. "No. I need you on the bridge."

A hand, more than humanly powerful, grabbed Kirk by the shoulder and brought him to a halt. "Then in that case I must insist. *I cannot allow you to do this.* One of my principal functions on this ship is to ensure that, where possible, reason and logic prevail in the making of all decisions. It would not be carrying out my duties if I failed to prevent you from acting in what is patently a self-destructive manner, something I believe you are doing at this moment."

Human and Vulcan stared at each other. Then Kirk nodded once and replied quietly.

"You're right."

Unused to agreement in such circumstances, Spock was uncharacteristically bemused. "Captain?"

"I said, you're right. Every call I've made since this whole business started has been wrong. We'd all be dead right now if it wasn't for Scotty—who's just one of the *ten* people who tried to warn me I was in over my head. So that's why it's now on me to go over there—because the one thing I know I *can* do for certain, and do really well, is punch people. And if that doesn't work?" He stared hard at his first officer—and friend. "The *Enterprise* and her crew need someone in that chair who knows what the hell he's doing. Nothing against Sulu or Uhura or any of the other senior officers, but—you know what I mean." He swallowed hard. "That's why you're captain now, Mr. Spock." As the Vulcan stared at him, speechless, Kirk stepped back. "I'm sorry I pulled you into this. I'm sorry I pulled the *Enterprise* and its crew into this. I'm sorry for—I'm sorry for a lot of things." He smiled wanly. "I don't know what a great captain would do in a situation like this. I only know what I can do."

Pivoting on his heel, he accelerated toward another part of the ship.

Watching him go, Spock considered hurrying after him. Surely more argument, more thorough reasoning, would persuade Kirk to change his mind. Careful dialogue with relevant points highlighted would see the captain back in his familiar seat in the command chair. But there was simply no time right now to afford such luxuries as extended contemplation. Turning purposefully, he headed for the bridge.

Lost in contemplation, it took Khan a moment to look up from his seat and meet Kirk's steady gaze. Once he was certain the prisoner was paying proper attention, Kirk snapped out a command.

"Tell me everything you know about that ship."

"To tell you everything I know about your opponent would require more time than remains to either of us, Captain," Khan replied. "Bearing that in mind, I will tell you that it would be considered a dreadnought class. It is far larger than the *Enterprise*—but you already know that. It is far more heavily armed than the *Enterprise*—but you already know that. Special modifications to its warp drive and engine nacelles allow it to exceed, for a short period of time, all accepted warp factors. Modified to be operated by a minimal crew. Unlike most Federation vessels, it is built solely for combat."

Kirk's mouth tightened. "I didn't know that. Listen to me, Khan. I am going to do everything I can to make you answer for what you did that night at Starfleet headquarters." He paused a moment. "But right now, I need your help."

"Of course you do. As your Mr. Spock would say, it is patently obvious. Very well. You need my help." His tone sharpened. "In exchange for what? Or do you think that I'll give you my assistance out of the kindness of my heart?"

What was it Spock had told him? *A man like Khan does nothing without a reason.* Wary as he might be, Kirk knew he had to act and act quickly before the maintenance crew of the warship succeeded in overturning Scotty's timely intervention. Survival first. Judgment later.

"You said you'd do anything for your crew. For your 'family.' Help me, and I can guarantee their safety."

His tone calmly contemptuous, Khan offered a pitying smile by way of reply. "Captain. You can't even guarantee the safety of your *own* crew."

Expecting something of the sort, Kirk was ready with a response. "Yeah, well, I'm working on it. I can't assure the safety of your people without first securing the safety of mine. That should be plain enough. If Marcus succeeds in destroying the *Enterprise,* the fact that your crew is cryogenically packed into torpedo frames won't save them. They'll be blown to bits just like the rest of us and their component pieces scattered across the solar system."

Kirk tried not to show the tension he felt. He had the uncomfortable feeling of being engaged in a deadly serious game of chess and always three moves behind. The prisoner's damnable self-assurance was infuriating, the sense that he was always right. What was worse, a part of Kirk felt that might be the case.

Unable to stand the prisoner's continuing silence, Kirk glanced across the room at where McCoy was busy at a work station. "Bones, what are you doing with that tribble?"

"The tribble's dead. A standard medical specimen. I'm injecting Khan's platelets into the deceased tissue of a necrotic host. You wanted me to figure out what makes the sunuvabitch tick? I'm figuring."

Kirk turned back to Khan. "So—are you coming with me or do I have to try and do this alone?"

After what seemed like several lifetimes, but in reality was only a moment, Khan's expression changed from taunting to thoughtful.

The security team Kirk speedily convened was comprised of the best the *Enterprise* could offer. Armed and ready, they quickly followed the captain and his strangely silent companion down the corridor while Uhura was busily trying to reconnect with the ship's absent chief engineer. The security team's presence was to ensure that Khan, now free of the confines of the ship's brig, did not attempt to veer off on some impromptu venture of his own. If that was his intent, Kirk mused as he studied the man striding along beside him, the prisoner was concealing it well.

On board the ebony warship, Montgomery Scott kept constantly on the move as he strove to evade what had become a remorseless pursuit. Only the vast size of the ship, coupled with the fact that Marcus had crewed it with the absolute minimum of personnel, allowed him to avoid capture. And even though it was of a new and advanced design, much was still familiar to him. There were, after all, only so many ways to lay in service corridors for the engines, only so many options for placing life-support systems. Despite several near encounters with his pursuers, Scott managed to stay several steps ahead of them. On more than one occasion, he had activated an empty survival suit or its support framework, fooling ship security's sensory detection apparatus into making it appear he was on a deck he had only recently vacated.

Listening intently for any sign that those on his trail might be drawing close again, his nerves more than a little on edge, Scott nearly jumped out of his boots as his communicator beeped for attention. Flipping it open, he all but hissed into the pickup.

"Oi, Captain . . . give a man some warning!"

"Sorry, Scotty. I take it you're still free to cause trouble?" Kirk asked him.

The chief glanced over a shoulder. The corridor behind him was still deserted—though for how much longer, he had no way of knowing.

"Doin' me best, sir—and still waitin' to be beamed off this *galla*."

"There's still going to be a delay in that, Scotty. We don't have adequate power to the transporter room yet. Maybe not for some time. So we're planning an alternative. We're coming over there."

The chief's eyes grew wide. "Excuse me, sir. Must be some problem with the communications link. I dinna think I heard you clearly. You wanna do *what?*"

"We're coming over there," Kirk repeated into the communicator, "even though we're going to have to do it without the use of the transporter. All the *Enterprise* has left that's still functioning are the independently powered maneuvering thrusters. Not enough push to get us to the moon, much less Earth. But enough to fine-tune ship position inside a spacedock—or move us closer to where you are. Sulu's shifting the *Enterprise* into position even as we speak."

"To this ship?" The incredulity in the chief's voice came over clearly via the communicator. *"How?"*

Kirk looked over at Khan. The prisoner spoke without hesitation. "There's a cargo door: hangar seven, access port 101A. This hangar is equipped with an internal manual override system. You need to locate the manual override to open the airlock."

Audible via the communicator's speaker, the chief's response was thick with suspicion. *"And who is this I'm supposed to be taking orders from? Are you crazy?"*

Quickening his pace toward the shuttle bay, Kirk fought to contain his anticipation. "Take my word for it, Scotty: Just listen to him. It's gonna be all right."

"Oh, I'm listenin', Captain," came the engineer's reply. *"You bet your mas I'm listenin'. Let me see if I heard this straight: You wanna shoot out of the* Enterprise's *garbage chute, then I'm supposed to open an airlock—to space—whereupon I dinna know what happens to you because before you get inside I freeze and die and explode!"*

Instead of disputing the chief's breakdown of their intentions, Khan replied in a reasonable but firm manner. "And yet it will be your captain and myself who are speeding towards you at four hundred meters a second. If you don't find and activate that manual override, it is we who will smash into the outer hull like insects on a windshield."

"Och, aye," Scott responded, his tone dry as moor heather on an August afternoon. *"Well, I certainly don't want* you *to get hurt."*

On the bridge, Spock leaned close to where Uhura sat at her station.

"Lieutenant, from our current position is it possible to establish contact with New Vulcan?"

She stared back up at him, ensuring she had heard correctly. "I'll do my best."

"Thank you." Moving away, he slid into the vacant command chair without hesitation. "Mr. Sulu, where are we?"

Trying to monitor a dozen readouts at once, the helmsman replied succinctly. "Almost there. I'm aligning our ship now."

"What is the status of the enemy ship?"

"Their main systems are still offline," the helmsman replied, "but sensors indicate gradual restoration is in progress." He glanced back at the command chair. "I can't predict how much time we have until they've reestablished weapons or drive capacity."

Spock nodded once, tersely. "Let us hope their ability to reinstate onboard functionality is exceeded only by Mr. Scott's uniquely individual aptitude for inducing chaos."

Having donned the silvery EV suits, Kirk and Khan now could only wait in one of the side personnel airlocks for clearance from the bridge. It was not long in coming.

"Captain," Sulu declared over their suit comms, *"your departure vector is now aligned with the specified cargo door on the other vessel. But there's nothing we can do about the intervening debris field."*

Debris field, Kirk reminded himself with a start. Of course. While much of the wreckage resulting from the warship's assault on the *Enterprise* would have been blown away into space by the violence of the attack, some would have become trapped between the two vessels, bouncing back and forth until the momentum imparted to the fragments by assorted explosions had dissipated. It would drift there until drawn off by the moon's gravity or knocked away by collision with other bits of drifting rubble or some other solid object.

Such as outward-flying EV-suited bodies. EV suits equipped with backpacks capable of only minimal maneuverability. Since the packs were designed to provide only a limited amount of propulsion, the distance between the two vessels required that they rely on the boost they would get from the garbage chute's own expulsion capability. Otherwise it would take so long to reach their target that the gigantic warship would likely have restored power and weapons capability before they even got to her. They had to make the crossing as fast as possible—which meant incurring the risk of contact with the intervening debris field.

"We'll have to maneuver around anything we encounter." As Kirk spoke, he was staring at the circular door in front of them. Outside, beyond, lay an unknown amount of detritus of varying size and potential danger, a hostile vessel—and a great, great deal of nothing.

Frantic yet somehow reassuring, Scott's voice reached him, neatly patched through by the ever-competent Uhura. *"Stand by. Stand by."* There was a pause, then, *"Yeah, okay—I'm here."*

In case someone was now eavesdropping on the frequency, the chief did not elaborate. Kirk knew it could only mean that Scott had successfully reached and entered hangar seven.

On the *Enterprise* bridge, Sulu continued his masterful manual tweaking of the ship's maneuvering thrusters. While the alignment he was seeking was actually easier to secure than that required to back a starship into dock, knowledge of that fact didn't prevent him from perspiring. Only when one readout turned green and the word LOCKED appeared on its neighbor did he allow himself to relax even slightly.

"Captain, the trash exhaust you are presently occupying is aimed at the personnel portal of hangar seven on the other ship. You are good to go. Provided the other vessel does not alter its current position, I should be able to hold this alignment as long as necessary."

"Copy that," Kirk replied. *"Scotty, you ready for us yet?"*

★   ★   ★

On the warship, the chief slowed before the very door he was supposed to open. Even though he knew he was in one of the smaller hangar entrances, the barrier's size still gave him pause.

"Whoa, hold on a sec now. This airlock door I'm lookin' at is very wee. I mean, it's small. Only four meters or so in diameter. And you're comin' straight across this way? It's goin' to be like jumpin' out of a movin' car, off a bridge, an' into a shot glass."

Back on the *Enterprise*, Kirk tensed as he prepared himself for the forthcoming release from the airlock. "That's okay," Kirk assured the chief via his suit's comm. "I've done this before."

Turning to him, Khan raised an eyebrow in a disarmingly Spock-like manner. "You've done this before?"

"Yeah," an increasingly tense Kirk told him, "it was vertical. We jumped onto a . . ." His words trailed off, along with the memory, and he returned his attention to the barrier directly in front of them. "It doesn't matter."

Khan eyed him a moment longer, then gave a mental shrug and addressed his own suit's comm pickup. "Mr. Scott. Did you find the manual override?"

On the massive warship, Scott was racing frantically down the empty, disarmingly vast corridor that was hangar seven. "Not yet, not yet! I'm in the hangar. Give me a minute. A lot o' this is famil- iar, but there's a lot that's new to me, too. Too much that's new!"

Looking to right and left, he searched desperately for a manual control panel. It should have been . . . there. It wasn't. Turning in a frantic circle, he thought he saw the console. A quick check revealed plenty of differences from a panel with similar functions on the *Enterprise*—but enough that were familiar. Several in particular were virtually identical. They were all he needed—he hadn't come here to stand in a suit and manually bring a shuttle aboard.

So intent was he on studying the controls that he didn't notice a portal open at the back of the hangar and behind him.

On the *Enterprise* bridge, Spock felt he could no longer ignore reporting what he was seeing on the monitors. "Captain, before you launch, I feel I must restate that there is considerable debris still drifting between our ships. At your calculated departure velocity, contact with even a seemingly insignificant fragment would be cat—"

"Don't say 'catastrophic'!" Despite the best efforts of his suit's automated internal climate control, Kirk was sweating. "Are we good to go or not?"

"Yes, Captain. If you choose to define 'good' as taking into account—"

Kirk interrupted the science officer's unnecessary and decidedly unwanted explication by checking in with the chief. "Scotty, you ready for us?"

"Give me two seconds!" came the decidedly frenetic response. Under his breath and away from the communicator, the chief added to no one but himself, "Ya mad bastard!"

★　　★　　★

On the bridge, McCoy leaned toward the command chair and its occupant. "Tell me this is gonna work."

"I have neither the information nor the confidence to do so, Doctor."

McCoy's expression twisted as he straightened. "As always, you're a real comfort."

Lying prone in the disposal chute, Kirk heard what he desperately wanted to hear from the chief. "Okay, okay—I'm set to open the door."

Kirk glanced over at his companion. "You ready?"

"Are you?"

Damn the man! Kirk thought to himself. *How can he be so calm under such circumstances? How human is he?* Recalling McCoy's comment about the prisoner's blood summoned forth a host of questions—none of which Kirk presently had the time or inclination to ask. But later, when this was all over . . .

He addressed his suit's pickup. "Okay, Spock—*pull the trigger.*"

"Yes, Captain . . . launching activation sequence on three . . . two . . . one . . ."

The airtight door in front of Kirk and Khan opened. There was a silent blast of compressed air from behind them that was intended to ensure that no refuse drifted back into the circular opening, and both men shot out into space as if blown from a cannon.

Into space, where pure tangled menace awaited.

XIV

Funny thing about acceleration, Kirk thought as he and his companion were shot out of the refuse tube: Though wholly an external stimulus, it has powerful effects on the mind. While being unceremoniously blasted out of a garbage chute lacked the aesthetic of tromping on the accelerator of an antique sports car, both generated similar feelings. He would much preferred to have been in that car now, powering across the flat Iowa landscape instead of . . .

But that was a long time ago, and that bitch reality kept poking him in the side with the ugly stick of immediacy.

Looking to his right, he could see Khan speeding along beside him as together they rocketed toward the looming warship. Rapidly changing light and reflection made it impossible to clearly make out the other man's face. What was this warrior from the past thinking? Was he excited, energized, afraid, indifferent? On more than one occasion, Kirk had tried to read him, and failed. Having murdered Christopher Pike and too many others, Khan was now assisting Kirk in trying to save the *Enterprise* and its crew. Did a damaged psyche reside in that remarkable body? If McCoy couldn't tell, how could he, Kirk?

One thing at a time, he told himself.

The heads-up inside Kirk's helmet showed their destination. At first absurdly tiny, the faint outline of the hatch was growing steadily larger as they drew nearer. He addressed his suit pickup, hoping that communications on board the warship were still sufficiently jumbled by Scott's efforts to prevent anyone from intercepting his short-range tight-beam sending.

"Scotty, we're there real soon! You good?"

Alone within hangar seven, Scott was lamenting the number of readouts on a console that was only half familiar. The control he sought ought to be *there,* high up on the right side, but it was not. Why move it to another location, his engineer's mind wondered, when high-up-right-side was perfectly adequate? Searching, searching, he ran the fingers of his right hand along the board. He could of course try a verbal command, but if the console was programmed to respond only to specific voices, then it would refuse his request—or worse, lock itself down until local security could unfreeze it.

"No, I'm hardly good," he muttered into his communicator. "Good is *not* what I am. . . ."

★   ★   ★

On the *Enterprise* bridge, Spock and everyone else who could spare a glance observed the progress of the captain and Khan as they approached the warship. An anxious ensign spoke up the instant Kirk's projected trajectory turned from green to red.

"Sir, their path isn't clear! It was when they launched, but much of the remaining debris is still in motion and they're now on course to intersect! The captain is headed for collision at point four-three-two."

Spock hit the command chair comm. "Captain, you have debris directly ahead and immediately in your path."

"Copy that." *Bad luck the chunk of metal was right in front of him,* Kirk thought wildly. *Good luck that it was large enough to see.*

Firing his backpack, he just managed to veer away from certain death from a ragged fragment of the damaged *Enterprise*. Surrounded by hundreds of drifting shards of metal, plastic, and torn construction fiber, Kirk fought to stay on course while avoiding certain doom. As he pondered the details of his close call, McCoy's voice echoed in his helmet.

"Whoa, Jim, you're way off course."

"I know, I know—I can see that!"

At the Academy, he had spent far more time learning how to maneuver a multi-ton starship than a body in an EV suit. While the heads-up in his forward view continued its inexorable countdown 'til arrival, he gently adjusted the firing controls on his pack until he was back on course.

★ ★ ★

Inside the hangar, Scott continued his desperate attempt to un-scramble the controls on the console. Was he even standing be-fore the correct console, he asked himself? A rapid check of the hangar's interior had shown him no other likely candidates, but that didn't mean he might not have missed something. The war-ship was brand new, after all. Maybe the manual override was located somewhere else. Or worse, that particular control had been entirely eliminated from the massive starship's design. In which case . . .

No, the override *had* to exist. Right here in front of him, if only he could identify it. Hadn't Kirk's companion said as much?

"Very close now, Mr. Scott," came Spock's voice over the com-municator.

Damn, but Vulcans could be annoying! he thought. *Even the most well-meaning ones.*

"Uh, just having a slight issue opening the door."

There! At an experimental brush of his hand, a number of previously invisible readouts sprang to life. *Not perceptible until they're needed*, he realized. Now that it had made itself visible, the control he had been frantically seeking plainly stood out. To ensure that it was functional, he adjusted it ever so slightly, intending to crack the hangar door as little as possible.

Nothing happened.

Frowning, he pushed against the control a little harder, then more forcefully. Still nothing. It struck him that it, and possibly this entire console, had been affected by his own hand—by the sabotage he had inflicted shipwide. Now that power was coming back online throughout the vessel, it was likely that certain ele-ments would have to be manually reactivated and reset—perhaps this console among them?

Well, if he had caused the console controls to shut down, he could damn well get them back online again. Ducking down, he probed beneath the console board, moving cables around until he could get at the solid-state components he sought. The designer portion of the engineer in him automatically took over.

Let's see . . . power in here, overflow there, emergency interrupt should be here . . . Bending down while holding his open communicator between his teeth, Scott began wrapping one end of a loose length of thick binding strap around one of the console's supports and the other end around his left wrist. In seconds, he was once more standing up and facing the console. A few last preparations and all would be ready. He didn't have time to be pessimistic.

A voice sounded behind him: cool, confident, controlled.

"Don't move."

"Use your display, Captain," Sulu told him anxiously. *"You must correct precisely thirty-seven-point-two degrees."*

"Got it," Kirk told him as he dodged still another chunk of floating debris. "I'm working my way back. Scotty, you're gonna be ready with that door, right?"

There was no response.

"Turn around. Slowly."

Dammit. Trying to keep his left hand out of sight, the chief complied, keeping his back against the control board while letting his communicator fall to the deck. The uniformed security officer glanced at it, his gaze narrowing as he returned his attention to its owner.

"What the hell are you doing?" The pistol the new arrival wielded was pointed directly at Scott's chest.

The chief smiled engagingly. "Wee bit o' maintenance on the airlock console. You're big." His expression brightened. "Poch Mahon, right?"

The officer blinked. "What?"

"Sorry," the chief replied. "Thought you were someone I knew. Fellow named Poch Mahon."

Time, Scott knew. Unless he could do something, it was a quantity the captain and his companion would very soon be out of.

"Mr. Scott, where are you?"

Uhura's voice sounded in his helmet. *"Captain, he can't seem to hear you. I'm working on getting his signal back. Stand by."*

They were very close to their destination now, Kirk saw. Almost close enough to . . .

Crack.

Generating a sound all out of proportion to its minuscule size, the impact startled Kirk. Traveling at full velocity, he had struck the seemingly insignificant particle head-on. Neither the *Enterprise*'s sensors nor those built into his suit had managed to detect its presence in time. The spiderwebbing cracks that had suddenly appeared on the front of his helmet were spreading in multiple directions in uneven jerks and bounds.

Dammit.

The warship lay just ahead, beckoning. Unable to see anything except the diffusing cracks in his faceplate, he hardly heard Spock's words as they reached him from the *Enterprise*.

"*Captain, what is it?*"

"My helmet faceplate was struck. Uhura, tell me you have Mr. Scott back!"

"*Not yet—I'm still working on a signal.*"

From the communicator Scott had dropped onto the hangar deck, Uhura's voice sounded plainly.

"*His communicator's working—I don't know why he isn't responding.*"

His attention drawn toward the voice, the security officer glanced sharply down at the communicator. "What the hell is that? *Who* the hell is that? What's going on here? What are you up to, mister?" His gaze shifted back to Scott. "I don't know everyone on this mission, but I sure don't recall seeing you in the line when we boarded."

Scott smiled. "I'm in general maintenance. We're not very memorable, we're not. Not like you brave *caileags* up front. Are you private security? Because you sure look like private security."

"Imminent collision detected," Sulu declared sharply.

"Khan," Spock informed Kirk's companion, "use evasive action. There is debris directly ahead."

"*I see it,*" came the prompt reply.

On the forward screen the words "Transmission Lost" appeared.

"Mr. Sulu," Spock inquired, "did we lose Khan?"

"I don't know, Commander." Used to tracking the movements of other ships, the helmsman was more than a little frazzled trying to maintain contact with two fast-moving but extremely tiny objects as they darted in and among thousands of individual scraps of ship debris.

Kirk glanced to his right, but he might as well have been trying to spot a bullet flying through a barnyard. "Was Khan hit?"

"We're trying to find him now," Spock reported.

"Captain," Sulu interrupted, giving Kirk no time for further contemplation, *"you need to adjust your course to target destination to one-eight-three by four-seven-three degrees."*

Kirk complied. The complex instructions didn't trouble him. Concentrating on Sulu's instructions helped to keep him from noting that his faceplate continued to crack and splinter.

"Mr. Spock, my faceplate display is down. I'm flying blind."

"Captain, without your display, hitting your target destination is mathematically impossible."

"Mr. Spock, when I get back, we really need to talk about your bedside manner."

Sulu whirled in his chair. "Commander—he's not gonna make it."

Another voice; one not heard for a while.

"I see you, Kirk."

Khan.

*   *   *

"My display is still functioning. You're two hundred meters ahead of me at my one o'clock. Come to your left at two degrees and follow me."

In a couple of seconds, the other man was in view, and soon Kirk was flying along almost parallel to him.

There remained the small matter, however, of whether or not they were about to smash themselves into the unyielding flank of the massive ship directly in front of them.

"Scotty," Kirk declaimed into his still-functioning helmet pickup, "we're getting close. We're gonna need a warm welcome. Scotty, do you copy—*Scotty!*"

"If you can hear us, Mr. Scott," Spock commanded, "open the door in ten . . ."

"Scotty!" a desperate Kirk yelled.

". . . nine . . . ," Spock continued to count down.

On board the warship, Spock's voice continued to spill from the open communicator on the floor. A nervously innocent Scott gazed pleasantly at the man holding the phaser on him while the chief's free hand slid back and down to steady himself against the console.

"That person counting down," the man demanded, "what is that?"

"What?" Scott feigned ignorance. "I don't hear anything."

". . . *seven* . . . ," Spock's voice declaimed clearly from the device.

"Mr. Scott, where are you?" Kirk queried as the distance between himself, his companion, and the warship continued to shrink rapidly.

". . . *three* . . . *two* . . . *one* . . . Now, *Mr. Scott,*" Spock said tightly.

Eyeing the security officer, Scott shook his head slightly. "Sorry about this."

Frowning, the guard gestured slightly with his phaser. "Sorry about what?"

Even Spock could not keep his voice from rising slightly. *"I said, Scott, open the door!"*

"Open the door!" Kirk shouted.

Spinning sharply to his left, Scott slammed his right hand down on a very large yellow-tinged button near the center of the console behind him, putting all his force into the gesture.

At the far terminus of the hangar, a small door snapped open. Instantly, a substantial quantity of air was sucked outward into open space—taking the unfortunate security officer along with it. With his left arm strapped to the console, a grimacing Scott found himself stretched out full-length, like a flag in a hurricane, in the direction of the open port.

Kirk barely saw the wide-eyed figure go sailing past him as he entered backward, both he and Khan having reversed position at the last moment so that their full-firing backpacks could slow their momentum. As they crossed the outer boundary of the now-gaping hangar, they also entered the warship's artificial gravity field.

Flailing with his right hand, Scott quickly hit the control again, repeating in reverse the gesture he had made a moment earlier. He fell flat on his front side as the hangar's outer door slammed shut and was all but out of breath when the ship's automated life-support systems rapidly filled the open space around him with atmosphere. Air pressure in the hangar swiftly returned to normal. Thankfully, the atmospherics were one component of the warship's life-support system that did not require a manual reset in order to operate.

Dropping to the deck, Kirk and Khan skidded, rolled, and tumbled down its length, slowing steadily—though not fast enough for Kirk. They came to rest close to where a gasping Scott was now sitting up.

"Welcome aboard," the chief wheezed, delighted and more than a little surprised to find that he was still alive.

"It's good to see you, Mr. Scott." Kirk found he was in no hurry to stand.

The chief smiled. "Don't you maybe mean 'relieved' to see me, Captain?" The engineer looked questioningly at the other arrival, who was in the process of rising to his knees. "Who is that?"

Having managed, with difficulty, to get onto his knees, the heavily breathing Kirk performed cursory introductions. "Scotty, Khan. Khan, Scotty . . . best engineer in Starfleet."

"Hello," Scott offered.

Khan did not waste time on pleasantries. "They'll know we're here. Marcus will have all approaches to the bridge secured if only as a precaution, but I know another route."

The two men regarded each other wordlessly as Kirk removed phasers from his backpack and handed one to each of them. "They're locked to stun."

Khan pursed his lips. "Theirs won't be."

Kirk responded with a wan smile. "Then try not to get shot."

Though it was confirmed that Kirk and Khan had successfully boarded the warship and made contact with Mr. Scott, everyone on the *Enterprise* knew it was far too soon to take anything, including hope, for granted. The three men were out of harm's way, but only for the moment. At any time, with a single wrong turn or move, they could be swept up by the warship's roaming security personnel.

As Spock was trying to analyze all possibilities, a loud acknowledgment sounded from the Communications station. Uhura looked back at him.

"Incoming message from New Vulcan, Captain. That call you had me try to place? The necessary relay links finally fell into position and it went through. You have the transmission you requested."

Spock acknowledged the exceptional technical achievement with a precise nod. "On screen, please. I would acclaim you a wizard at your specialty, Lieutenant, except there are no wizards."

"The correct term is 'sorceress,' Mr. Spock—and thank you. Putting through visual."

All eyes on the bridge turned to the main viewscreen forward, where an ancient and wizened visage appeared without preamble or fanfare. Behind the familiar figure could be seen signs of extensive activity. An old civilization was rising afresh on a new world, and the figure who gazed back at those on the bridge was a critical part of that resurrection.

"Mr. Spock," declared the image matter-of-factly.

"Mr. Spock," the science officer responded.

The security escort seemed excessive for a single woman, even one who had been beamed aboard the warship unceremoniously and involuntarily. Aware of Carol Marcus's identity—and what the consequences would be for each of them if anything happened to her before she could be delivered—the guards treated her with the utmost care. Although none of them showed it, they were very much relieved when they finally arrived on the bridge. The leader of the security team advised Marcus of their arrival.

"Admiral."

Through the hive of activity, as sweating technicians strove to restore full power and service to every corner of the massive warship, father and daughter locked eyes. When he finally spoke, Alexander Marcus's words weighed like lead on his offspring.

"I'll deal with *you* in a minute."

Carol had other ideas. Stepping forward and away from her escorts, who were hesitant to intercept her while in the admiral's presence, she drew back a hand and smacked her father across the face. He mutely stared at her, eyes wide.

"I've been trying to prepare what to say at this moment," she snapped at him. "I thought of a lot of things and discarded them. Hateful things, sad things, words grounded in moments and times past. What it all finally comes down to is fairly simple, however. I'm ashamed to be your daughter."

Spotting an empty seat at an unutilized station, her escort took her aside. She sat there in silence, glaring at him.

Whatever the admiral had in mind was forced to take a back-seat to a sudden report from one of the other officers on the bridge.

"Sir, we just recorded an unscheduled opening and subsequent closing of an outer door on deck thirteen. It appears to have been initiated manually."

Marcus looked resigned, not surprised. "Khan."

The officer eyed him uncertainly. "Sir? I don't understand."

"Hope that you won't." Marcus proceeded to let fly a string of orders directed at ship security. Now that Khan was here, the admiral intended to be ready for him. Despite being fully aware of the revived warrior's talents and abilities, Marcus was not afraid of him. At the same time, he intended to take every precaution possible.

Where Khan was concerned, hubris could prove more lethal than any gun.

"They're gonna have full power and we're walking," Scott was whispering as he trailed Kirk and Khan down yet another corridor.

Pausing at a control console, Khan quickly entered a series of brief commands. "This path we're taking runs adjacent to the engine room. They know they won't be able to use their weapons here without destabilizing the warp core, which gives us the advantage."

Moving closer to Kirk, Scott readily expressed his bewilderment. "Where'd you find this guy?"

"It's a long story," Kirk muttered as he hurried to keep up with Khan.

Empirically, Spock had grown used to conversing with his elder self. Philosophically and, dare he think it, emotionally, there were still moments of uncertainty. None of those were apparent in the ensuing conversation, of course. He had no more wish to unsettle his colleagues on the bridge than he did himself. "I wish I were contacting you under better circumstances, but . . ."

The older Spock took over. With time (in multiple senses of the term), his appearance had come to match his voice: sage, knowing, almost comforting, etched with more lines than any Rembrandt drawing.

"Given our unique relationship, it would be illogical to make such contact unless the situation were grave enough to demand it. And since you find yourself in the captain's chair, I can only assume that it is. I am aware that a most complex alignment of multiple relays was necessary in order for this present exchange to take place. Am I correct in assuming that Lieutenant Uhura continues to be responsible for such Communications expertise?"

"You are." From her position at the Communications station, she smiled at the image of the famous savant.

"Your conclusions are both correct," the younger Spock confirmed to his elder self. "Therefore I will be brief, so as not to waste time neither of us has to spare. In your many travels and experiences, did you ever have occasion to come across a man named Khan?"

While his face could not show shock, certainly not to a degree any human could detect, a slight shiver seemed to pass through the elder Spock's entire frame. He paused for a long moment, plainly composing his intended response. Unusual for him, it was prefaced by an exception. "As you know, I have made a vow never to give you information that could potentially alter your destiny. Your path—whatever it may be, wherever it may lead you, and however it may differ from the one I walked—is yours to walk and yours alone. I can and should have no influence over it. I always felt that way would be best for you."

"As do I," admitted his younger self.

"That being said, I have to tell you that the individual called Khan is the most dangerous adversary the *Enterprise* and her crew ever faced."

Not only young Spock but everyone on the bridge was now attending upon the words of the older Spock to the exclusion of all but the most inescapable tasks.

"He is a psychotic despot," the senior Spock continued, "whom we—I and my chronologically pertinent colleagues— once made the mistake of trusting. He is brilliant, ruthless, and will not hesitate to kill every single one of you in the pursuit of whatever personal goal he has set for himself. Nor will he spare others, including innocents and unknowing civilians. Wherever he is, I urge you to stay as far from him as humanly possible. And if you do not? I can all but guarantee you—lives will be lost."

The subsequent silence on the starship's bridge was complete. Nothing could be heard save the automated beep and hum of instruments.

"Did you defeat him?" the younger Spock finally asked.

A nod from a distant place and an even more distant time. "At great cost, yes."

The acting captain of the *Enterprise* stared forward, his voice and posture fixed, as he uttered a single word in reply.

"How?"

"I don't mean to tempt fate here," Scott muttered as they moved quickly along the newest corridor in Khan's wake, "but where is everybody?"

"The ship was designed to be run by a minimal crew," Khan told him. "One, if necessary."

"One!" Scott blurted. "I don't see how—"

The three boarders took the oncoming security team equally by surprise.

With bodies slamming into one another, there was no time to make use of phasers. All the rules of hand-to-hand combat Kirk had studied at the Academy were brought into play. Caught in high, constricted corridors, he also made use of earlier, less academic techniques he had acquired in the course of too many less-disciplined fights in too many bars.

Fists and the occasional leg flew, taking down first one of his opponents and then another. Nearby, Scotty was giving a vibrant if slightly more desperate account of himself. Their tight surroundings actually worked to the chief's advantage, as his better-trained opponents had less room in which to operate. Elaborate martial-arts techniques gave way to sharp elbows and simple punches.

Meanwhile Khan was demolishing everyone with whom he came in contact. The ease with which he dispatched members of the security team was at once impressive and disconcerting. One moment a blur, the next an implacable and irresistible force, Khan paid only minimal attention to whatever was being brought against him.

Two of their opponents tried to jump him simultaneously. Khan slammed one into a far wall, then turned and lifted the other before throwing him down the corridor. At no time in the course of the confrontation did he break a sweat. Indeed, Kirk saw, the former prisoner did not even appear to be breathing hard.

The fight was over much sooner than the captain expected. Every member of the security team was down: unconscious or too badly hurt to offer further resistance. Arms of certain individuals had been twisted absurdly far behind their backs, breaking them at the shoulder. Khan's work. As efficient as it was brutal.

And speaking of their guide . . .

"Where's Khan?" Scott managed to gasp out.

Tension on the *Enterprise* bridge was palpable as everyone awaited a word from their acting captain. Spock did not acknowledge their apprehension. Seemingly oblivious to the fact that all eyes were on him, he sat quietly in the command chair, thinking.

Dammit, man, McCoy thought, *say something. You're in command: Act like it. Issue an order, present an analysis, make a statement.* Had Spock said anything as soon as Uhura had terminated the complex exchange with New Vulcan, it would have reassured everyone on the bridge.

It was what Kirk would have done.

But Spock was not James Kirk. He was not like anyone on the bridge—a fact that was reflected in his continuing quiet contemplation of what his elder self had told him, combined with the facts as they presently existed.

But perhaps the Vulcan's patience stood in direct contrast to Kirk's tendency to act immediately.

With a start, the doctor reflected on what a perfect team this made the two of them. Except that one half of that team was not here. He was on that warship, no doubt in deadly danger. Which made Spock's ongoing lack of action all the more frustrating.

When the science officer finally spoke, his first words were for Uhura. "Lieutenant, I need you to assemble all senior Medical and Engineering staff who can be spared from critical positions and have them gather in the weapons bay."

Her expression twisted. "The weapons bay, Mr. Spock?"

A curt nod. "Weapons bay. At haste, if you please."

"All right."

With an uncertain shake of her head, she moved to comply. As soon as she did so, the science officer turned to the watching McCoy.

"Dr. McCoy. You inadvertently activated a torpedo. Do you think you would be able to replicate the process?"

McCoy gaped at the Vulcan. "Even assuming that I could, why the hell would I want to do *that*?"

As always, Spock's lack of expression offered no clue as to what he intended. "Can you or can you not?"

McCoy wasn't sure whether he was more stunned or outraged. "That thing almost ate my *arm*. And I wasn't even trying to arm it. *Dammit*, man, I'm a *doctor*, not a torpedo technician. Why would you want *me* to have anything to do with a torpedo of any kind, much less something new, untried, and partially cannibalized for another purpose entirely?"

Spock was, if anything, understanding. "Believe me, Doctor, I both recognize and sympathize with your concerns. However, the fact that you *are* a doctor is precisely why I need you to listen very carefully . . ."

"Where is he?" Scott murmured as he and Kirk made their way forward. Surely he hadn't been taken down?

"Shit," Kirk mumbled as he searched one side corridor after another. Then, from behind them . . .

"This way."

Khan's voice had come from farther up the branching corridor, his tone impatient, as if he expected them to be fully recovered and ready to go. He did not appear winded or stressed in the slightest. As soon as he received an acknowledging nod from Kirk, their guide resumed the way forward.

Hanging back slightly, the captain murmured to his chief engineer. "The minute we get to the bridge, *drop him*."

Scott was understandably confused. "Khan? I thought he was helping us."

Despite some lingering uncertainty, Kirk had no hesitation in explaining: "On the contrary, Scotty, I'm pretty sure we're helping *him*."

Alexander Marcus was smart and aware enough to know that the immediate danger to his health and intentions came not from the *Enterprise* or even from the fact that Khan had somehow managed to get himself aboard the warship, but from his rising blood pressure. This dropped immediately the instant the warship's main systems began to snap back online, one at a time. Full illumination, scanners, internal sensors: All he needed to do was swing around in his command chair to see them flare to life. Even so, he was glad when a senior ensign confirmed the informal visuals.

"Power coming online, sir."

"Excellent." Marcus once more felt secure in directing his full attention to the forward screen. "Retarget the *Enterprise* now." From her seat nearby, a helpless Carol could only continue to glare futilely at her father.

"Weapons charging," a second ensign reported calmly.

Marcus nodded to himself. It would all be over soon. Then even the presence of Khan on board the warship would be nothing more than a minor annoyance to be dealt with.

"Fire all weapons, phasers, and torpedoes—on my order."

The doors to the turbolift snapped open and the three men who burst from within were firing before anyone on the bridge could react.

First to go down was the ensign in control of the warship's weapons systems, struck in the back of the head by a stun blast from Kirk's phaser. Throwing himself to one side, the captain brought down another crewmember before he could draw his sidearm. As the crewman looming over Carol moved to engage the intruders, she put him down with a precisely placed elbow to his chin.

Though intense, the melee on the bridge did not last long. With all three men firing rapidly and Khan dealing with those who managed to avoid the phasers, it was only a matter of moments before the trio had gained complete control of the ship.

Before Khan could say or do anything else, Kirk nodded to the chief. Scott fired once. The stun blast hit Khan square in the back, and he went down. Moving to the body, Scott knelt to feel it, looked up, and nodded at Kirk.

"Breathing's regular. I hit him hard, like you said. He's alive, but he should be out for a while."

"Make sure he stays down."

Keeping his own phaser aimed at the admiral, Kirk now moved to stand closer to Carol Marcus. The two men regarded each other across the open space of the bridge: one behind his weapon, the other behind his ire.

"Admiral Alexander Marcus, by authority granted me under the relevant Starfleet regulations governing the use of unauthorized and excessive force, I hereby relieve you of command and place you under arrest."

Marcus sounded more exasperated than upset. It was plain that he was not about to go quietly. "You're not actually going to do this, are you? Do you still really think Starfleet is about exploring 'strange new worlds'? That's a fantasy, Kirk. The galaxy is wide, dark, and dangerous, populated by sentients who are collectively paranoid, warlike, and sometimes both. Their quest for species superiority has nothing to do with stealing other worlds' resources or enslaving an entirely different populace—it's all about bragging rights. About who is superior and who should bow down. If you think Starfleet was put together as a scientific enterprise, that's another fantasy. There are plenty of other organizations based on Earth and its colonies capable of exploring and studying. Fortunately, there are some of us who believe that all the do-gooding, glad-handing scientists might need a little protection while they're out there—not to mention that there's a need for defending the species itself. That's what Starfleet really is about."

Kirk considered the admiral's words before replying quietly.

"Anyone who knows me will tell you that I'm the last person on the planet to back away from a fight, but . . . that's your Starfleet, Admiral. It's not mine. It's not what I signed up for, not what I vowed to defend, and not the philosophy I plan to use in guiding my career." He glanced to his right. "Scotty?"

More than a little astonished to be asked to comment on such a philosophical difference of opinion, the chief engineer responded with a smile. "Dinna ask me, Captain. I just keep things running. But I'd rather be workin' with engines than with weapons." He shifted his gaze to the hard-staring Admiral Marcus. "You kinna make friends with others, Admiral, if you focus your energies on blowin' 'em up. As you say, the galaxy's a big place. Folks with whom you can share a few drinks are few and far between. Meself, I believe in doin' all we can to encourage that."

Kirk gestured at Marcus with the phaser he was holding. "Get out of that chair."

The admiral tried again. "I want you to stop and think about what you're doing, Kirk. Not about some imaginary future confrontation. About *right now*. Think about what you *did* on Qo'noS. Are you sure you weren't identified? That the Klingon patrol you wiped out—yes, I was able to access the preliminary report—didn't pass along the word that they had contacted and been forced into combat with humans? You were on their homeworld illegally, unauthorized. Not only did you not have permission to land on Qo'noS, you arrived and departed by stealth, having done nothing except resist interrogation and commit murder. That's how the Klingons will see it—as murder, not as resisting arrest and questioning."

Kirk smiled thinly. "If so, the K'normians will have some awkward questions to answer."

Marcus was shaking his head. "It doesn't matter who they blame, or if they blame anyone. It doesn't matter if you managed to make an incursion onto a hostile world without leaving a single trace of your visitation in your wake. Nothing changes the fact that war with the Klingons is *coming*. If your visit was discovered and reported to the authorities on Qo'noS, it will only hasten the inevitable. If it was not, then we have gained a little more time before the cataclysm arrives. And who's going to lead us? *You?*"

The admiral's tone changed to one of furious desperation.

"If I'm not in charge when that happens, our entire way of life, not to mention the very survival of our species, will be at risk. So I ask you, I beg you, one more time: Lower your gun. Report back to your ship. You have my word I'll allow the *Enterprise* to depart unharmed, or if you prefer, remain on station here in lunar space until such repairs have been completed as will allow you to transfer to Earth orbit."

He nodded in the direction of the prone body sprawled on the deck close by Kirk's feet.

"All I ask is that you leave *him* with me. The fact that you had him stunned shows that you don't trust him any more than I would. I used him and his knowledge; I admit that. Now you've used him to recover your ship. You and I are even. I've said from the beginning of this confrontation that it's him I wanted all along. Leave him with me so I can deal with him, and let's pretend none of this happened."

Scott made a disgusted noise. "Two Federation ships engage in near-fatal combat with one another, and we're to pretend none o' it happened? I'd like to see the final report on *that* one!"

Admiral Marcus favored the chief with a faint smile. "You would be surprised, Mr. Scott, on what can be made to disappear through the use of appropriate language. Obfuscation is the primary weapon of bureaucrats. What has happened here will be put down to mistakes in communication, deficient electronics, and whatever other scapegoats can be fabricated. It will not be the first time in human history that armed vessels engaged in accidental combat. If you are not familiar with the ancient term 'friendly fire,' I suggest you educate yourself when you have some free time." He turned back to Kirk. "That is my proposal. I suggest you think it over carefully in light of what you may have to do. Because if you think I'm abandoning this ship and leaving quietly with you, you're going to have to kill me."

"I'm not going to kill you, sir." Neither Kirk's determination nor the muzzle of the weapon he held had wavered. "But I could ignore everything you've said, stun your ass, and drag you out of that chair, but I'd rather not do that in front of your daughter." He looked toward her. "You all right?"

Though shaken, she replied immediately. "Yes, Captain."

For an instant, Scott had taken his eyes off the figure on the floor. It was more time than Khan needed. A single blow put the chief on the deck.

"Jim!" Carol shouted.

It would not have mattered how fast Kirk reacted; Khan was so much faster. A leap, a grab and squeeze, and a body slam put Kirk down. He tried to avoid the punch that followed and could not. Lifting the captain as if he were weightless, Khan threw him against the far wall.

Carol Marcus scrambled to intercept him. "Listen . . . wait!"

Contemptuously, Khan threw her to the floor. Though he pulled the kick he delivered to the right thigh of the prone science officer, it was enough to bring forth a high-pitched scream of pain. Advancing steadily, he cornered Admiral Marcus.

His lips tightened ever so slightly as he placed an open palm on either side of the admiral's head and began to squeeze. "You— you—should have let me sleep."

The snapping sound that followed was overwhelmed by Carol Marcus's horrified scream. On the deck, a stunned Kirk could only look on—and listen.

XV

Spock was as close as he could come to expressing genuine anxiety.

"Where is the captain, Mr. Sulu?"

While the same question had been bedeviling the helmsman for some time now, he could provide only the same maddeningly uninformative response as previously.

"Our sensor array's still down, sir. We can't probe the interior of the other ship. I've been trying some workarounds, but even they went down suddenly. I can't find him."

The science officer frowned. "Suddenly? Suddenly 'when,' Mr. Sulu?"

The helmsman looked toward the command chair. "Just now, actually, sir. I was starting to make some progress, and everything just went—"

Spock didn't wait for him to finish. "Divert all noncritical power to shields."

"Shields, sir?" Sulu looked uncertain. "According to what I can see, they're still working to finalize the restoration of their own systems over there. The only ones that I can see are running a hundred percent at the moment are life support and artificial gravity."

"Shields up," Spock tersely reiterated. "*Now.*"

From another station an ensign monitoring the referenced systems called across to the command chair. "Sir, our maximum capability is twenty-one percent, and that's only if we drop all—"

"Do it, Mr. Bradley. Extrapolating from what Mr. Sulu says, I have the feeling that . . . Captain?"

Without preamble, the view forward of the black warship had been replaced by one of James Kirk. Standing straight but looking more than a little battered, he was edged to one side to reveal Khan standing beside him. The former prisoner held the business end of a phaser against the captain's neck. Spock did not need higher resolution to tell him that the weapon was likely not set on stun.

"I'm going to make this very simple for you, Mr. Spock," Khan told him softly.

"Captain." There was almost a hint of emotion in Spock's voice.

"Your crew," Khan continued, "for my crew."

Well behind Khan, Spock could make out Chief Engineer Scott and Dr. Carol Marcus. They appeared to be weaponless, though the Vulcan was coming to believe that where Khan was concerned it would not have made any difference if both the chief and the admiral's daughter *had* been armed.

"You have betrayed us," Spock said evenly. "The captain

trusted you. Trusted you enough to make you an ally against the renegade Admiral Marcus." Spock tried to peer deeper into the corners of the viewscreen image. "I see only Engineer Scott and Dr. Marcus behind you. Where is the admiral?"

"At peace," Khan replied without hesitation. "And if we're going to throw around the term 'betrayal,' *I'm* the one who should be outraged. I'm the one who was betrayed." He nodded back in the direction of Scott. "Once the admiral and those around him had been dealt with, your man *shot* me. On the direct order of the same captain you claim made me his ally."

Spock replied with equal coolness. "And would we now be in a different position if he had *not*? Would this exchange be taking place under different circumstances? Or was having you put down—inadequately, it would appear—merely a momentary interruption in your predetermined plan for regaining control of your crew once the admiral had been dealt with?"

There was a pause, and then Khan smiled. There was pleasure in it, but no amusement. "Oh, you *are* smart, Mr. Spock. It takes true intelligence to see beyond the immediate and into the future. Most men have thoughts only for the moment. It would be interesting to play chess with you."

"Isn't that what we are doing?" Spock shot back.

One of the game pieces chose that moment to speak up, as the dazed Kirk tried to pull away from Khan. "Listen to me, Spock! Don't do—"

Khan cut Kirk off in mid-sentence with a blow from the butt of the phaser he was holding, dropping him to the deck. As the stunned Kirk struggled and failed to rise, Khan turned back to the vid pickup. It was evident he was tiring of games of any kind.

"No more discussions. No more meaningless, time-wasting banter. I've waited three hundred years. Give me my crew."

Khan was brilliant, devious, and physically overpowering, but he was not omnipotent. If that were so, he would have known that one cannot hurry a Vulcan.

"Suppose I comply with your request," Spock replied calmly, and not in the least intimidated. "What will you do when you get them?"

"Continue the work we were doing before we were banished."

"Which is?" One eyebrow lifted quizzically.

"Making the world a better place." There was not so much as a suggestion of irony in Khan's reply.

"'Better.' Meaning, more like you," Spock surmised.

Giving the lie to what he had said a moment earlier, Khan showed himself willing to continue the conversation . . . provided it might lead to a worthwhile conclusion on the part of a respected opponent.

"Would that be such a bad thing?"

"As I understand your position, and extrapolating from what I have subsequently learned about you, it would involve the mass genocide of all beings you found to be less than superior specimens. With you being the arbiter of such decisions, of course."

Khan turned simultaneously wistful and philosophical. Or maybe he was just insane. "One must first destroy before they can create anew. There is no point in sowing fresh seed on a field thick with weeds." His expression was almost sad. "Shall I destroy you, Mr. Spock, or will you give me what I want? Come: Here is an opportunity for you to demonstrate your own personal superiority. Not to mention simple good sense."

Though the Vulcan term for it differed from that of the human, stalling was a tactic not unknown to the science officer. "We have no transporter capabilities."

Khan favored him with a thin smile. "Fortunately, that is

not a problem, as mine are perfectly functional." He glanced to one side. "Dr. Marcus can personally attest to that. Drop your shields."

"If I do so," Spock responded, "I have no guarantee you will not kill the captain and destroy the *Enterprise*."

"Ah, so it seems we are back to gaming again. As you like. Let's play this out 'logically.' Firstly, I *will* kill your captain to demonstrate both my resolve and my seriousness. That will eliminate your first concern from the equation, as he will then be dead and no longer a factor in our discussion. As to your resolve, if it continues to hold firm, I *will* have no choice but to kill you and your entire crew. So you see, you can turn over my crew to me and subsequently trust me to let you live, or I can kill you and your colleagues and recover my crew afterwards. Whether you live or die, I will have my people back."

"And yet," Spock replied, "*if* you destroy the *Enterprise,* you destroy your own people as well."

Khan's smile widened. "You forget, Mr. Spock. Your crew requires a continuous supply of fresh air to survive. Mine, being frozen in stasis, demands only a minimal energy draw to remain as they are until such time as they can be properly revived. Each stasis pod is individually powered, so that even if one or two of my companions should be lost, the rest would survive until re-vivification." He nodded in the general direction of the warship's instrumentation.

"Obviously, obliterating the *Enterprise* in a paroxysm of destruction would risk my crew's survivability. Do you still wonder why the former admiral Marcus desired it? In contrast, I will selectively target the life-support systems located in the vicinity of the engine nacelles. Once everyone aboard your ship has suffocated, I will walk over your cold corpses until I recover my people. Should a few of you manage to slip into EV suits, I will deal with those resourceful individuals one at a time." For emphasis, he pointed the end of the phaser toward the dazed Kirk's neck. "Game over. Now, shall we begin?"

Time was indeed up, Spock knew. Aware that he had done all he could, he looked toward the helm. "Lower shields, Mr. Sulu."

"Mr. Spock, sir, are you sure that . . . ?"

"Now, if you please, Mr. Sulu."

Exhaling heavily, the helmsman complied. Relevant instrumentation confirmed the execution of Spock's command. Defeated murmuring rose from those on the bridge. No one could blame the science officer. He had tried his best to dissuade a creature who had proved remorseless as well as cunning.

Still on the viewscreen, Khan could be seen accessing a bridge display, scanning the now completely vulnerable *Enterprise* while he nodded to himself with satisfaction.

"A wise choice, Mr. Spock. I had a feeling that when all was said and done, you would do the rational thing. Decision making becomes so much easier when an individual's choices are reduced to one."

Drawing back his leg, he delivered a kick to the prone Kirk's midsection that left him hardly able to inhale.

"I now can see that your weapons bay is filled with a variety of photon torpedoes. Including, interestingly, six dozen of an entirely new type." His voice darkened. "If none of them are mine, Commander, I will know it. At which point there will be no more discussion—of anything."

"Vulcans do not lie," Spock replied solemnly. "You should know that. The ones to which you allude are indeed your torpedoes."

Khan stared into the vid pickup a moment longer, as if trying to penetrate the science officer's thoughts despite the space that separated their respective vessels. Then he nodded once, pleased. Activating the warship's military-grade transporter system, Khan began retrieving the torpedoes and the precious cryopods they contained one by one.

Although Khan operated the applicable controls with super-human speed and skill, it still took several moments to complete the multiple ship-to-ship transfer. As soon as all seventy-two torpedoes had been transported to the warship's main cargo bay, Khan commenced a unit-by-unit deep probe utilizing the warship's main sensor scan. It promptly revealed their interior specifications—and contents. After completing half a dozen of these, he appeared to relax ever so slightly.

"Thank you, Mr. Spock."

"I have fulfilled your terms," Spock told him stiffly. "Now fulfill mine."

"Why not? It will make no difference, in the end." Looking over at a revived Kirk, who was struggling to keep his balance, he spoke condescendingly. "Well, Kirk, it seems I have to return you to your crew, as mine has been returned to me." Seated now in the warship's command chair, he prepared to manipulate the available controls. "This isn't a transporter room, but if one has a mastery of simple physics and general starship engineering, it's not so very difficult to manage the reverse of what brought the three of you on board."

As he rose weakly, Kirk felt a familiar sense of displacement take hold. The light swam before his eyes, shifting and changing colors. Nearby, similar dislocating swirls of luminance enveloped Dr. Marcus and Mr. Scott. Just out of reach, an indifferent Khan eyed Kirk speculatively as the captain began to vanish.

"After all," Khan continued as he worked the relevant instrumentation, "no ship should go down without her captain."

On board the *Enterprise*, silent alarms began to appear on Sulu's readouts. A worried Sulu looked toward the command chair. "He's locking phasers on us, sir!"

"Evasive maneuvers," Spock snapped. "Full impulse—whatever we have."

Deep within the *Enterprise,* a tripartite swirl of radiance and color shrank and solidified until three figures emerged from within them. It took a disoriented Kirk a moment to realize where Khan had sent them. They were in a holding cell in the ship's brig—the very same one Khan had occupied while on board. Even a madman, it appeared, could have a sense of humor. Next to him, Carol Marcus looked about to collapse. As Kirk hurried to support her and keep her from falling, Scott rushed to the transparent barrier and began pounding on it. While it was doubtful the impact of his fists could be heard on the other side, his voice conveyed his exasperation quite clearly.

"Och, man," he shouted at the guard on duty, "let us outta here now!"

The concussion that rocked the brig area along with the rest of the ship knocked all three of them off their feet.

★　　★　　★

Battered by a flurry of firepower, the *Enterprise* was driven toward Earth. Controlled by one man, the warship followed.

Even given the great warship's deliberately simplified command and control system, it was still a remarkable feat of piloting on Khan's behalf: operating the ship, pursuing, and engaging with weaponry all at the same time and all by himself. One could almost believe he might have surreptitiously planned for such a contingency in the designs and suggestions he had provided to the late Alexander Marcus's Section 31.

"Shields at six percent!" Sulu barely managed to make himself heard above the screaming alarms and repeated explosions that filled the bridge.

In contrast to everyone around him, Spock was strangely calm even for a Vulcan caught in such dire circumstances. "The torpedoes: How much time, Lieutenant?"

The officer he had addressed checked a readout. "Twelve seconds, sir!"

Nodding once, the first officer leaned toward the command chair pickup. "Crew of the *Enterprise,* this is Commander Spock. All decks prepare for imminent proximity detonation."

Freed from the brig by the duty guard as soon as everyone had recovered their balance, Kirk and Scott shouldered the injured form of Carol Marcus between them while they struggled toward the nearest turbolift. As they advanced as fast as they could, the voice of the ship's science officer sounded its warning over multiple speakers.

The struggling chief made a face. "What the hell is he talking about? Proximity detonation? *What* detonation?"

As Kirk continued running, his eyes widened slightly. "The torpedoes. *He armed the damn torpedoes.*"

Beside him, Scott was disbelieving. "He couldna gotten away with such, Captain. Surely Khan would have checked them as soon as he got them on board the other ship?"

"As anxious as he was to get his crew back . . ." Kirk muttered. "No, you're right, Scotty. But he'd have to scan them one at a time. Besides, who would be fool enough to try and arm one *manually*, right? A photon torpedo is always armed by the sending of an electronic code. Once on the warship, they and their potentially dangerous warheads would be immune to interference from outside, safe behind the warship's shields. And if only one was manually armed . . ."

The chief engineer was nodding to himself. "Aye . . . then Khan would have to scan that one specifically to even suspect anything was amiss. One warhead a'tick-tocking out of seventy-two." He shook his head in admiration at the science officer's audacity. "I can see where to Mr. Spock those would be pretty good odds."

"Game playing." Kirk was nodding soberly to himself. "Even a superman should know better than to play chess with a Vulcan."

On the bridge, Spock leaned back into the firm cushioning of the command chair. "*Brace for impact,*" he commanded evenly.

This is going to work, he told himself. It *had* to work. He had computed the probability of success very carefully before deciding to go ahead with the plan.

Even so, he was grateful that none of his colleagues could see how his fingers tightened ever so imperceptibly on the arms of the command chair.

Kirk's supposition was correct—Spock had ordered Dr. McCoy to arm only a single warhead out of the seventy-two available in the hope that it would not be one that Khan would scan. Now it was inside the warship.

And upon detonation, there were no shields to dampen the force of its explosion, no external walls to absorb any flying fragments. The cargo bay took the full force of the blast. Anything within effective range of the discharge was blown apart.

Including the remaining seventy-one functional warheads that were mounted on the seventy-one other torpedoes.

A gigantic hole ripped open in the stern of the warship. One powerful explosion followed close upon another, then yet more. Systems did not merely go down—they were entirely obliterated. Disruption spread throughout the great ship, affecting everything from life support in the rear four-fifths of its volume, to motive power, to shields and weapons systems. No corner of the crippled vessel was spared.

Igniting oxygen spread brief but intense flames to other parts of the ship. Huge fireballs flared into space as one section after another of the mighty vessel's structural integrity was violated. As might be expected on board a state-of-the-art warship, fire suppression worked miracles, but it could not prevent a chain of instruments from being fried, nor entire compartments from being reduced to shards of metal, plastic, and other materials that were hurled into the surrounding vacuum.

The bridge suffered horribly, but as the most heavily shielded and best protected section of the ship, it maintained life-support functionality. Barely. Much else went down. Fire and escaping gases filled the vaulted compartment. Consoles collapsed upon themselves. Nothing moved save flame and smoke.

Then a single hand could be discerned: rising, clutching at the still-intact command console. Pulling himself up out of the wreckage that now surrounded him, eyes blazing, Khan embarked on the first of innumerable necessary work-arounds in a determined attempt to keep the warship's instrumentation functional.

Sulu could not repress a grin as he reported to the science officer. "Sir, their weapons have been knocked out. Not bad, Commander."

"Thank you, Lieutenant."

Still supporting Carol Marcus between them, Kirk and Scott finally arrived at sickbay. No second explosions jolted them or otherwise threatened their balance.

"Bones— Nurse!"

At once startled and relieved to see them, staff swarmed around the new arrivals. Among those eager to help was Uhura, who assisted the captain in gently easing Carol onto a vacant bed.

"What happened?" she queried the other woman intently. "Are you okay?"

Striving to smile through the pain, Carol managed a weak nod at the communications officer. "I'll be all right. But my father . . ." Her voice trailed off as she turned her head away.

One day she would have to try and reconcile the man who

had raised her with the man she had known in his final moments. People changed with age, she knew. Some grew content, some bitter. Something similar had happened to her father. One day she would learn what that was . . . but not now.

Off to one side, an exuberant McCoy greeted Scott, who was being attended to by a pair of nurses, before moving on to express his joy at the return of his commanding officer and friend.

"Good to see you, Jim."

Kirk nodded tiredly. "I never thought I'd say this, but it's a relief to find myself in sickbay." He gazed earnestly at the smiling doctor. "It was you, wasn't it? You helped Spock arrange for the torpedo to detonate?"

McCoy nodded, proud and without shame. "Who else? After all, I'm the only one who knows how to manually arm that entirely new type of weapon. Even if I did learn how to do so accidentally." His grin widened. "As Spock would say, 'a fortuitous coincidence, Doctor.'"

Kirk still couldn't believe it. "He killed Khan's crew. Frozen and unknowing though they were, he killed them."

McCoy spoke up. "No, he didn't. Spock's cold, but he's not that cold. *I've* got Khan's crew." He nodded and pointed to his left.

As Kirk followed McCoy's gesture, he saw that the main recovery ward had been cleared out, all beds and other equipment either removed or pushed to one side. In its place and occupying the entire space were seventy-two cryoshells that had been removed from their protective torpedoes. Each one was occupied by a three-hundred-year-old genetically warped man or woman.

McCoy's grin widened. "Seventy-two human popsicles, present and accounted for."

Kirk could only stare. "Son of a bitch. How did you fool his internal sensors into convincing him that he had transported his crew over to the other ship? You must have known that he would run scans on at least some of them as soon as they were shipped over."

McCoy explained. "As soon as I learned on that planetoid near Qo'noS that there were cryogenically preserved individuals in those torpedoes, I had in-depth dimensional bioscans run on all of them in case the opportunity arose to attempt revival and also just as part of normal records keeping. When Spock originally proposed his idea, I had the ship's bio-repair system generate nominal simulacra of each of the frozen crew. You know—the same process we use to regrow lost or damaged body parts for personnel who have been injured but who aren't beyond repair and for whom for various medical reasons standard regeneration or prosthetics aren't an option. I then set the system to duplicate everything. The collagen-based simulacra weren't perfect—not enough time for that. But I felt they were good enough to fool a quick external probe. We froze the results and had them inserted back into the torpedoes in place of his actual crew. When Khan scanned his transported torpedoes for his people, the sensors he was employing indicated the presence of long-frozen human components within the torpedo bodies." He shook his head at the memory of it.

"If he had bothered to go and open one of the casings *manually,* he would have seen immediately how he'd been fooled. But Mr. Superman was in too much of a hurry to lord it over us lesser beings. He trusted the preliminary readings of his instrumentation instead of his own eyes."

★   ★   ★

On the bridge, a greatly relieved Sulu turned toward the Vulcan seated in the command chair. "Sir—the internal explosions have completely neutralized the other ship's weapons systems and shields, and quite possibly her ability to maneuver as well. It is my professional opinion that she is no longer a threat. At this point it should be possible to—"

The sound of power cutting out was immediately recognizable. Internal lighting failed for an instant, until it could be restored by emergency backup. From the Science station, a concerned ensign issued a hasty preliminary report. "Sir, we have inclusive warp core misalignment. The ship's internal power grid is down."

"Switch to auxiliary power," Spock ordered.

A second ensign compounded the bad news. "Auxiliary power is heavily depleted and failing, sir. All backup systems were dangerously stressed in the course of taking evasive maneuvers." She bit her lower lip. "There's barely enough to sustain the ship's life-support systems and minimal artificial gravity. We've nothing available for propulsion or maneuvering."

As Spock was deciding that the ship's status could not possibly get any worse, a third officer proved him wrong. "Sir, I'm afraid our final maneuvers brought us in to the point where we appear to be caught in the Earth's gravity well."

"Mr. Sulu: Position relative to orbital stations?"

The helmsman only had to glance at his readouts. "Given our present rate of descent, sir, there's nothing near enough to get anything big enough to us in time to halt our dive."

Spock absorbed this. "Can we change our angle of descent enough to enter a temporary orbit? Even a low one?"

Sulu stared at his helm controls, sat back. Red lights he could have dealt with, but . . . there were no lights at all. No readouts—

nothing. A situation unprecedented in his experience—but that didn't mean he was unaware of the consequences. Essentially, the ship's helm was . . . dead.

"Commander," he reported professionally, "given what I'm seeing here, I can't do *anything*."

As the *Enterprise* shuddered and bounced, Uhura arrived on the bridge and stumbled to her station, easing aside the ensign who had been attending to it in her absence. Meanwhile, Sulu voiced what everyone around him already knew.

In sickbay, McCoy rushed toward the bed on which Carol Marcus lay and began to strap her in position. "Emergency lockdown!" To the patient he added more softly, "I hope you don't get seasick."

She smiled up at him. "Do you?"

His expression was already reflecting his discomfort. "Yeah."

"If we can't get engine power or shields back online," Sulu declared as he worked his instrumentation, "we'll be incinerated on entry."

Calculating his options, Spock found that, yet again, fate had given him nothing worthwhile to work with. "Lieutenant," he said, addressing Uhura, "sound evacuation. All decks." Spinning the command chair, he addressed them all. "As acting captain, I order you to abandon the ship." A touch of a control set in one arm activated the seat's emergency harness. Like a pair of striking snakes, the twin segmented safety belts snapped into place across his torso, securing him in place against violent jolting as well as a potential loss of artificial gravity.

Although all eyes were on him, no one moved.

"I will remain aboard," he continued, "to re-route and reapportion remaining power to life support, gravity, and evacuation shuttle bays. Once again: I order you to abandon ship."

No one moved from their stations.

Spock repeated the command, more forcefully this time. "I order you all to abandon this ship!"

It was left, not for the first time, to Sulu to respond. "With all due respect, Commander—but we're not going anywhere." Turning in the helmsman's seat, he activated his own crash harness. All around the bridge the same sharp *snap* was repeated as one set of emergency braces after another was locked into place.

Observing the unauthorized activity surrounding him, Spock contemplated repeated the order for a third time and finally decided against it. Humans being the demonstrably stubborn species that they were, he felt certain it would have been a waste of time. Should he survive, he knew he would have to include the mass disobedience in his official report. For some reason, though, he was not quite sure he would be able to manage that entry. There was the thought that should he attempt to do so, his eyes might give him trouble.

At least the ship's computer spared him the need to speak any further.

"Attention, all decks. Evacuation protocols initiated. Attention, all decks, proceed to exit bays and report to your assigned evacuation shuttle. . . ."

XVI

Scott grabbed for a handhold as his feet momentarily left the floor and he started to slide up the near wall. The ship's gravity precessers were beginning to struggle against the competing pull of the Earth's own gravity.

"There's not gonna *be* an evacuation if there's no power to stabilize the damn *ship!*" he shouted at the captain. "We lose power to the precessers and artificial gravity will be all over the place. People will be literally climbin' the walls trying to get to their evac shuttles."

Kirk pressed him for a solution. "Can we restore it? Get back enough power to stabilize ship's gravity along with life support, at least until everyone is safely off?"

"Maybe, Captain. But only from Engineering—not from the bridge."

It only got worse as they raced for Engineering itself. Occasionally they found themselves running along walls. Once, the precessers flipped completely and they had to make their way carefully along the ceiling. It was the same for everyone else on board. As the situation grew more critically unstable it became increasingly difficult for personnel to make their way to the evacuation shuttle bays. Objects as well as personnel tended to cling one moment to the floor and the next slide up a wall. Hands hunted for something solid and unmoving to grip. Queasiness became the norm. Throughout the confusion, it was all the ship's compromised computer system could do to keep the artificial gravity on the wounded *Enterprise* from slewing crazily from one degree to another and slamming its crew around like ball bearings in a barrel.

There was apprehension but no panic on the *Enterprise* as anxious crewmembers scrambled to find and board their assigned evac vehicles. This close to Earth, the shuttles would require very little programming. There was no reason everyone could not get off and down to ground safely—provided they could reach their assigned stations. The difficulty arose from the conflict between Earth's intensifying pull and the increasingly erratic operation of the ship's artificial gravity system. While the crew was prepared to deal with an emergency that saw them walking on floors one minute and ceilings the next, the constant gravitational flux forced everyone to go very slowly to avoid injury. As a result, the majority of the crew had yet to make it halfway to their designated shuttles.

If conditions did not improve, they might not have enough time to make it at all before the *Enterprise* disintegrated on entry.

Well aware of the increasing danger, Kirk and Scott made their way toward Engineering as fast as circumstances permitted. They were almost there when the ship's gravity gave a sudden lurch. Scott compared it to floating in a giant bathtub that had just been given an abrupt shove. The unexpected gravitational switch saw him tossed over a railing toward a deck below. Only Kirk's rapid reaction in getting a hand on the engineer's forearm saved Scott from being smashed against the unyielding metal below.

The captain's grip was firm, but he could do nothing about the shifting forces beneath his feet. As they changed direction once again, he felt himself starting to follow Scott over the rail. Straining hard, he tried to wrap his other arm around the railing to stabilize the two of them, at which point their continuing survival became a matter of muscle. Charged with supporting the chief's weight, he felt his own strength ebbing. Even if he lost his grasp and went over, he told himself, he wouldn't let go of Scott.

At the last possible instant, hands grabbed his arms and gripped tight. "I've got you, Keptin!"

Strung out over the railing, the three of them stayed like that a moment longer. At the same time as Chekov began to pull Kirk back, and Kirk to pull Scott, the gravity shifted again, and Kirk's feet found firmer footing. Soon the three of them were standing on what, for the moment at least, was a solid deck.

Scott was grateful, but there was no time to waste on extended expressions of gratitude. Instead, he glared at the ensign.

"What'd you do to me core?"

"Nothing," Chekov stammered as the ship rocked around them. "You can have it back!"

Scott nodded vigorously. "I *intend* to. And once we get a minimum of power back up, you're gonna manually redirect it to impulse control so we can avoid smashing into Earth. Much as I'd like to see home again, I dinna want to do it by turnin' any o' the Highlands into lowlands. There's a separate, backup relay—"

"Behind the deflector shielding." Chekov was completely in tune with the chief engineer's plan.

"Exactly." Scott said no more, impressed with and now confident in the ensign's surprising knowledge of a department that was not his own.

"Then I had better get going," Chekov told him. "The relay's going to need some supplementary programming."

"Mr. Sulu," Spock exclaimed, "divert all remaining power to stabilizers!"

"Doing what I can, sir," the helmsman replied as he desperately fought to comply. "Doing what I can."

Spock tried his best to see that the *Enterprise*'s vanishing energy resources were parceled out meticulously among the ship's most critical active systems. While life support drew the most attention, he and Sulu attempted to steady the starship's wildly skewing and rapidly failing artificial gravity. If he couldn't stabilize it any better, there was a good chance a large percentage of the ship's crew would never be able to make it to their assigned evacuation stations. Yet if he shunted power from life support to the precessers, there was a chance atmospheric pressure would fall too low and kill everyone on board.

They kept at it, doing their best, each man and woman calculating and recalculating in their mind as they strove to create an equilibrium out of uncooperative difficulties.

★   ★   ★

It took Chekov longer than he'd hoped but less than he feared to reach the auxiliary engineering station. Heaving aside the protective cover to expose the controls beneath, he was confronted by switches that were as archaic as they were functional. Levers and switches might be old-fashioned, but there were times when something made of metal and composites could operate efficiently while pure electronics were down.

The double connector was dark red and labeled "Main Router." Closing it required Chekov to employ both hands and all of his strength. Straining, he threw it forward until it snapped into place—and hoped it would work.

The great warship tumbled, burning internally, weaponless, without shields—but not entirely without control. Dragging himself to the forward console, a wounded but still functional Khan fought to make his orders heard above the crackle and thunder of instruments exploding and structural elements failing all around him.

"New destination!" he roared. "Starfleet headquarters!"

"Engines compromised," announced the voice of the ship's computer. *"Cannot guarantee we will reach intended destination. Specified destination off-limits. Do you confirm order?"*

Khan's one-word response emerged as a snarl. "Confirmed."

Scott cried out when he and Kirk finally reached Engineering. He couldn't help himself. His beloved section was a mess. Devoid of staff, stressed by the abrupt shifts in gravity, and reflecting the serious damage that had been done during the violent encounter with the warship, to his engineer's eyes it did not look capable of generating enough energy to power a handcart, much less a starship.

"Oh, no," he cried as he studied the active readouts, "no-nononooooo . . . !"

"What?" Standing behind the chief and resting his hands on his knees, an exhausted Kirk's cry was a challenge, an expression of sympathy, and a desperate query all wrapped up in a single exclamation.

The longer he studied the available readouts, the deeper Scott's anguish grew. "This isn't going to work, Captain. Even if we can restore enough power to drive the ship on impulse power, we kinna redirect it. The main core power thread is decoupled, out of alignment. We could maybe get power back up, but we kinna send it where we want it. Och, with the decoupling the way it is now, we kinna send it anywhere! The ship's *dead,* sir. She's *gone.*"

While Kirk had been listening to Scott's technological lamentation, he had also been studying the main readout. Though lacking in complete familiarity with some of the technical terms on display, and even more so with the majority of numerical summations, he *was* able make sense of the schematics that methodically changed as relevant information was automatically updated. With his eyes he traced the central lambent outline.

"No, she's not." Turning to his left, he sprinted in the direction of the central core.

Scott followed. "Jim, wait! This isn't some child's puzzle game. We kinna actually *manually* realign it. It would take a whole tech team working with specialized equipment to do that, and *never* while the core's still active. Even if we had a team, we could not shut the core down, because in its present condition, we might not be able to get it restarted again. Not in time, anyway. Jim, will ya listen to me?!"

Kirk did not comment. Halting outside the core containment area, he reached for the door control panel, tapped out code on still-functioning keys, and then placed his open palm over the appropriate bioscanner.

"Captain, what are you doing?" Scott began, only to have an unwavering Kirk cut him off.

"I'm going in."

Verging on the apoplectic, the chief gestured at the transparent barrier. "As you well know, that door is there, Captain, to prevent us from getting fatally irradiated! We'd be dead before we ever finished the climb to the damaged area."

"You're not making the climb."

Kirk having made his intentions inescapably clear, Scott moved to block his friend's path. "No. Captain . . . I kinna let you. . . ."

"I understand, Scotty. I appreciate your concern, and you're probably right." Dropping his head, he half turned as if to lead back the way they had come—but it was only to allow him to put more force behind the punch he threw. It was possible Scott saw it coming. Realization did not allow him to dodge the blow, however, and he fell back, unconscious.

"On the other hand," Kirk murmured as he carefully sat the stunned chief safely down nearby and started for the entrance to the core cavity, "you might be wrong. I'm counting on it." Returning to the bioscanner, he repeated the hand press that would identify him. It promptly released the door handle. Pulling and turning on it caused the portal to slide obediently aside.

At least there was enough localized auxiliary power for the doorway to function, Kirk thought as it opened before him. As he stepped through, he lingered briefly in the portal to look back. Montgomery Scott, the best chief of engineering in Starfleet, remained unconscious and with eyes closed. It was not the memory of his chief that he would have preferred to carry with him into the core, but it would have to do. The door closed automatically behind him.

Once on the other side, he immediately felt the excess heat. It permeated his surroundings. Undirected, unchanneled, even the very limited amount of energy that was being produced by the damaged core was hard to tolerate. While he could not keep from feeling it, he could try not to think about it. Training and determination were all that kept him moving as he made his way deeper into the engine area and began to ascend the main generator complex.

With every step, Kirk knew the radiation swirling around him was poisoning his system. Already he was weakening, his muscles refusing to respond to the commands sent from his brain. Even if he were to turn back now, there was no way he would be able to make it back to the safety barrier. Fortunately that was of no concern, since he never did have any intention of retracing his increasingly irregular footsteps.

Emerging from the access tube inside the top of the generator complex, he looked upward. There. The critical core component that had been isolated on the engineering console schematic was plainly out of alignment, its lower half listed drunkenly to one side, its multiple focusing beams dark and unaligned with their matching counterparts looming above. Standing there, he knew he was losing strength by the second.

He started up.

The climb was grueling. He could feel himself growing weaker with every push of his legs, every strain on his arms. The unrestricted radiation burned into him. It was taking forever to get to the core center. The higher he climbed, the farther away it seemed to become, as if it was retreating not only from his increasingly flickering vision but from his failing body itself. More than once, he nearly fell.

Then there were no more conduits to surmount, no more cables to avoid.

He paused at the top, fighting for breath. Directly in front of him, the misaligned lower unit lay askew at an angle for which it had never been designed.

Reaching up, he gripped a section of the unit overhead and swung his body forward, slamming both feet into the lower projecting unit.

Seemingly frozen in place, the heavy device didn't budge.

He repeated the gesture, striking down and forward again and again, each time trying to project all his weight and strength through his feet as he kicked out. His quads trembled as his feet slammed into the immobile component. The shock of each contact ran upward through his legs, threatening to reduce his rapidly weakening muscles to jelly. Still he kept pounding away at the misaligned device.

It began to shift. A little.

He continued swinging and kicking, wondering whether his heart and lungs would give out before his legs. Soon his vision began to blur, and not just from the perspiration that was streaming down his face and into his eyes. He could barely see well enough now to focus on his target. It was still shifting, but not nearly enough, nor fast enough. Swing, kick, gather strength; swing, kick, hope for strength; swing, kick . . .

Giving way suddenly to one side, the projection component slid away from him—and cleanly into place. Its arrival there was greeted by a rapid succession of clicks, a rising whirr, and a flash of blinding white light as the proximate coupling beam reengaged. The force of it broke his overhead grip, sending him flying backward and down, to land heavily on the first access walkway below.

Engineering consoles and instrumentation that had long since gone quiescent snapped back to life.

On the bridge, a disbelieving Sulu found himself gaping at a string of messages as welcome as they were unexpected.

"Full power back online!"

"Maximum thrusters, Mr. Sulu," Spock ordered immediately.

"Stand by, stand by!" the helmsman shouted.

As the ship plunged through the first thick layer of cumulus clouds, the sudden and unexpected restoration of full sound and light took everyone on the bridge by surprise. Their Academy instructors would have been proud to see how quickly and professionally their former students reacted.

"*Hold on!*" Sulu ordered. With everyone cocooned in their emergency harnesses, it was a superfluous command, but fingers instinctively tightened on armrests nonetheless. Manually manipulating the helm controls like a pianist essaying Busoni, Sulu not only adjusted the ship's internal gravity while compensating for that of the ever-nearer planetary surface, he also managed while only employing impulse power to bring the shocked *Enterprise* back from the brink of what had become a toxic trajectory.

Unseen and unappreciated by anyone save its exhausted crew, the *Enterprise* began to rise slowly, bursting upward like some dragon of legend through the white clouds through which it had helplessly fallen only moments before.

Sweat pouring off him even as life support came fully back online, Sulu noted the attitude adjustment with satisfaction.

"Shields restored," declared one officer from his station.

"Commander, power online," added the ensign seated next to him, glancing back in the direction of the command chair.

"Gaining altitude en route to establishing stable orbit," Sulu announced. "Once we've done that, I'll try easing us farther out. Then we can see about limping to the nearest dock for repairs. Altitude is stabilizing."

"It's a miracle," insisted the officer at the next station over.

"There are no such things," Spock felt compelled to declare.

As everyone sat contemplating their near demise, each lost in his or her own thoughts, Scott's voice sounded over the fully restored intercom system. "Engineering to bridge. Mr. Spock?"

"I am here, Mr. Scott. Since it would appear that congratulations are in order all around, I am pleased to—"

The chief didn't wait for him to finish. "Never mind that now, Mr. Spock. You'd better get down here."

Everyone heard. Not just the words, but what was implied in the tone of the chief engineer's voice. All but ripping himself out of his emergency harness, Spock rose and raced for the lift. Everyone watched him go. Everyone, Uhura included, had the sense not to say anything.

Elsewhere, another ship, much larger and in far worse shape, trailing fresh flames as it struck atmosphere, plunged toward the surface below as huge chunks of torn and twisted metal, fiery internal components, and disintegrating pieces of its interior formed a wild trail of destruction. It fell rather than flew, almost completely out of control.

Almost . . .

It is one thing to expect the worst; quite another to have it confirmed. Rushing into Engineering and reaching the outer core maintenance area, Spock slowed as he saw Scott standing by the nearest operations console. It took the science officer a moment longer before his gaze picked out Kirk—on the other side of the transparent sealed emergency barrier. Having fallen from the upper level where his reckless effort had succeeded in restoring power to the ship, he had since crawled to where he now lay, just beyond the sealed doors.

He was not moving.

Eyeing the barrier, Spock didn't hesitate. *"Open it."* When Scott failed to comply, the science officer moved to enter the necessary coding himself. Reluctantly but firmly, Scott addressed the overanxious Vulcan.

"The decontamination process is not complete. We'd flood the whole compartment with radiation, Mr. Spock. You know that. We'd risk losing control of what we've regained." He nodded toward the barrier. "Of everything the captain regained for us." As Spock stepped back, Scott indicated another set of instrumentation. "I'm bringin' the radiation levels in there down as fast as is possible. It's not like moppin' up a water spill." There was not a hint of sarcasm in his explanation.

Turning back to the barrier, Spock moved closer and dropped into a crouch. Responding to the science officer's appearance,

Kirk somehow forced his gravely weakened body to respond. Internal pickups relayed his barely perceptible words to those on the other side of the transparency.

"How's our ship . . . ?"

Spock swallowed hard. For the first time in his life he wished fervently to deny the evidence of his eyes.

This could not be happening.

"Out of danger," he heard himself saying. "You saved the *Enterprise*. You saved the crew."

Kirk managed a smile. Feeble, but recognizable. Weakened, yet indomitable. "And you . . . used what he wanted . . . against him, Spock. Nice move."

There was an unfamiliar taste in Spock's mouth. "It is what you would have done."

A sigh emerged from the other man's lips. "And when Scotty indicated to me that if I came in here I was a dead man—I did what *you* would've done."

If not for the hum of recently revived machines, it would have been completely silent in the area. Uhura arrived, slowing to a stop beside Scott, and likewise said nothing.

"Any . . . advice?" Kirk finally managed to eke out.

Another difficult swallow. "Captain?"

Exerting a supreme effort, Kirk raised his head so that their eyes met. "I'm . . . scared, Spock. Strange sensation. Not . . . used to it. Help me . . . not be. How do you choose . . . not to feel?"

Staring through the glass at his commanding officer—at his friend—Spock replied as straightforwardly as he could.

"Vulcans cannot lie. I do not know." His voice cracked. "Right now I am failing. Because you are my friend."

Reaching up and forward, Kirk just did manage to put his open palm against the inside of the barrier. Spock did the same on the opposite side. It was as close as one man could get to the other.

"Take care of our ship, Spock."

A tear slipped from the science officer's left eye.

Kirk's hand held its position against the transparency for a moment longer. Then it slid downward, down, as the captain's eyes turned away from those of his first officer, to gaze upward. They stopped moving.

On the captain's side of the emergency barrier, there was no more movement at all. Spock studied the still form opposite him for a long moment as Scott and Uhura struggled to comfort each other.

Then the Vulcan's lips parted and a single sound, more of a roar than a word, erupted from the bottom of his throat as he howled at the top of his lungs.

A name.

"KHHAAAAANNNNNNNNN!"

XVII

Screaming past the *Enterprise*, the gargantuan metallic corpse that was the late Admiral Marcus's warship hurled toward Earth, leaving Sulu gaping at his monitors.

"Holy shit, that was close!"

Far below, the appearance of the plunging warship drew the attention first of a few, and then of everyone out on San Francisco's streets. Initially, people stared—and as the huge vessel drew nearer, smoke pouring from its crippled engine nacelles, they began to scatter in panic.

Though the consequences of his doomed ship's arrival were devastating enough, it did not strike precisely where Khan had hoped. As if by a giant hand, the ancient monument that was the prison on the island of Alcatraz was scraped clean from its rocky promontory. The collision was just enough to critically slow the vessel's descent and alter its intended trajectory. Instead of smashing into and through Starfleet headquarters, it plunged into the bay.

Its momentum, however, was sufficient to send it through the water and slashing into the city bayfront. Tower after tower succumbed to the sickening impact, crumbling before the on-rushing mass, until the wreck of what had not long ago been the most powerful vessel in Starfleet's arsenal finally came to a grinding, groaning halt.

The concomitant wave that rose out of the harbor swept across the low-lying harbor front, inundating facilities, smashing apart landscaping, and tossing vehicles about like toys. Caught in the surge, stunned onlookers struggled to stay afloat. Those who managed to ride out the wave or reach higher ground fought to save those who could not do so on their own.

In guiding the crippled ship to its end, Khan's suicidal act gave rise to a thousand acts of bravery. There were numerous injuries and unavoidable deaths, but the greater carnage he had hoped to inflict did not occur. The slightest of maladjustments that had affected the intended course of the warship's death dive meant that many more survived who would otherwise have perished.

On the bridge of the *Enterprise*, Spock and his colleagues had tracked the descending warship to its final resting place. Staring at the view forward, Spock snapped a crisp command.

"Search the enemy ship for signs of life."

Sulu studied his readouts for a moment before responding. "Sir, there's no way anyone could have survived that impact."

"*He* could." Vulcan though he was, the science officer still managed to make the observation sound like a curse.

"Yes, sir," a subdued Sulu replied, returning to his instruments.

Another pause, followed by a startled exclamation from Sulu. "Got something. One life-form." He looked back at Spock. "Whoa—he just jumped thirty feet!"

"That's him," Spock declared with confidence. "Can we beam him up?"

Try as he might to make it possible, in the crowded confines of the compound and the city below, the effort required exceeded even Sulu's exceptional skills.

"He's moving too fast, and there are too many other people around. I can't get a lock on him."

"Keep trying," Spock directed the helmsman as he turned.

Sensing a presence at his back, he turned to find himself gazing at Uhura. Their eyes locked. Hers were wet, but her voice was low and thick with anger. "*Go get him.*"

By the time Spock reached the transporter room, there was a tech team waiting for him. As he adjusted the phaser he was holding from *stun* to *kill,* he calmly addressed the officer in charge.

"Stand by for coordinates."

"Yes, sir!" responded the tech manning the console.

Hands poised over the console controls, the officer nodded expectantly. A moment later Chekov reported from the bridge.

"Enter T-one-five-seven by two-five-nine-eight. Target still in motion. I can track him, but I can't lock on him."

"Coordinates confirmed," announced the transporter officer.

"Energize," Spock ordered him.

There followed a rising whine, a coalescing of light and energy, and then Spock was gone.

He rematerialized amid smoking chaos. Emergency vehicles screamed only slightly louder than some of the injured as medical teams attended to wounded Starfleet personnel and civilians. Spock's eyes were scanning his immediate surroundings even before he had fully reintegrated. If he had been put down in the right place by the transporter team . . .

A moment later, he had picked out a stolid figure on the other side of the crowd, trying to make itself as inconspicuous as possible as it attempted to get farther from the crash site. There was no mistaking the individual outline or the determination with which it was moving away from the point of impact, despite its evident injuries.

Turning toward the sound of the transporter whine, a frustrated Khan locked eyes with the science officer. An ordinary man might have offered a derisive gesture or uttered a frustrated curse. Khan did neither; he simply turned and ran.

Holstering his phaser, Spock took off in pursuit, his legs pounding the ground beneath him with unrelenting ferocity.

Khan ran without looking back. But no matter how hard he ran, he was unable to shake the pursuing Vulcan. Spock's expression never changed. He was wholly focused on closing the distance between them. When Spock thought he might be faltering, the image of Kirk drawing his last breath sent a fresh surge of strength into his legs.

Turning to his right, Khan raced through an open doorway into an undamaged building, speeding past startled onlookers. Racing through the lobby, he headed directly for the opposite side and the street beyond. The fact that there was no exit on the far side of the lobby did not stop him, nor did the wall of glass that appeared to block his way. He went through it like a projectile, sending shards flying in all directions.

And still he could not lose his stolid-faced pursuer.

Kirk's eyes were closed, his body as unmoving as when it had finally become safe enough to enter the sealed-off core area and remove him. Now he lay on a gurney in sickbay, awaiting final disposition.

Among those present was Carol Marcus. She stood staring at the body of a man she had hardly known. Yet he had died to save her life as surely as he had done so to save those of his crew. Chekov looked on from a distance, unable to bring himself to move any closer.

Bereft of such choices, Dr. McCoy prepared his examination. A formality; part of his job. One he had to do.

Except that he couldn't. Not just then, anyway. Turning, he walked away from the gurney, away from Scott, who had been standing by his side. McCoy was angry at himself as he sat down. Kirk wouldn't have approved. Doubtless he would have chided McCoy about his failure, would have made some stupid, half-assed joke that would have . . .

Closing his eyes, McCoy struggled to regain control of his emotions. He was failing miserably when something distracted him.

Movement. On the worktable beside him.

That should not be. Things did not move independently on tables in the fully sterilized sickbay, especially things large enough to be seen without the aid of a microscope. Also, they did not purr.

Turning toward the table, McCoy looked on first in confusion, then in disbelief. As he leaned closer to the source of both the slight movement and the appealing noise, it was clear that the object of his attention was very much alive.

The tribble. The only one on board. It was, impossibly, alive. It ought not to be. But it most certainly was, which suggested that . . . which meant that . . .

His eyes widened. Turning to the officer in charge of the detail that had brought Kirk in from Engineering, he issued what was perhaps one of the more unusual requests in the history of the Starfleet medical service.

"Get me a cryotube. *Now*."

How determined was the Vulcan? Could he keep pace even with an enhanced human, albeit an injured one? What Khan needed, he realized as he raced across yet another busy city avenue, was transportation. He could have stolen a private vehicle, but that would mean being confined to the ground.

The battered antigrav garbage scow was just lifting off ahead of him, on the other side of the raised street. On board there would be no human operator to contend with . . . or report his position. A single leap carried him to the top of the dull red machine. He was finally able to momentarily relax, catch his breath. A small smile played across his perspiring face. It didn't matter where the automated collector was going, so long as it was anywhere but there.

Khan never saw the solitary figure that came pounding around a corner, running hard in the superhuman's wake. Executing a leap no human could duplicate, Spock managed to grab hold of a metal brace on the underside of the rising garbage scow. As the vehicle continued to ascend, preparatory to completing its daily round in the city, Spock slowly but steadily worked himself from the underside of the machine to one side, and finally to the rough edge that rimmed the top.

Khan now saw him.

Rushing to the side of the vehicle, he struck out repeatedly. One kick sent the science officer's phaser plummeting over the side toward the ground below. When Khan reached for it, Spock managed to pull himself onto the top of the self-piloting machine before his opponent could kick out again. The unmanned vehicle continued on its programmed path, indifferent to the life-and-death struggle that was taking place on its topside.

The two men continued to trade blows, each combatant searching for a weakness in his opponent. Spock had the advantage of Vulcan strength, speed, and martial arts training, but Khan was enhanced, modified, improved—no ordinary human.

Spock managed to apply a full Vulcan nerve pinch. Paralyzed, Khan somehow remained upright. Fury and pain fought for dominance in his expression as he refused to go down. Screaming *"Noooo!"* he did the impossible and broke free.

Sickbay swarmed with activity as multiple medical and engineering personnel combined their efforts and expertise to prep the motionless body. Refusing to be sidelined, Carol hobbled about on a cane and did her best to assist, even if only with advice.

Standing beside the cylinder that had been moved into the main bay, McCoy spoke anxiously to the techs who had brought it in as he referred to its present occupant.

"Get this guy out of the cryotube. Keep him in an induced coma." He turned back to the table on which rested the motionless form of James Kirk. "We're gonna put Kirk inside." With Carol Marcus at his side, he returned to prepping the body of the captain for insertion into the device. "It's our only chance of preserving his brain function: induced hypothermia."

She turned from contemplating the still body on the table. "How much of Khan's original blood draw is left?"

His expression tightened. *"None."* He whirled on a watching med tech. "I've already started cardiopulmonary support. Set up an automated maintenance system. Two beats per minute. You understand? *Two beats.*"

As soon as he was certain everything that could be done to support Kirk's remaining physiological functions had been put in place, McCoy rushed to a nearby communicator.

"*Enterprise* to Spock." What seemed like an endless wait but in reality was scarcely seconds produced nothing but maddening static. "Spock!"

On the garbage scow, the two men—one superhuman, the other half Vulcan—continued to grapple. Getting the science officer in the same skull-crushing grip he had applied to Alexander Marcus, Khan began to squeeze. Spock countered with another nerve pinch that, while still not putting his enemy down, forced him to release his grasp. Khan came around with a knee strike that sent the science officer onto his back but failed to render him unconscious.

Frustrated, backing away from both his opponent and the terrible pain he had again inflicted, Khan noticed a second garbage scow approaching below the one on which he was riding. Throwing his relentless opponent a look of utter defiance, he jumped.

The landing on the other vehicle would have shattered a normal person's legs, driving both leg bones upward into the pelvis. Unharmed, though, Khan was on his feet immediately, glaring up at the transport he had just abandoned.

The last thing he expected was for Spock to follow.

Spock landed hard on the second machine. Khan hadn't noticed him at first, but he did now. Reaching the science officer, Khan lashed out with a vicious kick that sent the Vulcan flying backward. As Spock lay on his back, Khan bent forward and began to pummel the helpless officer without mercy.

In sickbay, McCoy stood over the cryotube into which Kirk's body had been carefully inserted.

"Activate the cryogenic sequence."

This time it was Carol Marcus following McCoy's orders. Her fingers adjusted the relevant control on the top of the cylinder. The transparent cover slid shut over the recumbent captain. The procedure as complete as he could make it, he turned his attention to the nearest communicator.

"McCoy to bridge. I can't reach Spock from sickbay. *Listen to me*. Khan—I need Khan *alive*. You get that murderous sonuvabitch back on this ship right now." He took a deep breath. *"I think he can save Kirk."*

As he closed the communication, he found Carol gazing at him intently. "What about bringing one of the other members of Khan's crew out of cryosleep? Even if they don't revive . . . properly . . . it's not their opinions we need."

McCoy looked toward the prone form of Kirk lying motionless on the gurney, where he continued to be prepped and monitored by the team of medical technicians.

"Too risky. I *think* this might work with Khan. I don't know how much alike he and his crew are, and I don't have time to find out. If there's even the slightest unresolved difference between their respective physiologies, then we might be doing nothing but wasting our time and what little, if any, Jim has left. And I have to have Khan alive, because I don't know what death might do to his body . . . or the viability of its respective components." He shook his head in dismay. "It's Khan—or nothing."

The bridge was the scene of almost as much activity as sickbay as Sulu and his fellow officers sought to track the movements of two people in a crowded city far below. Beyond placing the *Enterprise* in a stationary orbit above San Francisco, there was little more the helmsman could do.

"Can we beam them up to the ship?" Sulu asked his current second-in-command.

Chekov studied his instrumentation. "I think they're on a transport of some kind. They keep moving too fast in and out of structural surroundings filled with people to still be on foot. I can't get a lock on either of them."

Looking over Sulu's shoulders, Uhura had already come to a decision of her own. And for once there was no one to contradict her as she spoke to the helmsman.

"You can't beam them up. Can you beam someone down?"

Training had made Spock every bit as good a fighter as his opponent, but Vulcan or not, he didn't possess the endurance of his artificially enhanced adversary. Khan continued to pound his prone opponent, until the science officer was sufficiently weakened so that his enemy was again able to apply his two-handed grip to the Vulcan's head.

And this time Spock was too beaten down and too tired to respond with a third nerve pinch.

With his prone opponent trapped beneath him, the fight was as good as over. But it was not in Khan's nature to dwell on this kind of victory. Killing the science officer was simply something that had to be done, a next step in securing the latest iteration of his freedom. Focused on his now-pinned foe, Khan continued to apply pressure to the Vulcan's skull. Pressure capable of breaking bone.

Only to be distracted by a glimmer in his prey's eyes. A flashing of light that ought not to be there.

Whirling, he saw Lieutenant Uhura materialize, phaser in hand. Taking aim with the pistol, she began firing. One shot after another struck home. They slowed but did not put him down.

Why isn't her weapon set on kill? the battered, injured Spock wondered as he struggled to clamber back onto his feet. Ignoring the contradiction as well as the pain that now racked his body, he staggered erect, stumbled forward, and reached Khan.

Slowed by the repeated hits from Uhura's phaser, Khan was unable to counter the punch Spock threw at him. It caught his opponent across the face, dazing him and spinning him around. As Khan staggered, refusing to go down, Spock grabbed the enhanced human's extended arm and executed a formal Vulcan martial-arts move. Only unlike in training, this time he did not stop himself halfway through the movement.

The arm snapped. As Khan cried out, Spock employed another move to lift him, spin him, and slam him to the metal deck. Crouching atop his now-helpless enemy, the Vulcan proceeded to throw a closed fist into his face. Again and again, harder than Kirk ever had on Qo'noS. Blood pouring from his wounds, Khan no longer possessed the energy to fight back—but he refused to pass out, refused to surrender.

That was fine with Spock, who continued to pummel his adversary with the steady determination of a machine, his right fist descending in pulverizing rhythm.

Strike after strike landed, sending more blood and then bits of flesh flying. If fortune was with him and the universe possessed any degree of fairness, Spock thought grimly, Khan would remain aware until the science officer could beat him to death. It was a most human desire, but at that moment, emotional control had long since fled from the science officer's mind.

It remained for someone else to remind him of who and what he was.

"Spock!" Uhura staggered toward the two men. *"Spock!"* Another crushing blow landed. *"STOP!"*

Overcome with fury and bloodlust, only a lifetime of training enabled Spock to make sense of what she was saying—much less pause in his assault to turn and blink at her.

Kill him, Spock told himself. *Kill him now, here. So he will never have the opportunity to harm anyone ever again. Kill him because of all he has murdered. Kill him because of . . . Jim.*

He drew back his right hand for the final, executioner's blow.

Then Uhura was there, kneeling in front of him. "Spock, Spock—stop! He's our only chance to save Kirk!"

What is logical in such a situation? he asked himself. *What would be the rational decision?* It might not necessarily be what he personally might want to do. It might not necessarily be what even might be considered justice.

Eyeing the beseeching Uhura, the Vulcan brought his closed fist around one last time to smash the recumbent Khan square in the face.

Kirk opened his eyes.

Sunlight. Surprising how, no matter how advanced the simulation, a human could always tell real sunlight. It meant that unless he had been placed in a very peculiar corner of the ship indeed, he was no longer on the *Enterprise*. He tried to sit up. That didn't work so well and, for now at least, he had no problem giving up on the notion.

He was surrounded, all but engulfed, by a concatenation of medical instrumentation. They beeped softly and flashed occasionally, flooding his surroundings with an assortment of color extensive enough to be more readily associated with a freshly decorated Christmas tree.

A white-clad figure appeared at the side of his bed to grin down at him. Since he recognized it, it was not, properly, an angel. He could not sit up, but it seemed as if his mouth worked well enough, so he grinned back. So hoarse were the words he formed that he almost did not recognize his own voice.

"I died."

"Oh, don't be so melodramatic." McCoy frowned down at him as he placed the instrument he was holding close to the side of Kirk's head. "You were *barely* dead. It's the full effects of the transfusion that really took a toll. Your body fought it right from the beginning. You were out cold for two weeks. Someday I'll give you a full list of the anti-rejection drugs and other medications we had to pump into you to make it work. Makes for extensive reading." The grin returned. "Tribbles handle it better."

His mind not working quite as well as his mouth, Kirk struggled to digest all that the doctor had said. "Transfusion?"

"Your cells were heavily irradiated. We had no choice. The radiation poisoning had begun to affect your organs."

It took a moment, but the slowly reviving Kirk gradually put everything together. The implications . . .

"Khan?"

McCoy nodded. "Once we caught him, I synthesized a serum from his super blood. Kind of like how an antivenin is produced from the actual venom? Once we got your body to accept the stuff, it . . . repaired you. Fixed damaged cells, protected healthy ones, replaced with astonishing speed those that had died. In all my career, I never saw an individual's immunity levels rise so fast. Very useful stuff, that blood. I anticipate an assortment of awards once I get around to publishing the results." He leaned closer. "As to possible side effects, none have been observed so far. How about it? Are ya feeling homicidal? Power mad? Despotic?"

When he could speak again, Kirk replied, "No more than usual." The image of the grinning doctor seemed to waver, then solidify afresh. "How'd you catch him?"

"I didn't."

As McCoy moved to one side, Kirk was able to see to the back of the hospital room. Another figure was standing there. As it now came nearer, it gradually moved into focus.

Captain and first officer regarded each other.

"You saved my life," Kirk murmured, gazing up at his friend.

"You saved *my* life, Captain. And the lives of the entire crew and . . ."

"Spock, just—thank you."

There was only McCoy present to bear witness to the Vulcan's reply, and to be shocked by it.

"You are welcome, Jim."

Already locked in cryosleep, the body of the individual known as Khan was lowered into the capsule. No words were spoken as the cover was shut and sealed and the interior filled with an appropriate mixture of common and rare gases. Through the single transparent port, the eyes of the man imprisoned within stared out at a universe with which he could no longer interact. Could no longer affect. Could no longer harm.

Bored technicians moved the tube through a number of corridors until they reached the vault. High and imposing, it was filled with similar capsules: some contemporary, some of more ancient vintage. Save for the fact that those entombed within were not technically dead, it had the feel of a massive and little-visited crypt. The new visitor was placed in line next to a number of similarly occupied capsules. All looked alike—all seventy-two of them.

The technicians paused to make certain that the instrumentation responsible for maintaining the internal temperature of the new capsule was identical to that of the many hundreds surrounding it. Once they were satisfied, they departed. There was another arrival scheduled for later in the day, and they did not want it to overlap and interfere with their afternoon break.

High, heavy doors closed automatically behind them, sealing off much more than they knew.

The squadron came in low and fast above the city, flying in the missing-man formation. Only when they had passed and the six-person honor guard had completed the ceremony of formally folding the blue-and-white Starfleet flag did the man at the podium begin to speak to the assembled Starfleet personnel and civilians solemnly seated in the open square before him. Clad in the full dress uniform of a captain of the fleet, a fully recovered James Kirk spoke firmly and without hesitation.

"We are gathered here to pay our respects to fallen friends and family. We take solace in the knowledge that we honor those who lost their lives doing what they believed was right. And no matter what path they took, we hope that in death they can find forgiveness."

Seated nearby, Carol Marcus raised a handkerchief to her eyes. Her father . . . Kirk's words evoked the memory not of what he had become, but of what he had once been. For that as much as for her life, she was grateful.

"There will always be those who mean us harm," Kirk continued. "We can never know from where or from whom those threats will emerge. But we have to take them as they come. Not long ago, Christopher Pike asked me what it meant to be the captain of a starship. At the time, I was unable to see that a captain takes responsibility for his mistakes as completely and wholly as he does his successes. That is the only way he can ever become—better." He paused a moment to look out across the sea of faces that gazed back at him, silent and respectful not only of what he was saying, but of the man who was saying them. It was a new sensation for the speaker.

"We can *all* be better," he went on, acutely aware of the importance of the moment. "That is the ideal upon which Starfleet was founded. It is who we are. It is what we must be again."

Maybe it was because of all he had been forced to go through. Maybe it was because he had actually died. But the James T. Kirk who solemnly greeted Starfleet personnel and civilians alike following the services was not the same man who had steered forth the *Starship Enterprise* on its most recent voyage. The boldness, the inescapable tendency to impetuosity: All of that was still there, but now it was leavened by a new maturity. It was a strange feeling, but it felt . . . right.

EPILOGUE

Entering the bridge, Kirk grinned at the sight of Hikaru Sulu sitting in the command chair. The lieutenant started slightly at the captain's salutation.

"Hard to get it out of your system once you've had a taste. Isn't that right, Mr. Sulu?"

Hurrying to vacate the seat, Sulu adopted a wry smile as he moved to the helmsman's station. "'Captain' *does* have a nice ring to it. Chair's all yours, sir."

Kirk settled himself into the now-familiar seat. There had been a time when he had been mildly reluctant to do so. No longer. Now he occupied the space as if he owned it. He would forever respect the chair.

Leaning slightly forward, he addressed the chair pickup. "Mr. Scott, how's our core?"

The response came back without hesitation. "Purrin' like

a kitten, Captain," the chief assured him, as nearby, Keenser moved to his duty station. "She's ready for a long journey."

"Excellent," Kirk replied. Leaving the command station, he favored McCoy with a friendly clap on both arms. "Come on, Bones— It's gonna be *fun*."

"Five years in space," the doctor growled under his breath. "God help me."

"Dr. Marcus," Kirk said to the woman seated at the secondary science station, "I'm glad you could be part of the family."

She smiled warmly back at him. Very warmly. "Nice to have a family, Captain." As he smiled broadly and headed back toward his chair, she followed him with her eyes, her thoughts her own.

Kirk halted beside his second-in-command.

"So. Where should we go, Spock?"

"As a mission of this duration has never before been attempted, I defer to your good judgment, Captain." Turning and walking away, he returned to his own station.

Taking a seat, Kirk gazed anew out the forward port.

"Mr. Sulu—take us out."

"Aye, Captain."

**SIMON &
SCHUSTER**

IF YOU ENJOY GOOD BOOKS,
YOU'LL LOVE OUR GREAT OFFER
25% OFF THE RRP ON ALL
SIMON & SCHUSTER UK **TITLES**
WITH FREE POSTAGE AND PACKING (UK ONLY)

Simon & Schuster UK is one of the leading general book publishing
companies in the UK, publishing a wide and eclectic mix
of authors ranging across commercial fiction, literary fiction,
general non-fiction, illustrated and children's books.

For exclusive author interviews, features and competitions log onto:
www.simonandschuster.co.uk

*Titles also available in **eBook** format across all digital devices.*

How to buy your books

Credit and debit cards
Telephone Simon & Schuster Cash Sales at **Sparkle Direct** on **01326 569444**

Cheque
Send a cheque payable to *Simon & Schuster Bookshop* to:
Simon & Schuster Bookshop, PO Box 60, Helston, TR13 OTP

Email: sales@sparkledirect.co.uk
Website: www.sparkledirect.com

Prices and availability are subject to change without notice.